TOO DEEP TO CROSS

ALSO AVAILABLE BY KERRI HAKODA

Cold to the Touch

TOO DEEP TO CROSS

A THRILLER

Kerri Hakoda

NEW YORK

Books should be disposed of and recycled according to local requirements. All paper materials used are FSC compliant.

This is a work of fiction. All of the names, characters, organizations, places, and events portrayed in this novel are either products of the author's imagination or are used fictitiously. Any resemblance to real or actual events, locales, or persons, living or dead, is entirely coincidental.

Published in the United States by Crooked Lane Books, an imprint of The Quick Brown Fox & Company LLC.

Crooked Lane Books and its logo are trademarks of The Quick Brown Fox & Company LLC.

Library of Congress Catalog-in-Publication data available upon request.

ISBN (hardcover): 979-8-89242-434-9
ISBN (paperback): 979-8-89242-435-6
ISBN (ebook): 979-8-89242-436-3

Cover design by Nebojsa Zoric

Printed in the United States.

www.crookedlanebooks.com

Crooked Lane Books
34 West 27th St., 10th Floor
New York, NY 10001

First Edition: May 2026

The authorized representative in the EU for product safety and compliance is eucomply OÜPärnu mnt 139b-14, 11317 Tallinn, Estonia, hello@eucompliancepartner.com, +33757690241

10 9 8 7 6 5 4 3 2 1

For Sherry

Prologue

He was first on the scene, screeching into a "No Parking" space as his takeout container of kung pao chicken capsized and spilled onto the passenger seat. Anchorage Homicide Detective DeHavilland Beans was out of the Ford Explorer almost before it came to a complete stop and lunged toward the corner store where there had been reports of shots fired.

At the cash register of Ma's Family Grocery, tiny Sophie Ma pointed her Smith & Wesson with rock-steady hands at the armed man standing on the opposite side of the counter. The glass cabinet that had been suspended from the ceiling, holding tobacco products, lay shattered, its contents strewn. Fragments of broken glass nestled in Mrs. Ma's dark hair and glittered on the nicked linoleum countertop like diamonds scattered in a jewel heist. Cigarette packs, loose cigarettes, and flakes of tobacco settled like aromatic confetti on the counter and the floor.

Ma's Family Grocery was an Asian market and convenience store owned and operated by Beans's college friend Frankie Ma and Frankie's mother, Sophie. The Government Hill store had fallen victim to numerous smash-and-grab incidents in the past, and Sophie Ma kept her dead husband's licensed pistol under the cash register like a loaded talisman.

The man across the counter, with his gun trained on Sophie Ma was Willis Helms, an informant the Anchorage Police Department occasionally used on drug cases, though not very often any more. Willis had become increasingly unreliable as his meth addiction had taken over his life. The last of his Afghanistan deployments had left him with a piece of IED in his leg, and he walked with a pronounced limp. Another souvenir he bore from his time in the service was crippling PTSD that often sent him diving into cardboard box bunkers, shaking, terrified of unseen enemies.

Although his mental acuity and personal hygiene had definitely suffered, he had never been violent before. Now Willis held a nine-millimeter gun in quivering hands, aimed unsteadily at Mrs. Ma. His long, greasy hair hung around his face like tattered drapes, and a scraggly beard framed his mouth. The faded and stained Carhartt jacket he wore was shredded at the elbows and frayed at the hem. Even from where Beans was standing in the open doorway, he could smell Willis' sour odor. The man's right leg twitched convulsively, and change jingled in his pocket in an eerily familiar cadence.

Beans held his Glock at his side as he called, "Mrs. Ma? It's Beans. You can put the gun down now."

Mrs. Ma gave her head a brief shake, sending glass tinkling to the floor. "*He* shot my cigarette case, Beans. You make *him* put the gun away."

"Willis? It's Detective Beans. Why don't you put the gun down, and we can talk about this?"

"She won't give me the Cheetos, Beans. Or the Marlboros. And how come there's no chocolate milk?" Willis, clearly high, wailed in a reedy voice.

"No money, no groceries, Willis." Mrs. Ma said. "And nobody drinks chocolate milk anymore."

"I do," Willis whined. "Beans does, don't you, Beans?"

"Come on, guys. Mrs. Ma, put the gun down." Beans slowly walked through the door that had been propped open, glad that it let out some of Willis' funk.

"He puts his down first." Mrs. Ma set her mouth in a thin line.

Beans was now in the aisle, forming an equilateral triangle with Mrs. Ma and Willis. "Willis, you don't want to do this. Come on, stand down, soldier."

The next events apparently happened in quick succession, but to Beans, it seemed to slow to half-time. Willis reluctantly lowered his gun. Mrs. Ma gave an exasperated huff and lowered the Smith & Wesson. Then, with speed that Beans didn't think was possible for Willis, he whipped his gun back up and aimed it at Sophie Ma's shocked face.

"No Cool Ranch Doritos," Willis announced, lunging forward.

"No!" Beans raised his Glock. It was too familiar. The man stinking of alcohol and sweat, with a jangling, ragged gait, threatening the life of a small dark-haired woman. Like his mother.

Like before, the protective reflex sent a bullet flying. But this time, his training directed his aim like a magnet toward center mass. The cop instinct, whispering in his ear like a devil on his shoulder, made sure the assailant wouldn't get off a second shot. Willis jerked sideways and his finger spasmed on the trigger of his gun. The shot went wide, hitting liter bottles of soft drinks that fizzed and bubbled on the floor, mixing with Willis' blood in a sweet, sticky cocktail.

1

Beans

Summer 2024

Beans folded a pair of jeans into his suitcase while Elwood, his black and white German Shorthaired Pointer, watched him glumly from the bedroom doorway. Like all dogs, Elwood sensed that the appearance of the suitcase meant that his owner would be traveling somewhere, probably without him. The dog smacked his lips and whined.

"Cheer up," Beans said, tossing Elwood a wadded-up sock. "Piper is going to stay here with you and Archie while I'm gone. You love Piper." Piper was Beans' younger sister studying for her MBA at the University of Alaska in Anchorage. Archie was the long-haired ginger cat that minced his way across the folded clothes in the suitcase. He stretched and clawed at the folded jeans. Archie had belonged to the first victim of the barista killer Beans had apprehended the year before. He had taken Archie in with the intention of rehoming him, but the cat had other ideas.

Beans couldn't blame Elwood and Archie for feeling unsettled. He had felt the same way since he had shot Willis dead in the brightly lit Asian market. Since he had knelt in the sickening slurry of root beer and blood, trying to keep Willis's life from pulsing out between his fingers while the light faded from the man's eyes and Sophie Ma screamed.

He barely remembered the other responders storming in, paramedics taking over from him as he slumped onto the sticky, sweet-smelling floor, staring at his dripping hands.

Beans had been a cop for more than ten years and until then had never killed a man. The first time he had even fired at a perpetrator was during the apprehension of the serial killer who had terrorized Anchorage baristas the year before. That time, he had wounded the suspect, a predator resisting arrest. This time was different.

A mountain of paperwork had ensued, endless meetings with Internal Affairs and the union. Beans was put on administrative leave and gave up his gun and his badge. CCTV from the store was being reviewed as part of the internal investigation. He was instructed to not speak to anyone, especially the media, about the shooting.

Worst of all was the doubt in his own mind whether or not the shooting could have been avoided. The night he had killed Willis Helms, he stood under the hot shower until it ran cold, scrubbing his hands and arms until they stung. After that, he lit a few sticks of incense and said a sutra for Willis, hoping that the tortured man would be reborn into a kinder, gentler life. He prayed for himself as well, that the taking of this life hadn't spent too much of his karmic currency.

Who am I kidding? It was the worst thing I could have done.

He ran the event over and over in his mind. Could he have avoided killing Willis? Deflected his aim? Talked him down? Disarmed him? Should he have waited for a hostage negotiator? But if he had, would Sophie Ma be dead instead of Willis?

Finally, a call from his mother, Mari, broke the endless, torturous loop. Mari was in the San Francisco Bay Area, helping Beans's grandmother clean out the family home. His grandfather had died a year ago of a stroke, and his widow, Mari's mother, was preparing to move into a retirement community. The old rambling house in Fremont held two generations of old furniture and memories, and Mari was spending summer vacation from her school librarian job in Galena helping her mother downsize.

"Fly down for a few days. You need a change of scenery, Havi," his mother said in a FaceTime call. "And we could use a strong back down here."

Beans' Asian sense of filial obligation battled his ambivalent feelings toward his grandfather. Mari's father, Ben Yamane, had been, for no reason that was adequately explained, cold and distant toward Beans and his siblings, and had absolutely detested Beans's father Jimmy. The buttoned-up Sansei accountant had no doubt envisioned a more appropriate match for his youngest daughter than the wild half-Irish, half-Athabascan bush pilot who had won her heart.

In the end, it was Beans's partner, fellow detective Ed Heller, who convinced him to go help his mother. "You're getting a paid vacation. Get your ass out of here."

So, that's what Beans was doing, packing a suitcase for a trip down to the Bay Area to help his grandmother with the heavy lifting for her impending move when his phone rang. "Unknown Caller" showed up on the display, and he was just about to let it go to voicemail when he noticed the 907 area code, which could be his union rep or the shrink he was supposed to see. So he picked it up.

"Hi, is this Detective Beans? Havi, I mean, DeHavilland Beans?" A youthful female voice, calling him by Havi, his childhood nickname.

"Yes, this is Beans. Who's calling, please?"

A familiar laugh. "Havi, Hi! This is Fee—Felicia Gunnerson."

He remembered her now, an image from the past—the skinny younger sister of his buddy Conrad back in Galena, a tiny but undaunted girl, annoying as hell since they seemed to never be able to shake her, dwarfed by the huge bicycle her brother had passed down to her. She was all knees and elbows with large dark eyes that never missed anything.

"Fee! Wow, how long has it been? Everything OK? Conrad OK?" His first thought was that something had happened to his childhood friend, and she was calling to pass on bad news. Being a cop always made him anticipate the worst.

"Conrad's fine. Still in Japan, you know. Still with the Army. Got a couple of kids, a boy and a girl."

"That's great." Beans tossed a pair of socks into the suitcase and watched Archie bat them away, all the while wondering why this young woman from his hometown was calling him.

"He told me you're a detective now, in Anchorage. Hey, the bigtime, huh?"

He decided he wouldn't share with her the details of why he was not an active detective at this particular moment. "Yeah, for a few years now." *Why was she calling?* It wasn't just to catch up.

"I'm in law enforcement too . . . not a detective, like you, but I'm a cop here in Galena."

"Cool, congratulations." He hoped he didn't sound too distracted as he fished the socks out that Archie had shoved under the bed.

"Yeah, well, thanks. I'm calling because there's been a development here that I think—I hope—you can help us with."

"What's happened, Fee? Your folks?"

"Dad died a couple of years ago—a sudden heart attack. I still miss him." She sighed. "Mom's still kicking though. No, it's not that." She paused, and Beans could hear the rustle of paper. "Remember, a few years back, after that ice jam down near Bishop Rock caused all that flooding?"

"Sure, I heard about it. Caused quite a bit of damage, even in New Town."

"Yeah, and that weird little inlet opened up downstream?"

"Right, I remember."

"And remember how spring melt was really high this year?"

"I guess." *Where was she going with this?* She hadn't called to give him a tide report.

"And then, once things dried out a little, there was a nice new little landing there at that inlet."

"OK." Beans brought the phone into the bathroom and started packing toiletries. It felt like old times, Fee following him around, telling long drawn-out stories.

"So, this morning Fish and Wildlife guys were out there on the landing, pulling out their skiffs. And you wouldn't guess what they found."

"Driftwood?"

Fee laughed, and he flashed again on the gangly girl with the scraped knees and the huge grin. "Havi! Still a funny guy!" She lowered her voice. "No, listen. They found an artificial leg, Havi. A prosthetic lower left leg, in a Nike shoe."

Beans felt like the air had been sucked out of the room. He stood, then sat down suddenly on the toilet. "Shit, You're kidding."

"Not kidding. No way. Now, who do we know—the only person we know—with a prosthetic left leg, Havi?"

"Shit." He leaned back against the toilet tank.

"No shit."

"Lloyd Paul. Fuck."

"Lloyd Fucking Paul. Roger that."

Lloyd was the son of the Yukon Commercial store proprietor Victor Paul, and a member of a large and influential family in town. Not much happened in Galena or any of the other surrounding villages without somebody in the Paul family knowing about it. Decades ago, when Lloyd was a teenager, he had lost the lower part of his left leg in a snowmachine accident and had been fitted with a transtibial prosthetic device, state of the art at the time.

Nothing too good for Victor's kid. "Have you told the family yet?"

"Not yet. I'm taking a skiff down to pick it up this afternoon. Gotta preserve the chain of custody and all that. But I could wait."

"Wait? Why? You don't want it sitting out in the elements longer than it has to."

"Shit, Havi, if it's Lloyd's, which I'm sure it is, it's been sitting either in the river or on the beach for almost twenty years. A day or two isn't going to mess it up too bad." She paused. "But anyway, I'm thinking I could run down and get it, see if there are more of Lloydie's remains around. But I could wait to see Victor until you get here?" Her voice rose in a hopeful lilt.

"Me? There?" Beans sat up suddenly. He was supposed to be on a flight to the Bay Area tomorrow morning.

"Yeah, you. You got nothing else going on, right?"

"I have a job, Fee." He realized that at the moment, he didn't, but how would she know this?

"No, you don't. Not right now. Not according to your sister, anyway."

"Goddamn Piper," he groaned. He had forgotten that Fee had been in Girl Scouts with his sister. "But I'm supposed to be going to California to help my grandmother with her move."

"You can go later." Fee lowered her voice. "Havi, you know this is a BFD. Everybody thought Lloyd left town. Everybody thought your mother broke Lloyd's heart—what, eighteen years ago?—and he took a charter flight out of the village."

"Of course. He shipped his skiff and all his stuff out, didn't he? Looked like he was leaving for good."

"Yeah, but he wouldn't have left without his leg."

Beans could hear the clink of a spoon in a mug as she stirred her coffee. Of course she was right. For years, he and pretty much everyone in the village were glad and relieved that Lloyd Paul had pulled up stakes and left. Lloyd's father, Victor, had been driving the snowmachine back when his son had lost his leg, and out of a sense of guilt or regret had coddled and overindulged him ever since. It was a town consensus that Lloyd was pretty much unbearable.

Unfortunately for Beans and his family, it had been hard to avoid Lloyd. Although he was at least ten years younger, he had taken a real shine to their mother, Mari, especially after their father had died crashing his plane. He'd appear at their house, uninvited, with his insulated flask of cranberry juice and Everclear, limping through the door while the change he'd confiscated from his family's coin-op laundromat jingled in his pockets.

"OK, but we need to confirm that this is Lloyd Paul's leg before we go jumping to conclusions. Don't they have some kind of ID numbers?" If he wasn't so stressed about changing his travel plans and the troubling notion that Lloyd would not have left town without his leg, he might have thought using "leg" and "jumping" in the same sentence amusing.

"Right. I'll fire up the skiff and pick it up this afternoon, as long as the weather holds. Piper says she's watching your dog and cat starting tonight, so I'll see you tomorrow. It's Taco Tuesday at the Greek/Mexican/Japanese place."

"Wait, I'm . . ." Beans started, but he knew it was a futile gesture.

"Havi." Fee's voice was suddenly serious. "You owe my family. You owe me."

And he knew she was right.

2

Beans

Summer 2024

Beans normally visited his hometown of Galena, a quiet Alaskan town of about five hundred on the north bank of the Yukon River, at Christmas. In winter, Galena from the air looked like jewels cast upon the snow, the river frozen and pristine, striped only by trails left by snowmachines or dogsleds. Now the river cut a wide serpentine swath across the wild tundra, following a meandering silty path through and around several wildlife refuges to the ocean. The small town of Ruby lay about fifty-two miles upriver, and the even smaller village of Koyukuk, at the confluence of the Koyukuk and the Yukon, lay thirty miles downstream.

Landmarks that were usually blurred by a veil of snow in winter were now vivid—the dike at the airport, the bulk fuel storage site, the New Town development at Alexander Lake. He could pick out a small tug and barge plying its way downriver on one of its seasonal journeys, and a floatplane skimming across the water and taking off. Tendrils of mist hovered and snagged in the pale fingers of new hemlock lining the shore.

Just as she promised, Fee was there to meet him at the airport, the rumbling idle of her pickup truck sending plumes of gray exhaust into the spruce-scented air.

A slim figure in a khaki uniform hopped out of the driver's seat, the familiar broad smile, her hand outstretched. "Detective Beans."

He took her hand in his and shook it, formally. "Officer Gunnerson."

She laughed, then enfolded him in an embrace. "Good to see you, Havi. Thanks for coming."

Did I have a choice? He tossed his bag into the bed of the truck and climbed into the passenger seat.

"So, I Googled him, just to make sure he didn't surface fifteen years ago as the CEO of some Fortune 500 company or something—no mention of Lloyd Paul anywhere. You want to go to the house first, or see what's apparently left of Lloydie?" she asked.

"Let's take a look at the leg."

Beans studied Felicia Gunnerson as she drove. She pointed out a portable addition to the school, the new coffee shop (*shitty coffee, brewed by Victor's granddaughter*), and the new fire truck to replace the ancient one that had mysteriously burst into flames last Fourth of July (*alleged Paul grandchild handiwork*, Fee said, rolling her eyes.) Like her brother, Conrad, she was slender and lanky with dark hair and eyes. Both were gifted athletes, as he recalled, strong and agile on the track field and the basketball court. Fee was pretty in a wholesome way and had matured gracefully, he thought. She wore little or no makeup, as far as he could tell, and had pulled her hair into a gleaming ponytail.

She noticed her watching him, and grimaced into the rear-view mirror. “What, do I have something in my teeth?”

“Nah. I was just wondering if this was the same kid with the SpongeBob Band-Aids on her elbows and the Dreamhouse full of headless Barbies.”

She smiled. “That’s me.”

He smiled back. “Yeah, well, looking good, Gunnerson.”

Before he knew it, they had pulled in front of the Public Safety Building that served as Galena police headquarters, among other municipal functions. Fee led the way into her office, where on a credenza against the window lay a large metal tray covered with a sheet.

“I borrowed a brownie pan from the school cafeteria,” she explained, as she pulled off the sheet. The prosthetic leg on the metal tray lacked any flesh-like covering and looked to Beans like part of a sad, defective robot wearing a faded black-and-white waterlogged Nike. The plastic receptacle portion of the socket, the part that would cup around the end of an amputated left leg had broken off, probably long ago, leaving what he thought were the dulled aluminum and fiberglass components miraculously clinging together like the wreckage of a small plane.

“Jesus.” Beans pulled on latex gloves and poked at the shoe. He had seen several dead bodies in his career, but this inanimate appendage for some reason rattled him more than any other. “Any other remains at the site?”

“Not a single bone. Anything organic would have been long gone, I think.”

Beans loosened the frayed laces and gently tugged on the Nike. The narrow foot attachment that he assumed was fiberglass or some other composite material, slid out, along with mud and silt from the river bottom. "All that mud probably held the foot in the shoe," he said. "We'd better bag it in case we need it to help ID Lloyd."

Fee stared at him. "Seriously? Who else could it be, Havi?"

Beans wagged the shoe at her. "Never assume. It makes an ass—"

"Out of you and me. God, did you have Mr. Pervert for Science too?"

"Purvis. And yes, I did." He sealed an evidence bag around the shoe. "I seem to remember that we'd lose a hunter or fisherman upriver every year. Could be a tourist."

"With an artificial leg? That just happens to be a left leg?" Fee held her hands up in surrender. "OK, OK. We'll have Victor look at all the moving pieces."

"I think prosthetic limbs are assigned identification numbers. Hopefully, we can get the manufacturer and some kind of barcode or serial number off the leg." It suddenly occurred to him that in all the times he'd run into Lloyd Paul in life, he'd never actually seen his prosthetic leg.

"I'll look for it. Still need to process it anyway. I know, it's kind of worthless for evidence extraction, but protocol, you know."

They agreed that it would be cruel, even considering it was Victor Paul, to burden him with the discovery this late in the day that they'd located an old prosthetic leg that might belong to his long-absent son. "Let's torture him in the morning," Fee said.

She dropped him in front of Mari's bungalow, promising to pick him up the next morning and take him to "the new shitty coffee place."

"Can't wait," he said, and waved at her. She had offered to take him for pizza at the "not so shitty pizza place" or Taco Tuesday at the Greek/Mexican/Japanese place, but he'd declined. Tonight, he preferred to fix a bowl of instant ramen he knew Mari kept around the house, then crawl into the lower half of the bunk bed he had shared with his little brother, Otter, when they were kids.

Ever since he could remember, his mother kept a spare key hidden under the cement guidepost near the front door. The living room was dark and cool, and smelled faintly of ginger and garlic. He turned on a few lights, and his childhood home sprang into focus.

The three-bedroom bungalow was achingly familiar. The old woodstove had been replaced with an oil-burning one after the last flood, but just about everything else was exactly as he remembered it. The leather sofa, scored and scratched by his dog Muktuk's claws. The faded plaid La-Z-Boy recliner that Jimmy Beans had acquired from floatplane passengers he had flown out just before a blizzard, a young teacher and his wife bugging out before the end of their contract. A glass case containing a Japanese porcelain doll in Girls Day attire, a strangely inappropriate gift given to tomboy Piper by her maternal grandparents. The ancient roll-top desk that slumped against the wall near the door, its surface scarred from endless rings of keys that had been flung there. The even older upright piano that no one had played since his oldest brother, Lindbergh, died—partly because only Lindbergh had ever had lessons, but mostly because it hid one of Jimmy Beans's treasured secrets, revealed the night Lloyd Paul disappeared.

While he waited for the water to boil for his ramen, his eyes drifted to the photographs hanging on the far wall. A time-bleached photo with his parents, Jimmy and Mari, and their young family—Lindbergh, the eldest, a gangly teenager; Hercules, a twelve-year-old with a shock of curly dark hair; young DeHavilland, holding the collar of a huge Malamute mix with a lolling tongue; round-faced Piper, looking like a tiny ivory carving, her pale face peering out of her muskrat collar; and the infant Otter, bundled in his mother's arms. All of them except the eldest named after airplanes.

Another photo of Jimmy, smiling and handsome, and Mari, fresh-faced and radiant, on their wedding day. Another of Jimmy beside his beloved DeHavilland Beaver floatplane, years before he and his plane would die together in a fiery crash. Beans swung the photo to the right, and there it was. The bullet hole, patched with sheetrock mud and painted over but still noticeable, that Beans had made with his father's Colt revolver the night he shot Lloyd Paul.

3

Beans

May 2007

Beans was sixteen the night it happened. It was unseasonably warm for May, the week before Mother's Day. That year, breakup was early, with the river thawed and swollen, occasional chunks of upriver ice breaking free and swirling by. He had worked up a sweat playing basketball at the gym with some of his teammates. He was very proud of his blue and gold Galena Hawks jersey and wore it every chance he got, which was probably way too often. Even Beans had to admit the jersey could use some laundering, and he rolled down the window of the old pickup to improve the air quality.

He parked the truck in front of the house and whistling, dribbled his basketball through the front door and tossed his keys on the battered rolltop desk.

He heard him before he saw him—the telltale jingle of change from his family's laundromat in his pockets, the annoying signature soundtrack of Lloyd Paul. Ever since the death of Beans's father two years ago, and maybe even before that, Lloyd Paul had shown what Beans thought was an unnatural interest in his mother, Mari. *Especially since she was quite a bit older than he was.* Lloyd was scrawny and small, not much taller than Mari, his shrewd brown eyes glinting from behind his bowl-cut bangs. This evening, he moved around the living room, pockets jangling, waving his Stanley thermos full of what Beans knew was a mixture of fruit juice and Everclear.

"Just say the word, Mari. I've loaded everything up—the truck, the skiff—the first barge'll take them out of here, but I'll be gone long before that."

A wave of relief washed over Beans. *Lloyd is leaving. He'll leave Mom alone.*

Mari, her arms crossed over her chest, leaned against the kitchen counter and murmured something Beans thought sounded like, "No, Lloyd, I'm staying here." Or maybe it was, "*No way*, Lloyd. I'm staying here." Beans could sense Mari inwardly cringe when Lloyd went near her, but she was careful not to show it. Lloyd Paul's family practically ran the village, and they were quick to let their displeasure be known. Lloyd's Uncle Carlton was the school principal and Mari's boss, and God knows she needed her librarian job.

Lloyd jingled and thumped over to Mari and raised a hand to her cheek. She backed away, pretending to check on the rice cooker that bubbled on the countertop. "Havi, go and wash up. Dinner will be ready soon."

Beans cast a sideways glance at Lloyd. "Where's Muktuk? Where are Piper and Otter?" His little sister and brother were eleven and seven, respectively, and didn't need to be subject to the drunken antics of Lloyd Paul.

"At Grandma's tonight. Muktuk too."

How did Lloyd know when his younger siblings would be away? Beans wondered. And their dog, Muktuk too, who could be very protective of Mari. Lloyd obviously hadn't planned on Beans being there, though.

"Jesus, you stink, Havi." Lloyd wrinkled his nose.

"So do you, ass—" Beans started to say.

"Havi!" Mari warned.

Seething, he retrieved the basketball from a corner of the living room and went to the bathroom to wash his hands and face. He stared at his reflection, and his mother's piercing eyes in his father's lightly freckled face stared back. From the living room, he heard his mother's muffled, "Lloyd, no!"

The bathroom door slammed behind Beans as he ran out. Lloyd had pinned Mari between himself and the counter, while she struggled to push him away.

"Hey!" Beans grabbed him by the shoulder and wrenched him off his mother. Beans was taller and outweighed the scrawny Lloyd by a good twenty pounds, but the man was ten years older and spry for a guy with an artificial leg. Quicker than Beans thought possible, Lloyd took a swipe at him, and a ripping noise tore through the room. Something tugged at his chest and he looked down. A long gash had opened on his favorite jersey, and under that, a gaping wound in his skin that stretched across his chest in a forty-five-degree angle. For a moment, Beans was stunned, frozen in place, not yet feeling any pain, not even feeling the blood that began to trickle down his chest.

Suddenly, Mari was there with the big yellow Grainger industrial flashlight, the one they kept on the kitchen counter in case of a power outage. She screamed something unintelligible, then hit Lloyd hard on the side of his head with the flashlight, so hard that Beans heard the glass crack. In the next second, Lloyd roared like a wounded bear and swung the Stanley thermos at Mari's face, striking her squarely in the right eye.

Mari made some kind of animal noise that scared even Lloyd. "Oh shit, I didn't mean it, Mari, I'm sorry—" He reached for her, but she pushed away from him, hissing and spitting like a cat.

Beans finally found movement in his feet and sprinted to the old upright piano. He flung open the top of the cabinet and groped deep into the case. Hanging from a wooden peg was Jimmy Beans's old Colt revolver hidden and out of reach of the younger kids. He grabbed it and slammed the top down with a dissonant thud.

He never thought the gun was loaded, nor did he think he would ever pull the trigger. But he held it in both of his trembling hands. "Get the fuck away from her, Lloyd."

Just as Lloyd turned toward him with a sneering "Or what, shithead?"—Beans pulled the trigger. It was a kneejerk reaction, he knew, not at all like the slow methodical squeeze that his father taught him. But Lloyd Paul's proprietary groping of his mother and the purple lump that bloomed on her cheekbone made his hand spasm with anger and frustration. The Colt's shot was deafening in the small house, and its recoil shoved him back into the rolltop desk.

Lloyd shrieked and grabbed his left shoulder, and the jagged-bladed knife that had cut Beans clattered to the floor.

For a moment, Beans was just as shocked as Lloyd, the Colt still trained on him.

Mari broke the silence. "Get out." It was barely above a whisper, then louder, "Get out! Get out!" She shoved at Lloyd, her small face, usually delicate and symmetrical like Piper's glass-encased doll, now broken and purple with rage.

Lloyd stumbled forward, picked up his knife and sheathed it at his waist. He was strangely silent. With just one furtive backward look, he staggered through the door, jingling, dripping blood in his wake.

Beans felt the Colt slip through his fingers and fall to the floor. He was suddenly exhausted, and the gash in his chest throbbed. “I’m sorry, Mom. When he hit you . . . I didn’t know what else . . . I’m sorry.” He was embarrassed to find tears streaming down his cheeks. He brushed them away.

Mari took him by the hand and gave him a crooked smile, the swelling at her eye giving her face a lopsided look. “So brave.” Her face grew serious as she looked at the gash at his chest, now soaking his jersey and dripping down his shorts. “Let’s get you to Doc Gunnerson.”

“But what about Lloyd?”

Mari shrugged and looked away. “Let him find his own doctor.”

Instead of taking him to the clinic in town, Mari drove them to the Gunnersons’ home in the chugging pickup, Beans holding a reddening dishcloth to the wound. Jens and Gloria Gunnerson’s house was only a few minutes away. Beans had ridden his bike down there to see their son, Conrad, so many times he could do it blindfolded.

Mari turned off the ignition and stared straight ahead. “Not a word about shooting Lloyd, OK?”

Beans nodded.

Doc Gunnerson’s house was the second biggest one in Galena, with a large detached garage where the doctor indulged his hobby of restoring antique furniture. The porch light flickered on a few seconds after Mari knocked. The door opened, emitting the warm aroma of some kind of stew, and framing Gloria Gunnerson, the doctor's wife and a teacher's aide at Mari's school. Even the typical stoic expression on Gloria's smooth round face couldn't mask her surprise when she saw the egg-sized bruise growing on Mari's cheek, and the bleeding teenager standing beside her.

"Good evening, Gloria." Mari said, smiling with one side of her face and speaking so pleasantly she might be discussing the weather. "I'm sorry to interrupt your dinner. Is Doc available?"

Gloria stared at the towel at Beans chest, and without changing her expression or moving her head, called out, "Jens. Patient."

Doc Gunnerson, a tall, long-limbed Swede with pastel hair and eyes, led Mari and Beans to the heated garage, where they were surrounded by rolltop desks, dining tables, and chairs that had been stripped for refinishing. Conrad had band practice and wasn't available to assist, Doc explained, so he enlisted the help of his twelve-year-old daughter, Felicia. Awkward and coltish, Fee had voluminous dark eyes that grew even larger when she saw the slash on Beans's chest and the lump on Mari's face.

Doc Gunnerson's watery blue eyes narrowed as they moved from Beans's wound to Mari's swollen eye. "Just hold the light steady, Fee. And remember about doctor/patient confidentiality. It extends to you, too."

Fee nodded, and pantomimed a key-turning-in-a-lock motion at her lips.

"That's a good girl."

Beans suppressed a wail when Doc Gunnerson cut the jersey off him and tossed it to the floor. *His precious jersey, cut to shreds.*

Under the cold blue light from the lantern, Doc Gunnerson methodically cleaned the wound with some kind of stinging antiseptic that made Beans's eyes water. "Not too deep, thankfully." He cast a glance to Mari. "I should report this, you know."

"I'd rather you didn't, Doc," Mari said, as pleasantly as she had addressed Gloria earlier. "I'd be in deep shit."

Beans started, surprised, and Doc Gunnerson paused in his stitching. His mother hated it when they swore, and normally wouldn't say "shit" even if she's had a mouthful of it.

The doctor nodded and gave her a small, kindly smile. "I know." He tied off the stitches then covered the wound with a clean bandage. He unwrapped a syringe and filled it with a clear liquid. He swabbed Beans's upper arm with an alcohol-soaked sterile pad, then poked the syringe into the fleshy part of his arm and pushed the plunger. "This is an antibiotic, but I'll give you some pills to take as well—one pill, four times a day. Take them all, you hear? And come back next Tuesday, and I'll remove the stitches." Beans nodded his thanks, then raised his arms to pull on the clean shirt Mari had brought with them. The stitches felt like tiny sharp teeth holding the wound closed, and he inhaled sharply.

"No basketball until at least a week from Tuesday, you hear? I don't want you ripping out my handiwork."

Doc tilted Mari's head toward the lantern light. He sighed, shaking his head. "Lucky it missed the eye, but could have broken that orbital bone, Mari."

Beans watched Fee's face, pale in the light from the lantern. The young girl looked as if she were about to cry. Mari was the school librarian, much beloved and respected by the students.

Mari noticed Fee's despair and smiled, even though Beans knew it must hurt for her to do it. "Just an accident, Fee. I'll be fine. You'll see me in the library Monday."

"I could ask you to come down to the clinic for X-rays." The doctor rummaged through his bag for a few foil-wrapped packets of sample pills. "These are a little stronger than Tylenol."

Mari shoved the pills into her pocket. "No X-rays, Doc. I'll ice. I know the drill." She held out her hand. "Thanks again. Send me a bill."

"I can do more than that, Mari. We can file a report with Arvid—"

"No." Mari's voice was firm. "No police. I'll take care of it."

Beans and his mother left Doc Gunnerson's cluttered garage. Mari was about to help him into the cab of the pickup when Beans remembered something. He loped back to the garage, as quickly as his stitches would let him, and retrieved the ripped blood-stained jersey from the floor. He wadded it up and stuffed it into his waistband.

As they drove away, the pickup's headlights swept across the Gunnersons' front yard and caught the small face and fawnlike eyes of Fee Gunnerson, still holding the lantern against the dying light.

4

Beans

Summer 2024

Fee Gunnerson was at his door the next morning in her crisp khaki uniform.

"Rise and shine, Havi. Come on, I'll buy you a shitty coffee at Victor's grandkid's place."

They drove the few blocks to a small strip mall that housed the post office, the washeteria, also owned by the Paul family, and the small coffee shop "Charbucks." The signage above the coffee shop's door was in the same blocky, sans serif typeface, with an almost identical green and white insignia used by Starbucks.

Fee rolled her eyes. "Charlene thought she was being *so* clever with the name. Still, if Grandpa owns the building and finances the operation, I guess you feel you can name it anything you want. And I don't imagine Starbucks's legal team has been up here lately."

A heavyset young woman with a pale doughy face and a halo of frizzy hair stood behind a hazy glass case housing tired-looking pastries with hand-written *sugar-free!* labels emerging from them like tiny tombstones. She nodded, but didn't smile as they entered the shop.

"'Morning, Fee. Haven't seen you in a while."

"Hi, Char. Got me a new Nespresso, you know, and it works great. But you can make me a soy latte. What'll you have, Havi?"

Charlene Mangold's small eyes, set deep in her face like currants in soda bread, blinked in recognition. "Havi? Mari's son? From Anchorage?"

"Yup, the middle one. Nice to see you, Char. It's been a while."

Char studied his face. "Your mom flew out a few days ago, didn't she? Down to California or some such?"

Beans wasn't surprised that in a town this size, everyone knew everyone else's business. But she left out the obvious question, *So what are you doing here, then?*

"That's right. Just an Americano for me, Char."

Fee insisted on paying for their drinks and got them to go. As she took her first sips of coffee, Beans noticed she barely suppressed a wince. "So, is your grandpa in town?" she asked.

"Yeah, got back yesterday." Char's shrewd eyes glanced from Fee to Beans.

"OK then. See you, Char."

As soon as she was out of sight of Charbucks, Fee opened her door and dumped the coffee from her cardboard cup into the dusty road. "Jesus, that's shitty coffee."

Beans tasted his. It was harsh and bitter, and he had to fight the urge to spit it back into the cup. "So if the coffee's so bad, why did we go there?"

She threw the empty cup on the floorboard at her feet and put the truck in gear. "Just to show you the efficiency of the Paul family's messaging network. I guarantee you by the time we get to the YC store, Victor will be waiting for us."

Sure enough, by the time they drove the three blocks to the Yukon Commercial store, Victor stood just inside, pretending to wipe smudges off the glass doors, fixing them in his glare.

Fee unbuckled her seat belt, smirking. "Faster than fiberoptics."

Not much had changed from the Yukon Commercial store Beans had known as a child. The store sold everything from wilted vegetables ("flown in fresh that day") to frozen meat to old Easter candy to propane to Carhartts, XtraTuf boots, mosquito punk, and condoms. The bell on the door jangled as Victor held it open for Beans and Fee.

Victor Paul was a big man, thick-set with meat-hook hands and a disproportionately large head. With his thick grizzled hair and belligerent glare, he almost looked like a buffalo about to charge. He stared at Beans first, then at Fee with eyes as hard as river rock. "Char said you were asking about me."

"Yeah, right, if you have a minute. You know Havi Beans, of course?" She nodded to Beans.

Victor squinted. "Sure. Mari's boy."

Beans extended his hand and after a second, it was engulfed in Victor's huge, dry one. "Nice to see you again, Victor."

Victor squeezed his hand harder than Beans thought necessary. "Yeah, Havi. You and your brothers, always sniffing around the candy—"

"Is there someplace we can talk, Victor?" Fee broke in. "Somewhere private?"

Victor turned his squint to Fee. "Why?"

"Because . . ." Fee hesitated. "You might not want the whole town to hear what we have to say."

Somewhere at the back of the store, a door slammed, and a woman's voice called, "Dad! Junior got called in, so you'll need to unload the propane yourself or wait until he gets back."

The woman who pushed a hand truck loaded with boxes of Brawny paper towels seemed like a taller, older version of Charlene, who ran Charbucks. Although it had been a few years and he guessed about twenty extra pounds on her part, Beans had no trouble recognizing Victor's daughter, Janelle Mangold.

Janelle blew a curly brown fringe of bangs from her forehead. "Hi Fee. And—Havi?" Her round face broke into a smile that made her almost pretty. "Lordy, it's been a while."

Beans smiled back. Unlike Lloyd and their father, Janelle had always been pleasant to his family. "No kidding. Hi, Janelle. How are you and Junior doing?"

Janelle snorted. "Look at me, fat and happy. Junior's fine, complaining as always."

Beans chuckled. "He still pumping fuel, then?"

"Pisses and moans, but I can't get him to do anything else." She set the hand truck against the ice cream freezer. "What brings you here from the big city in the summer? Can't be for the fishing." The much sought-after Yukon River King salmon had all but disappeared, and fishing for the prized catch had been prohibited for the last few years.

Fee cleared her throat. "We actually came to talk to your dad, Janelle, but you may as well hear what we have to say too. Can we go back to the office for a sec?"

"I gotta have somebody cover the store, or they'll be robbing me blind." Victor growled. "There's nobody here now. We can talk right here. Lock the door, Janelle."

Her brow furrowed with concern, Janelle locked the front doors. She turned back toward Fee and Beans. "What's this about?"

Fee took a deep breath. "A couple of days ago, hunters found something washed up on the beach at that inlet downriver. It was a leg—"

"A what?" Victor interrupted. "What does this have to do with—"

"A leg. An *artificial* leg." Fee raised her voice to be heard, and Victor was suddenly silent. "The prosthetic leg was wearing a black and white Nike, a left shoe. We're checking out the serial number with the manufacturer." She sighed. "But we are concerned that it could have belonged to your son, Lloyd."

Janelle gasped and brought her hands to her mouth. "Oh my Jesus."

Victor seemed to grow pale. "How can it—he left, almost twenty years ago. Shipped his truck, his skiff! Got the first barge upriver! Flew out with some charter!"

"Did you ever hear from him, Victor? Did you ever find out who he flew out with?" Beans asked.

"Well, no! He was going to travel, then take some hotshot job, he said. Took all of his money—"

"And a lot of yours, too," Janelle said under her breath.

"You shut up, girl!" Victor's great bulk seemed to shift toward Janelle, and for a moment, Beans thought he was going to strike her. He stepped between daughter and father.

"So he took his money, right?" Fee asked. "He said he was leaving town, never coming back. But you never heard from him again?"

Janelle shook her head. Fat tears rolled down her cheeks.

Victor began pacing up and down the aisle. "That policeman at the time, Arvid Straight—"

"Streeter," Fee corrected.

"What a worthless shit. I filed a missing person report with him, a lot of good it did me. He said he asked around and never found out who Lloydie flew out with. But he never tried hard enough. Drank like a fish."

"The Parkinson's was taking him, Dad," Janelle said.

"He was a drunk," Victor said bitterly.

"Did you ever wonder why Lloyd never tried to contact you?" Beans asked Janelle.

She sniffed, and her gaze darted between Beans and Victor. "He gave his cell phone to Junior before he left. He was on Dad's contract anyway. Lloydie said he'd be getting a newer, fancier one. But he never called. From any phone." She took a deep breath. "He cleaned out the washeteria machines, and the till from the store, and then some . . ."

Victor closed his eyes and turned his face toward the ceiling. "That was owed him, you stupid girl." His voice was quiet, seeming to barely contain his disdain.

"So if he didn't steal that money, Dad, why did he never call or visit? Why did he disappear?" Janelle wiped her cheeks on the back of her hand. "Why didn't he come back when Mom died?"

Victor swatted at his ear, as if Janelle's voice was an annoying mosquito whining at the side of his head. "So, how can you be sure this is my boy's leg?"

Fee stared at him, and in an eerie echo of her statement to Beans, said, "Who else do you know in the Middle Yukon with a prosthetic left leg?"

"Could be a hunter, or a goddamn ecotourist, for all we know. Could have come from upriver."

"This leg's been around a long time, from what we can tell. About as long as Lloyd's been out of touch," Beans said.

"No!" Victor pounded on the glass-topped counter with his fist and the cabinet shuddered. "Where's his head? How can you do a positive ID"—he thumped on the counter with each word—"like they say on those cop shows, without his head?"

Beans thought Fee used remarkable restraint, but she had a far less volatile history with the Paul family than he did. She put her hands in her back pockets, adopting a conversational pose. "Meaning no disrespect, Victor, but it's been, what—going on eighteen years? Hell, if it's still in one piece, Lloydie's head could be all the way down to Alakanuk by now."

Janelle pulled a paper towel from a roll on the counter and blew her nose. Victor chose that moment to fix his attention on Beans.

"And you? Why are you here?"

"Detective Beans is on loan from Anchorage PD," Fee answered without hesitation. "He has lots of experience with cold cases."

"Yeah, and his mother has lots of experience with Lloydie," Victor muttered.

Beans had expected that Victor would bait him, and he didn't rise to it. "Yeah, Lloyd was over a lot in the old days."

Victor snorted a laugh. "Might have been the last folks to see him alive."

"He certainly was alive the last time I saw him. All excited about leaving town, doing some traveling." Beans grabbed a pack of sugar-free gum from a rack and placed cash on the counter. "I think that'll cover it."

The big man snorted again, opened the register and handed Beans a few coins. "Now, there's a change. The Beans kids don't usually bother paying."

Beans jammed the gum and change in his pocket, trying to keep a benevolent smile on his face. "Now, Victor, Lindbergh and Herc paid you back, with interest." He had to admit that his older brothers had been petty shoplifters, especially when it came to candy. Mari had been livid when she found out about the stolen Milky Ways and made them apologize and pay the shopkeeper back from their allowances.

Victor waved him off. "Ah, they weren't the only ones. Everyone's trying to rob me blind, I tell you."

He was the only one in town, Beans knew, who refused to believe that it was his own son Lloyd who was doing the robbing. Small and delicately built like his mother, a passenger on the snow machine driven by his father in the accident that had cost him his leg, Lloyd had soaked up Victor's affection and guilt for most of his life.

Half-grunting and half-sighing, Victor pulled a ring of keys from behind the counter. "So, where's this leg?"

5

Beans

Summer 2024

When Fee removed the frayed towel that covered the remains of the prosthetic leg, all the bluster seemed to go out of Victor Paul, and he seemed to shrink to two-thirds his size, a scale model of himself. He reached out to touch it, then changed his mind, balling his hand into a fist and lowering it to his side.

Surrounded by the dented, gray file cabinets and the fake veneer of the battered credenza, lying on a scratched rimmed baking sheet the cafeteria ladies used to make brownies and pizza on Fridays, the broken Transformers-like leg and the waterlogged Nike seemed even sadder than before, like leftover pieces from a do-it-yourself project gone wrong.

Janelle broke the silence with a loud sob. "He's dead, Dad."

Victor used his balled-up fist to swipe at his forehead, like somehow that would help him understand. "It looks like his leg, and he had shoes like that—but how can it be? He's traveling, right? Touring Europe or South America or wherever. Or working at that fat-cat job."

Fee's voice was quiet, kind. "I'm tracking down the manufacturer of the prosthesis now—if you know the name of the doctor or clinic that fitted him with it, it would help. I can only make out part of a serial number, but I'm hoping that's all they'll need."

Janelle's face was streaked with tears. "He's dead, Dad. He must've gotten drunk and fallen in the river."

Victor shook his head in disgust and renewed anger, and pointed an index finger at his daughter. "Don't be stupid, girl! Your brother was a gimp, but he was a sure-footed gimp. No, I won't believe he's dead. Not until you show me his head."

Beans was starting to feel sorry for Victor. "After all these years, there wouldn't be much of anything left of him, Victor. The leg has survived because it's made of composite materials."

Victor turned and shook his finger at Beans now. "You listen to me, Havi. Lloydie had crappy teeth. He went to Fairbanks to get implants. Those would show up in his skull, right? We need to find the skull. Find me his skull!" Victor stormed out of Fee's office.

Janelle swiped her blotchy face with the back of her hand. She shook her head, staring wistfully at the wreckage of the prosthetic leg. "It's like he doesn't want to admit that Lloyd's dead, but he doesn't want to admit that he's alive either and never contacted us. I don't know which would hurt him more."

"Janelle! You gonna walk back or not?" Victor's voice boomed from the parking lot.

"Coming, Dad." She gave them a sad smile and left.

* * *

For the duration of his consulting gig in Galena, Fee told Beans, he could work out of the spare desk in the Public Safety Building, just opposite hers. The City of Galena was budgeted for two full-time officers, but were usually half-staffed, like now. It was hard to keep people in the village, she said.

"Sure you don't want to apply, Havi? It'll be like old times." Fee gave him a wide grin.

Beans shot a rubber band across the room at her, which she caught deftly with her left hand. "Nah, not me," he said. "Too many Pauls in town."

After he dusted the gray metal desk, supplied it with pens and pads of paper and logged onto the server, he grabbed his coat and asked, "Where's a guy go for lunch in this town?"

Fee's eyes danced. "I know just the place."

* * *

One of Fee's classmates, Andreas Kobayashi, had just opened up a Greek/Mexican/Japanese restaurant, a short, dusty walk from the Public Safety Building. Andreas, being Greek, Mexican, and Japanese himself, served a diverse fusion of ethnic cuisines, Fee told him—her favorite being the spicy miso pulled moose tacos.

They had missed "the lunch rush," as Andreas called it. They were the only two patrons in the small restaurant and took a table near the back. Friendly, bearded Andreas took their orders, while his husband Geno, a handsome Latino, called out greetings as he fired up the grill.

These tacos—his grouse, hers moose—really were spicy and excellent—grilled, marinated meat topped with jalapenos, cabbage, pickled vegetables and cilantro. One bite and Beans knew he would be frequenting Andreas K's more than once, maybe every day, maybe several times a day, while he was in Galena.

Fee squeezed lime on her tacos and asked about Piper and Beans's brothers. Beans asked about her brother, Conrad, and said he wanted to stop by and say hello to her mother, Gloria.

Fee took a bite of taco and chewed thoughtfully. "I was what, twelve, when you and your mom came by that night?"

Beans stopped, midchew, and nodded.

"That was the first time I saw that much blood, Havi. Sorry, I know it's not the best mealtime conversation. But I was scared you were going to bleed to death."

"Ah, Fee, come on. Even your dad said it wasn't very deep." Beans brushed her off, but he was suddenly uneasy. He knew this would come up at some point, but hadn't expected it so soon.

Fee swallowed hard and fixed him in her gaze. "I have to know, Havi. That night you came to the house—that last night—what happened?"

He set down his taco and wiped his hands on a paper napkin. He took a drink of Diet Coke and said, "Just like I told Arvid when he came around asking about Lloyd. Lloyd came after my mother. You know what he was like around her, especially after my dad . . . Anyway, Lloyd was drunk, going on and on about how he was leaving town and wanted my mom to go with him. I pulled him off her, and he slashed me with his hunting knife." *How many times had he told this story? How many times leaving out the part about the gun?* "I didn't even know he'd done it at first—just heard my jersey ripping. Then my mom got the big flashlight and whacked him on the side of the head. He hit her on the face with his thermos. He was stunned, I guess, and staggered out of the house, and that's the last time I saw him. Probably the last time anybody saw him."

Fee's eyes searched his face. She lowered her voice and kindly, as if speaking to a child, asked, "Did you kill him, Havi? I mean, I wouldn't blame if you did, after . . ." she pointed to Beans's chest. "It would have been self-defense. But I need to know."

He looked into the dark pools of her eyes. "I didn't kill him, Fee."

She nodded, an odd, expressionless look crossing her face, and in that moment, she looked a lot like her mother, Gloria. "I hope not." She picked up her taco and took another bite.

* * *

The long summer days made it possible for Beans to take a leisurely run after Fee dropped him off at the house that evening and be back with sunlight still glinting on the river. The breeze off the water kept the bugs down, and he enjoyed revisiting the school, library, and pool, and even waved at Victor (who pretended not to see him) as he ran by the YC Store. He jogged by the ditch where his eldest brother, Lindbergh, had rolled the family truck with Beans inside so long ago. He still had a recurring nightmare of hanging upside down, tethered by his seatbelt, while smoke from the fire under the hood filled the cabin and Lindbergh staggered off.

Beans jogged on, past the berm where they had found Lindbergh's body after spring breakup. These memories were vivid only in his dreams, and otherwise were like sepia photographs from another time. Running through the quiet evening, the cool air off the river refreshed him, and he returned to the house in better spirits than he had been since Willis' shooting.

Like most of their neighbors, they didn't lock their front doors, so he hadn't bothered taking a key. Whistling through his teeth, he checked emails on his phone as he ambled through the door and toward the bathroom for a long shower. The warm water made him sleepy, and he collapsed on the lower mattress of the bunk bed he had shared with his little brother Otter.

By the time he jolted awake it was dark. Yawning and scratching his still-damp head, he clicked on the light in the bedroom only to find that it didn't come on. None of the lights came on throughout the house.

"Goddamn it." This neighborhood was prone to power outages, so this wasn't an unusual occurrence. Using the flashlight app on his phone, he rummaged around in a closet until he found the yellow Grainger industrial lantern with the cracked glass, the same one Mari had used to clock Lloyd Paul all those many years ago. And it still worked. Not even the tensile strength of Lloyd Paul's missing skull could defeat the Mighty Grainger Industrial Lantern. Chuckling to himself, he switched it on and off as he moved into the kitchen.

Suddenly, the flashlight's beam caught something blindingly white on the kitchen counter. It surprised him at first, and the light caromed crazily across the ceiling. He brought the beam to rest on four white eggs in a torn-off section of cardboard egg carton, sitting just to the right of the sink.

6

Beans

May 2007

Beans jolted awake from the dream he had often, hanging upside down in Lindbergh's flaming truck. His sheets were twisted in a sticky wad around his waist and the wound on his chest throbbed. The local anesthesia Doc Gunnerson had administered had worn off and the pain seemed to roar back. He untangled the swaddled sheets and stumbled to the bathroom, looking for aspirin or Tylenol. In the harsh light above the medicine cabinet, he studied the gauze taped to his chest, now dotted with blood.

Now what? He was sure that any minute, Arvid Streeter would be knocking at the door, charging him with assault or attempted murder or something. The only reason he wasn't already here to make an arrest was probably because Lloyd couldn't awaken Arvid from his alcoholic stupor.

He rubbed his palm against the faint stubble on his cheeks. He was actually proud of this stubble, having shaved for the first time a few weeks ago. He knew it was unlikely that he would ever have a full beard—Japanese and Athabascan men were not known for a lot of facial hair, though he was still holding out for his one-quarter Irish side. But he'd be happy with an unkempt, scruffy goatee and mustache. *Yeah, like Mark Wahlberg—but I'd have to work on my pecs.* He smiled at the thought, and his almost-hazel eyes crinkled at the corners.

There was nothing in the medicine cabinet except his shaving gear, toothbrushes, toothpaste, mouthwash, and some of Piper's fruit-flavored lip gloss. He knew that his mother had a supply of Tylenol in her bathroom, and shuffled down the hall toward her room. Her door was ajar, so he pushed it open quietly, not wanting to wake her.

A shaft of moonlight beamed through her window onto the neatly made bed. Mari wasn't in the bathroom either. Beans felt a funny feeling in the pit of his stomach, like falling. He hobbled into the kitchen, feeling the stitches pull at his chest. Empty, counters clean, just the hum of the refrigerator.

The living room was unoccupied, and it was obvious that while he was sleeping, Mari had cleaned the blood off the vinyl flooring. Holding his chest, Beans threw open the front door.

The pickup truck was gone, the empty driveway bathed in moonlight. He had slept so soundly that he hadn't heard the familiar roar of the old Dodge starting up and rumbling down the road.

The Colt. He lifted the lid of the upright piano and reached into it, feeling for the gun among the tuning pins. His groping fingers found only the wooden peg it had hung from. *No Colt.* "Oh, shit." One hand under the keyboard and one gripping the case body behind the piano, he shook it, listening for the thunk of a gun dropping somewhere in the case. He winced as he thought he felt a stitch pop, and he clutched his chest, catching his breath.

He shuffled back to Mari's bathroom and looked through her nightstand and her drawers. The gun was gone.

He downed two Tylenol with a glass of milk and crawled into bed. He tossed in the clammy sheets for he didn't know how long, his head spinning with possible disaster scenarios involving his mother, until he finally drifted off to sleep. *I'll take care of it, she had said.*

Morning seemed to arrive only few minutes later. He groaned and rubbed at his eyes, sticky with sleep. He could hear the local NPR radio station on low, and Mari humming softly in the kitchen. The smell of bacon made his mouth water. Without stopping to brush his teeth, he marched into the kitchen and demanded, "Where were you last night?"

Mari's eye was ugly and purple this morning, but she smiled with one half of her face. "And good morning to you, too."

Beans collapsed in a kitchen chair and ran a hand through his thick dark hair. "Where did you go, Mom? I woke up and you were gone."

Mari looked at his spotty bandage and frowned. "I might need to change your dressing—"

"Where did you go, Mom?" he demanded.

Mari set a half dozen slices of bread on the counter. "Your grandma called. She said that Otter needed his inhaler, and she couldn't find it with his things. So I just ran it over there." Her voice was matter-of-fact.

"I didn't hear you leave."

"I looked in on you. You were dead to the world. I just let you sleep."

"You could have left a note."

"Sure, I could have, but Otter was having trouble breathing, right? I didn't want to take the time to compose something." Her voice dripped with sarcasm as her one eye glared at him.

"Yeah, OK. Sorry," Beans muttered.

"And I was coming right back, Havi." She put a frying pan on the stove to heat. "Little Fee was already here this morning."

"Fee? Why?"

"Gloria had her bring us a few eggs." She gestured to the counter at the four eggs nestled in a torn-off section of egg carton. "She said there'll be more where those came from, but the hens are just getting settled. French toast?"

Beans couldn't believe that Mari was so calm this morning, not after what had happened the night before.

"Mom, aren't you worried? Don't you think Lloyd might call the cops on us? On me?"

"Put a shirt on before breakfast, please. And really, you could use a shower." She wrinkled her nose. "Not sure how we can work around the bandage, though." She broke a few eggs into a bowl and beat them with a fork.

"Mom! Seriously? You're worried that I stink?" He stared at her in disbelief.

Mari set the bowl down with a loud thump. "If Lloyd was going to call Arvid, he'd have done it by now. And look at us!" She jabbed a finger at her eye and his chest. "I dare him to come after us, after what he's done to me and my son. I dare the little bastard!"

Beans and his siblings had been on the receiving end of Mari's temper often enough, but it was generally slow to reach boiling point. She was as angry as he'd ever seen her now, her lips pursed, her face fierce and discolored like an ogre from a Japanese fairy tale. He thought it best to let her subside to a simmer and went into his room to put on a shirt.

By the time he returned to the kitchen table, Mari seemed to have calmed down, dipping slices of bread in the egg/milk mixture. "How many do you want, Havi?"

"Three, no, four. Please." He brought forks and knives to the table, and went to the refrigerator for maple syrup and jam.

Smelling the French toast and the bacon reminded Beans that he hadn't eaten since a microwaved Hot Pocket the previous afternoon, and he was starving. He poured on a healthy dollop of maple syrup, while Mari set a paper napkin on her lap.

"Havi?"

He looked up, his mouth full of French toast.

"If anyone asks, and they will—here's what we'll tell them. It'll be the truth, but with some parts left out. Lloyd came over, drunk. He attacked me, you defended me, and he stabbed you. I hit him with the flashlight to defend you, and he hit me back reflexively with the thermos. There was no gun, OK?"

Beans nodded and wolfed down a piece of bacon. He swallowed hard, then asked, "Mom? Where is the gun?"

She gave him a quick glance then said, "Pass the syrup, please."

"OK, we don't have to talk about it anymore, but I need to know—where's the gun?"

She sighed. "It's gone. Just leave it at that."

* * *

Ironically, it was the day before Mother's Day. The Beans family was going to have a smaller than usual celebration, with just Mari, Beans, Piper, Otter, and their paternal grandmother, Daisy. His older brother Hercules was fishing Copper River salmon this year and sent his mother his regrets, along with a generous Alaska Airlines gift card.

Beans realized, at the last minute, that dinner preparations for the Mother's Day celebration would fall on him, with help from his eleven-year-old sister, Piper. The store in town with the largest selection of grocery items was, unfortunately, Yukon Commercial, where there was a good chance he would run into Lloyd Paul.

Kicking himself for procrastinating, he drove down to YC, Piper beside him on the passenger seat, studiously reviewing their shopping list from behind her dark-framed glasses. He pulled in the last parking spot in front of the store and turned to his sister.

"Do me a favor, Piper?"

Piper looked at him askance. "It'll cost you."

Being the family's only girl had taught Piper at an early age to be suspicious of any possible "deals" made with her brothers.

"This is an easy one. Go into the store first and see if Lloyd is there. If he is, just get back in the truck. If he's not, give me a thumbs-up."

She wrinkled her freckled nose, and tossed back her long black hair. She didn't like Lloyd any more than anybody else in the family did. She got out of the car and leaned in before closing the door. "A Twix bar."

He nodded. In a few seconds, Piper was at the door giving him a thumbs-up.

The YC store was bustling with Mother's Day shoppers. Everywhere, there seemed to be hand-lettered signs advertising turkeys and hams flown in especially for the occasion. Russet potatoes spilled from display boxes, and almost-fresh-looking bouquets of asparagus sat in shallow trays of water. Wall freezers were stocked with Sara Lee cheesecakes and Marie Callender frozen pies.

Beans picked up a small Hormel cured ham, encased in plastic. "Think we can figure out how to cook this?" he asked Piper.

"I think you just heat it up. It says it's already cooked. It's not like you're going to get worms or anything." She picked up a jar of orange marmalade and shrugged. "I think we can put this on as a sauce, maybe?"

Above the white noise of shoppers' conversations and the jangling of the bell on the store's front door, Beans heard the rough, angry voice of Victor Paul, calling across the store.

"Where's your brother?"

Janelle was lifting frozen turkeys from a tote into the freezer case. She was a big woman, could probably bench press the same as Beans could, and handled the turkeys with ease. "I'm sure I don't know, Dad. We could use the help here today."

"Maybe he's at the washeteria," Victor grumbled. "He'll have to answer to his mother if he doesn't show up for dinner tomorrow." He looked up from ringing up a customer and met Beans's eye. "You!"

Beans and the customer Victor was cashing out at the time just about leaped out of their shoes. "Yeah?"

"Don't touch the candy unless you're paying for it," he growled. "I know what you Beans kids are like."

Piper's face was red with indignation and she opened her mouth, about to let loose a string of obscenities she had learned from her light-fingered brothers. Beans grabbed her arm and pulled her aside. "Not now, Piper. Let's just get our stuff and go."

They left the YC store with the ham, the marmalade, a few potatoes that they would probably bake, and two bunches of asparagus that it was going to be Piper's job to figure out what to do with. Piper already had dessert handled—she'd made an angel food cake from a box mix and iced it with canned frosting.

Despite the unpleasantness in the store with Victor, Beans was relieved. Victor obviously didn't know about his and Mari's run-in with Lloyd, and Lloyd appeared to be keeping a low profile. *Maybe we "dodged this bullet."* He smiled to himself, enjoying his pun and the load off his mind. He put his hand in his pocket for the truck keys and realized that the Twix bar he had promised Piper was in there with them. "Shit." He closed his eyes and rocked his head back.

"Holy crap, did you just lift that?" Piper's eyes were round with amazement.

"Just shut up, don't tell Mom." He tossed it to her and started the car.

"It'll cost you." Piper grinned with self-satisfaction and unwrapped her candy bar. She took a big bite, then stopped and frowned, midchew. "What the hel—heck is poking me in the ass?" She reached behind her and from between the car seat cushions, pulled out Otter's albuterol asthma inhaler.

7

Beans

Summer 2024

While he waited for his mother's ancient Black & Decker coffeemaker to finish brewing, Beans called Fee to tell her that it wasn't necessary for her to pick him up this morning—Mari had left her pickup truck parked there at the house, and the keys were in a lacquer candy dish on the rolltop desk.

"Suit yourself," she said. He could hear the hissing and bubbling of her Nespresso machine in the background and was envious. Black & Decker-brewed coffee was tolerable at best. *How could you expect a company that made lawnmowers and battery-powered drills to make a decent coffeemaker?* "I gotta give a little talk for Career Day at GILA this morning—want to come with me? I could introduce the hometown boy made good, and all that happy horseshit." GILA was the Galena Interior Learning Academy, a residential vocational school for high school-aged students.

"I'll pass, thanks."

"Chicken." A spoon clinked in a ceramic mug.

"Speaking of chickens, thank your mom for me for the eggs."

"What eggs?

"The eggs she left on the counter. Like she used to when we were kids, remember?"

A long pause and a heavy sigh. "She's not supposed to do that—just walk into people's houses when they aren't home."

"What's the big deal? Nobody locks their doors anyway." He pulled a pint carton of milk out of the refrigerator.

He heard a chair being pulled out. When Fee spoke again, her voice was hushed. "This was a couple of years back. You weren't here then. Neither was I. My dad had died suddenly that winter, and I think that really affected Mom. She continued egg deliveries to her friends, which everybody appreciated. But then people started noticing that the days she left the eggs, the water was left running, or the TV left on in the house. Then she brought eggs to the Robinsons—a nice schoolteacher couple. She not only brought them eggs—she turned the stove on high, with a pizza box on the burner."

"Jesus."

"The house wasn't a total loss, but it did quite a lot of damage. And their cat died."

Beans heard scraping on the floor again, and water running.

"So that's why I'm here. I was a member of a nice little police force in McMinnville, Oregon. My boyfriend was—and still is—an up-and-coming winemaker in Yamhill County. But he just couldn't make himself follow me here when I told him 'I gotta go home. My mom is losing her mind.' I don't blame him. It just wasn't part of his ten-year career plan. I know it wasn't part of mine."

Beans dropped into a kitchen chair. "Sorry, Fee, I didn't know."

"Most of the time she's OK. She feeds her chickens. She takes care of herself, bathing, toileting. A couple of CNAs from the clinic who want to make a few extra bucks keep an eye on her during the day. She must have snuck out at the changing of the guard."

"Maybe she saw me on my run and thought I needed eggs."

"You have a distinctly underfed look." A jangle of keys. "Just kidding, I told her you were here. It probably jogged something loose in her memory. Oh, there's Anita for her shift with Mom. OK, I'll see you at the shop."

* * *

Beans brought the old Dodge pickup to a chugging stop in front of the Gunnerson house. The oversized garage, previously stacked floor to ceiling with furniture waiting to be refinished, was now sealed off with a garage door. Geraniums overflowed from planter boxes lining the front walkway. Fee, like her mother, obviously kept the house well-maintained. A slightly built middle-aged woman in blue nurse's scrubs and a knit cardigan sat on an Adirondack chair near the front door, smoking a cigarette. Gloria's CNA caregiver Anita, Beans assumed.

She eyed him warily until he introduced himself, then she gave him a tentative smile. "Oh, right, you're Mari's son. My girl, Tiffany, was in school with your sister."

He smiled to himself. *Small towns.* Everybody defining themselves in time against who they knew and the year they graduated. "Yeah, and Tiffany's cousin Lonnie was in my year."

She nodded, taking a deep drag from her cigarette. "Well, Fee's already left . . ."

"Right, I was wondering if I could talk to Gloria for a minute."

Anita flicked ash from her cigarette into a broken terracotta pot. "Uh, you know that . . ."

"Yeah, Fee's filled me in. I won't take too much of her time. Just want to say hello."

Anita shrugged and opened the front door for him to enter. "Gloria. You have company," she called after him.

The living room was exactly as Beans remembered it from when he and Conrad were growing up. The furniture was old but comfortable and tidy, and the room had the familiar smell of Lemon Pledge and sausages. Gloria Gunnerson shuffled into the living room from the kitchen, wiping her hands on an apron.

When she saw Beans, her broad face broke into a huge grin. "Havi!" She opened her arms and gripped him in a bear hug that almost left him breathless. Gloria was mostly Athabascan "with some Inuit thrown in" she used to say, and was warm and open, like his own Native Alaskan grandmother.

He had almost forgotten how many hours he and Conrad had spent in each other's homes, opening each other's refrigerators, eating each other's food. And Gloria was always here, baking cookies, making berry jam, keeping secrets.

He hugged her back, at once happy and sad to see her. She was heavier, and seemed to carry the excess weight like a burden. Her hair had grayed and she wore it in a neat bob. "Mrs. G., how are you?"

She made a shooing motion. "Oh, you know. Just the same as always." She gestured toward the sofa. "Sit, sit. You want a Coke?"

Beans thought it might be a little early in the day for a Coke, even for him. "No thanks, I'm good."

She sat on the sofa next to him. "You only come at Christmas time, so I never get to see you. We usually go to my sister's place in Fairbanks for Christmas." She took off the apron and folded it in her lap. "And we almost never see Conrad anymore. He's in the service in Japan, you know."

"Yes, that's what Fee tells me."

She raised her hand and set it gently on his chest. "And you? You OK?"

He knew she was asking about the wound Lloyd Paul had inflicted on him so long ago. "Yeah, I'm fine, Mrs. G. Doc fixed me up good as new."

She shook her head. "So much blood for a young boy. And Mari—Jens thought she had a broken bone in her face."

No X-rays. I'll take care of it. "She's doing OK too, Mrs. G."

"Your mother, such a pretty lady. But not the same after that." She patted his hand. "Sure you don't want a Coke? Coffee?"

"No, no thanks, Mrs. G. Just had coffee at the house." *Sub-standard Black & Decker-created brew.*

"Oh, you're staying at the house? That's good. Mari could use the company."

"She's out of town now, helping my grandma in California."

"Havi, Daisy died years ago." She slapped his hand as if to say, *Don't be silly.*

"Oh, not my Grandma Daisy, this is my mother's mother, in California."

Gloria looked confused for a moment, then smiled. "Why didn't your mother ever remarry, I wonder? She was still so young when Jimmy died, so pretty, even after Lloydie bashed her face."

Beans had been looking at a poster of an Iditarod race on the wall and started.

She saw his surprise and continued. "Oh, everyone knew he was sweet on her, even before Jimmy died. But Mari wouldn't have anybody but Jimmy, and that's a fact. That's probably why Lloydie bashed her face." Gloria began wiping the top of the gleaming coffee table with her apron.

Beans had just planned on thanking her for the eggs and leaving, but was intrigued by the direction this conversation was taking.

Gloria stretched her mouth into a line and shook her head. "So much blood. Jens wanted to report it to Arvid, but your mother wouldn't have it." She stopped cleaning the table top and looked at him, her gaze suddenly clear and intent. "If someone had hurt my boy like that, they would pay for it."

"How?" The word was out of his mouth before he could stop it.

"I saw your truck that night, you know. It was late. The chickens made a fuss, and I thought it was a fox, so I got up. I saw the truck then. Your truck had a bad timing belt—my dad was a mechanic, I should know—and it made a kind of squeal. So I knew it was yours."

"My little brother was at Grandma's and needed his inhaler. Mom was bringing it to him, that's all."

She gave his hand a "silly boy" slap again and said, "Havi, I know where Daisy Beans lives. The truck was heading in the opposite direction, toward the fuel dock."

The front door swung open and Anita came in, bringing with her the smell of her cigarettes. "Having a nice visit, Gloria?"

"Oh yes," Gloria beamed.

Beans took this as his cue to leave. "And thanks so much for the eggs, Mrs. G."

She smiled at him blankly. "What eggs?"

* * *

His cell phone barked. The screen read *Heller*, his colleague and partner at Anchorage Homicide Division. He took his hand off the wheel for a second to press the speaker function.

"Hellboy."

"Beans. How goes it? Basking in the California sun?"

"Uh, no. Actually, I'm in Galena."

"What? Everything OK with your mom?"

"Yeah, yeah. I got roped into consulting on a cold case here."

"Anything juicy?"

"Not really. A missing person that might be more than that now."

"Oh, yeah? Who is it?"

Beans envisioned Heller, a forty-something career cop, his eyes lighting up at the thought of a new, intriguing case, especially one that could be a homicide. "I'll fill you in later. What's up?"

"Thought I'd give you a heads-up. Internal Affairs is getting a lot of heat from homeless advocates. The techs are going over Ma's CCTV with a fine-toothed comb. But I got our boy Cam on it too."

Cam was Cameron Kristovich, a bus driver on the autism spectrum who had been instrumental in solving the barista serial murder case that made Beans and Heller Anchorage household names, at least for their fifteen minutes of fame. Cam had an eidetic memory, one that served him well viewing hours of video footage and ultimately helped identify the perpetrator.

"But they got nothing to stand on," Heller continued. "Willis fired first. He looked like he was going to shoot Mrs. Ma. You did what you had to neutralize the shooter. I would have done the same."

"What are they saying? That I didn't need to shoot him? That I was too quick to shoot?" Was he? Wasn't Willis raising his gun again toward Mrs. Ma? He ran through the scene again, spooling it back and forward in his memory. *Mrs. Ma, shards of glass glittering in her hair, holding the Smith & Wesson in her steady hands. Willis lowering his gun, then, inexplicably, raising it again, saying something about Doritos?*

Heller emitted a dismissive grunt. "No cop alive would have done any different. But, you know, they gotta do their due diligence, especially after the Begay incident."

Before Willis Helms, Joey Begay was the latest casualty of the spate of police violence. Begay, high on bath salts, had threatened a couple of teenagers with a knife. The police officer who had responded had shot and killed Begay—unnecessarily, some claimed.

"Just saying, and the lieutenant agrees—don't be in any rush to get back here."

The cup of Maxwell House coffee from his mother's ancient Black & Decker roiled in his stomach as he pulled in front of the Public Safety Building.

8

Mari

Summer 2024

Mari hated the incessant commotion of California. Even at night, especially at night, the rumbling drone of the freeway (*was it the 880, or the 84, or some other number?*) was an endless grinding background noise that kept her awake. So unlike the almost deep space quiet of nights in Galena, interrupted only by the bark of a dog or a fox or the scream of a dying animal.

The first few nights in her parents' home in Fremont in the Bay Area were not restful ones. The relentless groaning of the freeway wore at her. It was too hot in the house, even with the windows open. And there was a certain level of irritation with her siblings—who were "conveniently" on vacations—Roy and his family on a European trip, Naomi and her family on a cruise—when their mother needed help packing up the house. And there was her mother, who after the death of her extremely decisive husband seemed to be cast adrift, even less decisive than before.

Michiko Yamane was stressed out about the impending move to her apartment in the retirement community, and was totally scattered in her approach toward cleaning out the house. Mari's father, Ben, had died over a year ago, and there was still his stuff to go through—but his belongings were only the top layer of the archeological dig that was The Yamane House in Fremont.

Michiko was distracted to the point of paralysis by the sheer immensity of this task, spending hours poring over a single junk drawer or a box of photos, and it fell upon Mari to plot out the most basic plan of action. Anything making the move to the new place was boxed, marked, and stacked in the house. Anything that was to be given away or donated to charity was to be packed up, labeled, and held in the garage. Her brother, Roy, once he returned to the country and his filial duties, would haul these to the dump or Goodwill in his pickup truck. Mari figured her mother, even in her distracted state, could follow these simple designations.

It was still slow going. Some days it seemed like she'd work all day and only have four boxes to show for it by dinner time. On these days she wondered if she'd be finished by the time she had to return to Galena for the start of the school year.

She had to admit that returning to Galena now made her uneasy. How could Lloyd Paul's leg appear after all these years? *What does that mean? And what does it mean that Havi is on the case?* She stopped in the middle of taping a box closed. *How much does he remember?*

Havi and Piper, she knew, were the most level-headed of her children. Lindbergh the eldest, dead at seventeen, after rolling the truck with Havi in it, then wandering off to collapse into a snowdrift. Hercules, or Herc, the most like his father—handsome, jovial, a lovable drunk. Divorced now with two daughters, he lived in Sitka when he wasn't on a fishing boat. DeHavilland, "Havi," was the proverbial middle child—serious, observant. No wonder he became a cop. Piper was the brightest of the bunch, excelling at her studies, quick to anger, but also quick to forgive. Otter was still a work in progress, she thought, but was clever and self-reliant, an IT consultant with the State of Alaska in Juneau.

Mari had been new to Galena, a recent college graduate with a two-year contract to teach at the village elementary school, when she stumbled into the washeteria and realized she didn't have change for the machines. The only other person in the steaming, Tide-scented room was smiling, hazel-eyed Jimmy Beans in grease-stained Carharrts, a duffel bag full of dirty clothes over one shoulder and a pocketful of change. Her life had never been the same since that snowy evening when he pressed eight warm quarters into her waiting hand.

Her father had been incensed that she had hooked up not with another Asian, but with the "drunken half-breed" Jimmy Beans, and apoplectic that she was pregnant with Lindbergh when they got married. She then had four more children, all named after airplanes, and Ben Yamane avoided all contact with Jimmy Beans. It still surprised her that she managed to pop that many seven-pound infants out of her five-foot, hundred-pound frame—but she did so without a single C-section, and with little or no help from her parents.

Despite the tension with her father, she had loved Jimmy, and they had a good marriage, except for the two times that almost broke her. The first was when Lindbergh rolled the truck and Havi was trapped in the cab, the engine ablaze. Villagers rescued Havi and he survived, while Lindbergh, her firstborn, did not.

Maybe it was because she had almost lost him that Havi was special to her. She knew that as a mother, she wasn't supposed to have favorites, but he was the "old soul" in the family, and the one his siblings turned to when they needed guidance.

The second time that almost broke her was when Jimmy Beans crashed his floatplane. She felt like part of her had shattered and burned, like the blackened fuselage of his precious aircraft. Twenty years had passed now, but the reckless joy and beauty of Jimmy in his youth was as vivid as when she had first met him. What had begun to dull, very gradually, was the pain of his loss. For this, she was grateful. The emptiness, she was sure, would never go away entirely.

She had been able to keep the loneliness at bay while she was busy raising her family. It was only after all her children had left home that it prowled around the bungalow like a caged animal, restless and hungry. Over the years, she had fed the loneliness with unsatisfying affairs with a tugboat captain and a married teacher at her school. Now that she was older, the loneliness was not so much a hungry animal as an annoying gnawing at her gut that she was resolved to live with, like acid reflux.

Still, she was proud that she had survived two of the most devastating events of her life—the death of a child and the death of her life partner—the two of them forever frozen in time, ageless.

* * *

Mari finished boxing up some fabric remnants from the sewing room and carried them out to the garage. Her mother's Toyota RAV4 was parked in the driveway. *It's going to be Roy's job to take the keys from her, lucky bastard. Paybacks can be brutal.* She smiled to herself as she shoved the fabric box in a corner with her foot.

It was then that she noticed a small white nightstand, the little table that had held her lamp at her bedside when she was growing up. It had first belonged to her sister, Naomi, and after she'd outgrown it, her father had refinished it and painted it little-girl-white. Mari had loved it. *What's it doing here in the Goodwill pile?* It was still in good shape, and with a little paint, one of Herc's girls might want it for her room.

She bent to pick it up and noticed that it rocked. Flipping it over, she saw that one of the legs had a missing end cap. *Typical of California's disposable lifestyle. One little missing end cap, and you throw it away, then you burn a half tank of gas on the freeway to go buy a new pressboard piece of crap from Ikea.* She was just thinking that she could probably get a new end cap from Home Depot, when she noticed something taped to the bottom of the nightstand.

A key. Stuck onto the nightstand with a strip of yellowed masking tape. *Odd.* She pulled it off and stared at it. None of the drawers in the nightstand locked, and she certainly hadn't put the key there when she owned the little table.

Mari dropped the key into her pocket. It probably went to one of the dressers in the bedrooms, or maybe to one of the trunks up in the attic. She returned to the sewing room, where her mother was contemplating a drawerful of spools of thread.

She showed her mother the key. "Do you know what this is for? I found it taped to the bottom of my old nightstand, the one in the garage."

Michiko stared at the key and shook her head. "Doesn't look familiar. Why was it taped to the nightstand?"

"I'm sure I don't know." *Another of Dad's secrets.*

"Do I need all this thread, Mari?"

"It's up to you, Mom." *It was going to be a long day.* "Either take all of it or none of it."

"Oh, I just don't know." Michiko prodded the spools with her finger. "How's Havi doing?"

'He's fine, Mom. He's helping out on a case."

"So, he'd rather do that than help out here, huh?"

"Probably. Do you blame him?"

"Ha ha." Michiko pointed to a lower drawer of an antique tansu. "Look in there."

The drawer appeared to be full of tissue paper, but smelled of mothballs. "What's this? Wrapping paper? You already have enough wrapping paper." *So help me, I'd sooner burn it in the fireplace than pack another freaking roll of wrapping paper.*

"No, it's not wrapping paper, silly" Michiko said. "Reach in there."

Mari pulled out what felt like a bolt of fabric, covered with tissue. Unwrapping it, she found a beautiful purple kimono with a pale gold obi folded on top.

"It was my mother's," Michiko said. "It's way too long for me, and probably for you, too. It should be a good fit for your Piper."

Mari held the rustling fabric up against her. Piper was a good three inches taller than she was—the color and the length should fit her perfectly. "Mom, this is . . . wow, Piper will be so stoked to have something of her great-grandmother's! It's beautiful! Thank you!" She gave her mother a hug, pressing the kimono between them.

"It's nothing." Michiko's round face flushed with pleasure. "I've been wanting to . . . it's about time"—she looked flustered, then embarrassed. "I've wanted to do more, you know, for your kids, your family, but . . ."

Mari gave her mother another hug. "I know, Mom, it's all good."

Michiko sniffed and gave her a return squeeze. Then she stood, slammed the thread drawer shut decisively (for her), and announced, "I've decided. They're all going." Michiko sniffed. "And if they're going, I'll need to bring my serger."

"Your what?" Mari asked. *Something else to pack.*

"My serger. You know, for making all those nice overcast seam allowances. For sewing knit fabrics."

Mari suppressed a sigh. "How big is it?"

"Don't worry, mine is not as big as a sewing machine. Kind of looks like a small sewing machine, with multiple spindles for the spools of thread."

This time Mari sighed. "Where is it? And is it light enough for me to lift?" *Maybe, I'll leave it for Roy to do.*

Michiko chewed her lip thoughtfully. "If I still have it, it'll be in the attic. And it's very light. I can carry it with one hand."

She would have to venture into the attic sooner or later, Mari said to herself as the narrow stairs descended from the ceiling. She pulled on a mask, a remnant from Covid, and ascended the steep incline, more like a ladder than stairs. It had been years since Mari had been in the attic, and from the thick layer of dust on all surfaces, her parents hadn't ventured there recently either.

With a gloved hand, she flipped on the light switch and a bare bulb flickered to life. The attic was packed with labeled boxes and plastic bins, and Mari's spirits sank with the sheer volume of stuff to go through. "But first—serger, whatever the hell that is," she muttered.

Miraculously, one of the first Rubbermaid bins she came across was labeled with a magic marker in her mother's unsteady hand: "*Michiko—sewing.*"

"Hallelujah." A cloud of dust rose in the stale air as she lifted the lid.

In the bin was a small machine she assumed was her mother's serger, with multiple spindles and a sewing foot. Also in the bin were several odd-sized bundles protected with yellowed pages of old newspaper. Mari unwrapped one of them to find a small carved wooden figure of an otter, lying on its back with a shell between its paws.

9

Beans

Summer 2024

"Got it!" Fee was jubilant. "The Fairbanks clinic called back—they were able to confirm that the leg with the partial serial number was fitted to one Lloyd Victor Paul. DOB matches."

Beans popped a couple of Tums and chewed. "Who's telling Victor?"

Her face fell. "What a killjoy."

"So what does this tell us? Just that Lloyd is most likely dead. It could be an accident, not necessarily a homicide." *And I could pack up and go home to face an internal inquiry.*

"Come on, Havi. What are the odds? More than half the people in this town hated Lloyd!"

Beans swiveled in his desk chair, which did nothing to help his acid indigestion. "Still, he could have fallen in and drowned."

"What—a 'sure-footed gimp' like Lloydie?" Fee made air quotes, rolling her eyes.

"Yeah. Always a possibility, since he was in the bag a lot of the time. Where's the original missing person file?"

She handed him a worn manila file folder. "Knock yourself out. I'll make the call to Victor."

As far as Beans could tell by reading through the missing person report, former police chief Arvid Streeter had done things by the book. Lloyd had made arrangements for Chena Barge Lines to ship his Ford Ranger pickup, his skiff on a trailer, and a tote of personal effects on the first upriver barge back to Nenana in June. The cargo was consigned not to Lloyd, but a third party, Tundra Moving and Storage.

The pallet of personal effects was loaded into a small container, and the pickup truck and skiff onto shipping platforms by Chena Barge's agent in town, Bernie Waterman. Bernie, Beans remembered, was also the postmaster in town.

Bernie told Arvid that he had received Lloyd's cargo and with Junior's help loaded it, filled out the appropriate paperwork, and secured the cargo on the landing with the other upriver cargo to await the first backhaul barge. According to Bernie, Lloyd had prepaid his freight charges and said he wasn't in any big rush for the cargo, just wanted to get out of town. He talked about hitching a ride out with a floatplane charter.

Beans noted an addendum to Arvid's report dated July 2009. A fire at Tundra Moving and Storage had destroyed the office and warehouses that had housed their customers' goods and paperwork. The company went out of business shortly after that. Even if he wanted to, Beans wouldn't be able to find out if anyone had picked up Lloyd's cargo.

Beans's review of Lloyd's file was interrupted by Fee's intense one-sided phone conversation across the room.

"I'm sorry, Victor. This is Lloyd's leg. The clinic in Fairbanks that fitted him with it confirmed it." A pause, and then, "That'll prove nothing, Victor." Another pause, this time with an eyeroll. "Well, that's certainly your prerogative." She drummed her fingers on her desktop, clearly impatient. "We've gotten all the evidence we're going to from it. You can pick it up at any time." She hung up, then leaned forward and thumped her forehead on her desk. "He still thinks we need Lloyd's skull. He says he's going to hire divers to look for it."

"You're shitting me, right?" Victor's refusal to consider that his son was dead defied belief.

"He says he knows some salvage guys out of Anchorage who would be willing to do it." Fee sighed, reached into a desk drawer and pulled out a Hefty lawn bag. "I'd better get Lloydie bagged up. The cafeteria ladies are getting impatient for their brownie pan."

Beans grabbed his phone and keys. "Looks like Bernie Waterman was one of the last people to see Lloyd. I'm going to run by the post office and see what he remembers."

Bernie Waterman was stacking Amazon returns in a rolling bin when Beans entered the small post office. A bachelor for as long as Beans could remember, Bernie was a fit, middle-aged man, around fifty-five years old, but slender and wiry. Other than a receding hairline, Bernie was much the same, neatly dressed in khaki slacks and an Oxford button-down shirt. He peered at Beans over the top of his reading glasses. "Havi! I heard you were in town." He came around the counter to shake Beans's hand.

"Can't stay away."

Bernie shook his head. "Heard about the leg. I guess there's no question that it's Lloyd's."

No keeping that quiet, I guess. "I don't think there's any doubt."

Bernie's long face lengthened into a frown. "I bet Victor's beside himself. Such a shame. It really did look like Lloyd had been leaving to make a fresh start for himself."

"Right, I'm helping Fee out, you know, reviewing the old case files, making sure we covered all our bases. When was the last time you saw Lloyd?"

"Wow, that's ancient history now. The Friday before Mother's Day that year, I think. I met him at the landing to load up his stuff. He prepaid the freight charges."

"What was he like that day?"

Bernie eyed him shrewdly. "There's no way he was suicidal, if that's what you're thinking. He was positively giddy. He was going to blow this doghole, he said, travel, start anew somewhere else. Ask Junior. He was there too, and we laughed about it after Lloyd left."

"Arvid's file said that the cargo was consigned to Tundra Moving and Storage in Nenana?" Beans inspected the display of commemorative stamps.

"Yeah, Lloyd said he had planned on doing some traveling first, so made arrangements for them to store his goods. Too bad about the fire."

Beans looked from a commemorative stamp of endangered species back to Bernie. "How did you get along with Lloyd?"

Bernie blinked in surprise behind his readers. "Me?"

"Yeah, well, he wasn't universally liked here in town, you know."

"Wait," Bernie crossed his arms over his chest. "I'm a little slow, but I get it now. Of course, you're here—a homicide cop from Anchorage. You think Lloyd was killed?"

"With the discovery of the leg, the case has changed from a missing person to a possible accidental death or homicide. Given what everyone has said about his state of mind before he went missing, it's unlikely to be a suicide. I've got some time off, so flew in to help out, seeing as Fee's shorthanded right now."

Bernie smiled knowingly. "Sure, right. Since you asked, Lloyd and I got along fine. Like everybody else, I thought Victor spoiled him and let him get away with—if you'll pardon the expression—murder. But I am sorry that the family hasn't had any closure."

Closure. Beans hated that word. He wondered if Willis Helms' family felt a sense of a meaningful conclusion to his life.

He realized that Bernie was still talking to him. "It's a pity you're missing your mother this time. Mari's in California, I think she said?"

Everybody knows everybody's business. "She's visiting her mother in the Bay Area."

"Be sure and give her my regards when you talk to her." He shook Beans's hand again. "It's been, what, almost twenty years since . . ." Bernie looked genuinely mournful. "I was really fond of your dad. My dad was a pilot too, you know. Jimmy was one of the best."

Fourteen-year-old DeHavilland and his four-year-old brother Otter had been browsing the candy aisle in the Yukon Commercial store under Victor's watchful eye when a distant boom sounded. Everyone in the store thought it was miners using dynamite until the town's only fire truck wailed down the dusty street. In minutes, Piper appeared, tear-streaked and breathless.

"Come quick, Havi. It's Papa."

He tucked Otter under his arm and followed Piper out of the store, saying to himself, "Please God, don't let it be Papa. Please God, don't let it be Papa."

That was the day he became a Buddhist.

* * *

Beans called Piper and put her on speaker as he drove down to the fuel dock on his way to talk to Junior Mangold.

Before he could say anything, Piper said, "Before you ask, Elwood is doing well with his G/I diet, and I'm giving Archie his thyroid meds twice a day, although he's not happy about it." From the sounds of it, Piper was also in her car.

"You driving?"

"Business Law to Starbucks. What's up?" In addition to studying for her MBA, Piper had a part-time job as a barista.

"Just checking in. The boys behaving themselves?"

"They are *excellent* boys," Piper gushed. "I'll really miss them when you get home. When are you getting home, anyway?"

"I don't really know yet. It's a little more complicated than I thought."

"Is that really Lloyd's leg?"

"Yup. That's all we got of him, though, after so many years."

He heard her shudder on the phone. "I just remember him being really creepy. And remember, after Papa died, he would just show up, whenever."

"I remember." He remembered a lot more, but Piper didn't need to know. "You talk to Mom lately?"

"Yeah, she's busy shoveling all that old shit out of Grandma's house. She's just starting on the attic. Nobody's touched that stuff in ages, since Grandma can't get up those steps. OK, I'm here at Freddy's. Gotta go."

* * *

The fuel dock appeared to be deserted when Beans pulled up a few minutes later. He got out of the pickup and strolled to the water's edge. The river was still high and silty from the spring melt, but he could never remember being able to see its muddy bottom. *Where did Lloyd go in? Here?*

"Hey, Havi."

He turned and saw Junior Mangold striding toward him with his spidery gait, pausing to crush out a cigarette under his work boot. "Can't be smoking around the pumps, you know, kablam!" He chuckled, reaching out to shake Beans's hand, then remembering that his hand was black with grease and stopping to wipe it on an oily rag.

Junior was as unlike his wife, Janelle, as anyone could be. By Beans's assessment, she had him by three inches and at least twenty pounds. He had thinning red hair that he pulled back into a wispy ponytail and squinted at the world through smudged bifocals. He was active, jittery, with a nervous laugh. Beans remembered him as being almost overaccommodating, but he knew that Junior had a minor juvenile record and was probably squirrely around cops. Beans felt a little sorry for Junior, surrounded by much larger and domineering family members.

"Hey, Junior, how's it going?"

"Same shit, different day, you know." Junior giggled. "So, Lloydie's leg, huh?"

"Yeah, I'm just reviewing the old case file. When was the last time you saw Lloyd?"

"Well, let's see . . . would be that Friday before Mother's Day? Yeah, that's it—he came down to the landing with his truck and skiff, and Bernie and me loaded them up."

"What was he like?"

"Like? It's like he won the lottery, man. He was going to ditch Galena, see the world, fuck you all, et cetera, et cetera." Junior chuckled, but there was bitterness to it.

"Do you know if he did? Come into some money, I mean?"

Junior stared out over the river, tapping his foot on the dock, startling a pair of mergansers into flight. "Sure, sure. He was always into some money. Always walking around with his pockets jingling with the change from the washeteria machines. Or the register at the store. After he went missing, we found out that he withdrew a bunch from a joint account he had with Victor and Dolores. Oh, yeah, he planned on getting out of town."

"What did Victor say about that?"

Junior's giggle turned into a snort. "For Victor, the sun rose and set out of Lloydie's ass. The old man would hear nothing against him. You'd never hear Janelle say anything either, but I never was so glad to see the back of him leaving town."

"Did you see him leaving town?"

"No, course not. Nobody did. It's a figure of speech, like."

"What do you think happened to Lloyd?"

"The way he mainlined Everclear, he probably got drunk and drowned, don't you think?"

An aluminum skiff motored up to the dock, and Junior nodded to Beans apologetically as he loped forward to help its occupant.

10

Beans

Summer 2024

When Beans returned to the house, he found a sealed Tupperware containing four eggs sitting on the wrought iron bench on the front porch. With it was a note on a yellow Post-It: "From Gloria. She wants the container back. Anita." Smiling to himself, he brought the eggs in and put them in the refrigerator with the other four.

He scrolled through his emails on his phone as he devoured the takeout ptarmigan yakisoba he had bought at Andreas K's. His stomach full, he tapped on the FaceTime app to talk to his mother. Almost instantaneously, Mari's image appeared on the screen. She looked drawn and exhausted. It was obvious that she was in the family room, with a Japanese travelogue blaring from the television.

"Hold on, let me go to the other room." She jiggled the phone as she walked. "Your grandmother's hearing is really getting bad." She entered what appeared to be a formal dining room and sat in one of the upholstered chairs.

It saddened Beans to realize that he had never visited his maternal grandparents in their home. He knew that Mari's father had considered Jimmy Beans an uncivilized half-breed, and by extension, his children a litter of well, mutts. But now, with the silent remains of Ben Yamane in an urn on the mantel, Beans had had a chance to see his grandmother for the last time in this environment. Had he let that chance slip by? *Maybe I'll visit later.*

"So," Mari said, "what do they know?" When his mother was tired, the broken orbital bone in her face made it look like she had suffered a minor stroke, or was the subject of a cubist painting.

"It's definitely Lloyd's leg, Mom."

"I guess that's good. Maybe Victor will abandon that ridiculous fiction of Lloyd leaving Galena and becoming The Most Interesting Man in the World."

Beans chuckled. His mother had a way of being frank to the point of absurdity. She could be outrageously funny or scary—one or the other—and sometimes both. "He's still refusing to admit that Lloyd is most likely dead. Thinks that we need to produce his head in order to convince him."

"Well, that's not going to happen." Mari sounded relieved.

"No, I guess not." He decided not to tell his mother about Victor's independent efforts to find Lloyd's skull. "Hey, you never told me about Gloria."

"Her dementia, you mean? Sometimes she's just fine, and sometimes in la-la land. I think it's Alzheimer's or vascular dementia, poor thing."

"She brings me eggs, then forgets she brought them."

Mari laughed. "Knowing you were in town must have reminded her of the old days, when she brought us eggs every day, remember?"

"One thing she does remember—she remembers us going over to their house that night. I was bleeding all over the place, and you had that black eye."

"Nobody was likely to forget that night, especially Fee, I should think. She was just a kid."

"But Gloria remembers seeing your truck that night."

"Of course, that's what I drove to their place—"

"No, later. Probably the same time I got up and saw that you were gone."

"Yeah, sure. I went to Grandma's to bring Otter his inhaler."

"That's what's weird. Gloria said you were heading in the opposite direction, toward the dock."

The slightly cubist look to Mari's face intensified. "Oh really? Gloria Gunnerson, the 'reliable witness'? She obviously has it backward. Oh hey." She switched the phone's camera to face a menagerie of wooden objects on the dining room table. "Look at these."

A half dozen or so intricately carved wooden figures were arranged on the table—a bear, a whale, an otter, a small Native person in a parka, a salmon, and a few birds. While Beans was annoyed at the sudden change of subject, he was fascinated by the little figurines. "Where did those come from?"

She picked up the otter and held it to the phone. "Aren't these remarkable? I found them in one of the boxes upstairs. With your grandmother's serger."

"What's a serger?" Beans asked.

"Some kind of sewing gizmo. This one will have to go to your little brother, of course. Each one of these is carved with the initials 'BY.' I asked your grandma if your grandfather had carved these, but she said she thought *his* father had carved them."

Beans was reminded of the delicately carved wooden pistol that his grandfather had left him after his death. It was the same worn wooden gun that young Ben Yamane wore in a child-sized holster in the black and white photo, the one with which he had dueled an unseen adversary under the hot sun at the Minidoka War Relocation Center.

"Grandpa's father? He was the woodworker?"

"Kazuhiro Yamane. I think he died years before your grandparents got married. He apparently spent some time in Alaska fishing—you can probably tell from the subject matter."

"Are there more of these?

"I'm not sure. These were in the attic—in just one of the several boxes and chests up there. No one's been up there in years, as far as I can tell, so the dust is inches thick. I wear gloves and mask up—it's like Covid all over again."

"What else is up there?"

"Most of it is dumpster fodder, probably. There's tons of my stuff, and Naomi and Roy's . . . but maybe more treasures like these."

"Sorry I'm not there to help."

She gave him a teasing smile. "No, you're not. It's nasty, dirty work, and Jesus, you could get hantavirus"—she lowered her voice—"and you hardly knew them anyway." In that instant, Mari sounded apologetic, sorry that her children hadn't had the same warm relationship they had with their father's parents.

"Not your fault, was it?"

"I don't know. Maybe." She rubbed the little wooden otter between her fingers. "So, you're probably going back to work soon anyway, right?"

"I don't know. It's less straightforward than they thought. They're saying I should stay away longer until things cool down."

"What?" Anger flashed in Mari's eyes. "Don't they know you, Havi? Shooting somebody would always be your last resort."

"It's different this time, Mom. I killed a man."

Mari set the otter on the table and picked up the figure of the bear rearing up on two legs, seeming to sniff the air around it. "You did it because you had to. As Mom would say, *Shikata ga nai*. It couldn't be helped."

In the background, Beans could hear the thin, querulous voice of his grandmother.

"Coming, Mom." Mari turned back to the screen. "She can't figure out how to work the closed captioning. I'll say goodnight, then." She smiled her cubist smile and signed off.

The conversation with his mother left Beans restless. He got in the truck and drove out the road to the small cemetery where his father's parents, Harold and Daisy Beans, were buried. His brother Lindbergh's marker was beside theirs, more weather-worn by far than those of his grandparents, as he had predeceased them by several years. His father, Jimmy Beans, had been cremated and his remains released into the river.

It was after 9 PM but still daylight, so he could easily find the headstones. Noisy mosquitos swarmed around his face and he swatted them away.

Why hadn't he ever asked his grandmother while he could whether she had called for Otter's inhaler that night? Otter was too young to remember, and Piper was a sound sleeper. Grandma Daisy could have confirmed his mother's account of that night. Or not. Had his mother delivered the inhaler as requested? Or had she gone out looking for Lloyd Paul, the Colt beside her in the cab?

It suddenly struck him, at the same time a whining mosquito bit him on the neck. He slapped at it way more angrily than warranted.

He hadn't asked his grandmother because he didn't want to know.

11

Mari

Summer 2024

Another thing Mari hated about California was the traffic, hundreds of thousands of cars packed onto miles of concrete snaking across the dried landscape. She slowly (way too slowly for the cars behind her, apparently) merged the RAV4 onto the freeway toward San Jose and one of the two H Mart Korean markets in the area. She admitted that after living for years in a small Yukon River village, freeway driving had ceased to be one of her more practiced skills. Not even in the Top Ten, in fact. Behind her, someone honked, and she waved in what she hoped was interpreted as a friendly and not gunfire-inducing manner.

She settled into a middle lane and kept up with traffic, which turned out to be an uncomfortable twenty miles an hour above the speed limit. Beside her, Michiko applied lipstick and pressed her lips together, seemingly unalarmed at their breakneck speed. She patted at her gray bob.

"H Mart first, then we can stop at Osaka Marketplace for fish and 99 Ranch if there's time."

Although Mari hated California for its noise and traffic, she loved the Asian food and markets in the Bay Area. Paper-thin beef for *shabu shabu* or *sukiyaki*, *kasuzuke*-marinated black cod. Fresh tofu. Smoked duck. Hum bao and dim sum. Fruit and vegetables that didn't look like they'd been flown in by carrier pigeon. Fresh ahi for *poke*. Andreas K did pretty well at his Greek/Mexican/Japanese place in Galena, but it was still a far cry from an *omakase* sushi dinner in the city. She loved her life in Galena, but the downside was that the YC store was the most exotic (seriously?) grocery store in town, and she would have to order bonito flakes, dried dashi, nori, and other ingredients online to prepare some of the dishes she liked.

Stay in the right two lanes, the female GPS voice said. Thinking about the YC store and its failings made her think about Lloyd Paul's leg, and she found herself gripping the steering wheel. Someone behind her landed on the horn again, and she glanced into the rearview mirror.

Her asymmetrical face stared back at her. *What did Gloria Gunnerson see?* Dementia had made the usually tightlipped Gloria uncharacteristically chatty. *And would anyone believe her*?

* * *

Michiko busied herself unpacking groceries, burbling on about how she was going to make sukiyaki tonight, but not with the beaten raw egg because eggs are so expensive, and what about the bird flu? Or salmonella?

With her mother occupied preparing dinner and unpacking groceries, Mari decided to head into the attic to organize the following day's cleaning schedule. The pull-down stairs creaked more insistently under Mari's weight—she could see why her parents hadn't been up there in years. She carefully climbed up into the musty attic. This is where she had found the carved wooden animals, but there was much more to excavate.

Once again the overhead naked bulb flickered to life. Several moving boxes lined one wall, labeled "Naomi" or "Roy"—no doubt holding her siblings' 4-H ribbons and sports trophies. She would haul those down to the garage and make them go through them and decide what to keep. She had already sifted through her boxes and found nothing to save except a few high school yearbooks.

Behind a nested stack of shredded lampshades (*why would anyone save shredded lampshades?*) were several boxes of books, many of them moth-eaten accounting textbooks that had belonged to her father. She shoved them in a corner for the "to be junked" section in the garage. Not for the first time she wished Havi was with her so he could shlep these heavier boxes down that narrow ladder.

In the far corner of the attic was a battered olive drab foot locker with "Yamane" stenciled on its side. The hardware was corroded, and it was clearly locked. She tried lifting one end. She wouldn't be able to haul it down that ladder herself, that's for sure, not without taking a header and breaking something. "Havi, where are you when I need you?"

Then she remembered the worn key in her pocket. She pulled it out and squinted at it. She sighed and pulled her readers down from the top of her head. Not expecting much, she was surprised when the key fit in the chest's lock and turned. She coughed as a fine dust rose from the contents when she lifted the lid.

It contained a young boy's belongings, well-worn and loved—an old baseball, a fielder's glove with its leather dried and cracked, kid-sized cowboy hat and holster, a homemade slingshot, and a rainbow of marbles that she could hear rolling around randomly at the bottom of the foot locker. She would ask her sons if they wanted any memorabilia of their unapproachable grandfather—she doubted it.

Earlier, she had brought several bankers boxes to the attic, anticipating the possibility of having to haul things down in smaller, lighter increments. She set what she assumed were her father's toys in one of the bankers boxes.

Under the toys were bundles of letters, still in their yellowed envelopes, and held together with rubber bands crumbling with age. Most were addressed to Setsuo Sawada at a San Francisco address, but a few were addressed to Kazuhiro Yamane, her grandfather, at the Minidoka Relocation Center in Idaho. Intrigued, she stacked them up to look at later.

The only other contents of the footlocker were a dozen or so black and white children's composition books and sketchpads of varying sizes. Some of the composition books seemed to be journals, written in a careful cursive. Others appeared to be filled with drawings of birds—some in flight, some on branches, all labeled. *Tufted puffin, Pacific Loon, Osprey, Snow Goose.* Another sketchbook contained what looked like cartoon drawings with whimsical tales of a cat, a coyote, and a rat. In yet another lined book were landscapes—a small village on the water from across a bay, boats moored at a dock, and a simple church with an onion dome captioned: Saints Peter and Paul Church, St. Paul, Alaska.

She ran her fingers over the images, willing them to tell her their stories.

* * *

It's not for nothing she became a librarian, Mari thought, as she arranged the rows of yellowed documents on her mother's dining room table. She had painstakingly shuttled down in a bankers box the contents of the battered foot locker in several trips down the rickety ladder. Kazuhiro Yamane, her father's father, had dated and labeled every journal, drawing and cartoon—so diligently that Mari could establish a timeline of Kazu's activities and locales from 1941 through 1953. She knew that somewhere in this paperwork was history that to date had remained unexplored.

12

Kazuhiro Yamane

August 1941

The light was beautiful this time of every endless summer day. Kazuhiro Yamane, a child's composition book propped on his lap, watched the ripe persimmon hue of early evening glint on the onion dome of the Russian Orthodox Church on St. Paul Island. He sat on a rusted crab pot in the tall grass across the church, pencil in hand, making tentative strokes, trying to capture the contrast of the simple white clapboard structure with the ornate domes that adorned it. *I wish I had watercolors.*

The long summer days gave him ample opportunity to sketch not only the stark but beautiful landscapes, but the diverse population of birdlife on the remote island. One of the two major Pribilof Islands in the Bering Sea, St. Paul was a seasonal stop for migratory birds, some so exotic he'd never even heard of them growing up in Seattle.

One composition book was already full of drawings of puffins, auklets, cormorants and kittiwakes. In the next few days, he thought he might venture to the other side of the island to where there were rookeries for fur seals and get a few drawings of them.

A slender, serious young man of twenty-six, Kazu was a perfectionist. His drawings were precise and lifelike, even with the distracting blue lines going across the pages. He never succumbed to flights of abstraction. The bird drawings gave the impression of realistic motion—even those posed on branches seemed like they were poised to take wing at any moment.

As he used his fingertip to texture the pencil lines, he thought to himself with surprise, that he was content. For the time being, on this faraway island in the middle of nowhere, he was happy. It hadn't started out that way.

A few weeks ago, he was halibut fishing on a boat that seemed way too small for the mountainous swells of the Bering Sea. The skipper of the *Lisa Jo* was Dan Harkonen, a burly but softspoken Finn, and a friend and neighbor of his wife Hoshi's family. He had taken Kazu on as deck crew, along with men from Louisiana and Texas, who like Kazu, had thought they could make a lot of money fast. It was brutally hard work and dangerous, with baited hooks flying off the bulwark on coiled lines with alarming speed. Huge slabs of flailing halibut were pulled up equally quickly and dangerously. But the pay was good and it was just for the season, he told himself when he fell into his bunk, aching and exhausted.

Most of the crew did the work and minded their own business, with the exception of one scrawny white man from Baton Rouge, who never missed a chance to call Kazu a "Nip" or "Jap" or "slant-eye." Everyone told him to ignore the asshole, so Kazu usually called him "scrotum face" in Japanese under his breath while his insides roiled.

They were setting gear on Kazu's last night on the boat, farther west than they should have been, practically in Russian waters, when the skipper came on deck and told "Scrotum Face" he had to take his turn at galley duty. The crewman whined, "Ah, Skip, get the Jap houseboy to do it."

Maybe it was the stink of fish guts sliming the deck, the nights of too little sleep, or the lip-curling sneer on the crewman's bearded face, but Kazu had a sense of something popping inside him. He shoved the crewman hard against the wall of the wheelhouse, the hollow metal sound of the man's head like a temple gong. The crewman shoved back, and it took the skipper and another man to pull them apart. Scrotum Face grabbed a gaff, and swung it wildly, roaring something about "hairy-carey." Kazu tried to spin away just as the crewman plunged the hook into Kazu's thigh. White hot pain detonated in his leg, and the deck lights on the boat grew dim.

* * *

What he noticed first, lying on a narrow bunk, was that it wasn't moving under him. No rolling of the ocean, or slapping of water against the hull of the ship. His eyes stinging and gummy, he pried them open in the milky light. He felt for his glasses, and his hand groped an unfamiliar surface, one with a lamp on it. *A lamp? A glass of water? Where am I?*

Now in focus, his eyes took in the wooden ceiling of a small building. Pulling himself up into a seated position, a strange warmth spread through his leg. His right thigh was encased in a thick bandage and other than that and a flimsy faded green hospital gown, he was naked. He sank back in the bed, sighing. It came back to him then, the fight on the *Lisa Jo*, the gaff hook. He heard the soft murmur of conversation somewhere and thought about calling out until he heard a door open.

A brisk patter of footsteps and she suddenly stood at his bedside. Barely taller than a child, her round, serious face peered at him from under a flowered headscarf.

"Good, you're awake. Do you speak Japanese?" She spoke loudly and slowly.

"Yes, I do." He smiled. "And I speak English, too."

She laughed, embarrassed at her mistake, and Kazu joined her. It was a full-throated chuckle, embellished by two deep dimples on her cheeks. "Sorry. I'll get the doc."

She left the room, still chuckling to herself, then reentered with a white-coated Native Alaskan man, stethoscope around his neck, beaming at him.

"I'm Dr. Otto Laskin. This silly thing," he gestured fondly toward the young woman, "is my daughter and reluctant nurse, Adelaide."

Before he could say anything, Dr. Laskin continued, "And you're Kazuhiro Yamane." He consulted a file folder and pronounced the syllables slowly. "Did I get that right?"

Kazu nodded, impressed. Not too many non-Japanese got the pronunciation right the first time.

"You're lucky to be alive, young man." Laskin sat on the end of the bed. "That gaff hook just missed your femoral artery. Your skipper got you here plenty fast, left you with me, then went on to Dutch Harbor to turn that murderous bastard who gaffed you over to the authorities. He said he would get in touch with your family as well, and let them know where you are."

"Where am I?" Kazu looked from the doctor's face to his daughter's.

"Oh, didn't Addy tell you? You're at the clinic on St. Paul Island."

Of course. Practically in Russian waters. "How long have I been here?"

"You got here last night. Been in and out of consciousness since. I cleaned up the wound and stitched you up the best I could, but to be honest, it's pretty deep, and there's always the danger of infection. You're on a pretty hefty dose of sulfa right now, and we'll keep an eye on it."

"I need to get home." He started to stand, then fell back again, his head spinning.

"Whoa, take it easy," Laskin said, settling him back in bed. "You're getting a hefty dose of morphine, too."

For the next few days, Kazu drifted in and out of consciousness, sometimes seeing the smiling dimpled face of Adelaide in front of him as she fed him spoonfuls of broth, helped him negotiate the bedpan, or administered pills the size of large caliber bullets, it seemed.

More often, behind his closed lids, he would see the face of his young son Ben, apple-cheeked and chubby, with his arms raised, laughing and shrieking, running towards him with the unsteady syncopated gait of a toddler. The image of his wife, Hoshi, was her head bent over the store's ledger, her brow furrowed as she stared at columns of numbers. Intelligent and driven, Hoshi was the daughter of a local Seattle merchant and had inherited her family's business acumen.

Kazu, unlike Hoshi, did not have the taste or aptitude for numbers. Before his parents had died a few years ago—his mother from influenza and his father from cancer—they had both been teachers, and he shared their love of reading, music, and painting. At the time, both Kazu's parents and Hoshi's father thought that their children's complementary personalities would make for a productive and harmonious marriage, so approved the *nakodo*'s—the go-between's—match. Neither Hoshi nor Kazu deluded themselves that their marriage was a love match: it was a contractual agreement entered into by both families. Kazu was grateful that Hoshi for the most part was a hard-working and even-tempered wife.

After Ben was born, Hoshi impressed upon Kazu the need to earn more money—the boy would need things that a simple shopkeeper wouldn't be able to supply. She had a family friend, she said, who knew how he could make a lot of money in a summer. Which is how Kazu became a deckhand on the *Lisa Jo*.

Since he had arrived on St. Paul, he had written one letter to Hoshi and received one back. He was still taking a lot of medication, he wrote, and couldn't walk well yet, but would be home as soon as he could, and he missed them both.

Her return letter was as factual and personalized as the newspaper. "Dad got up this morning and found the word 'Jap' painted on the delivery truck. The roof leaked in last week's storm. Ben started preschool at the Hongwanji. His teacher is Tanaka Sensei."

Kazu had started taking tentative clomping steps with the aid of a cane after five days and began making plans to return home. A tramper was due to call on St. Paul within a week, then dock at Dutch Harbor in Unalaska. From there he could catch a steamship to Seattle. He could be home within a few weeks, depending on how he caught the connection in Dutch Harbor. He was worried that he had nothing to bring Ben for an *omiyage*, a present—he would need to find something in Dutch. Maybe a toy puffin or fur seal.

He awoke the next morning with his damp bedclothes wrapped around him, his right leg hot and painful. Dr. Laskin's kind face creased with worry after he saw the swollen leg, the skin tight and red. Kazu's temperature soared to 102 degrees. As the doctor had feared, the leg was infected. He had heard of an experimental drug called penicillin that looked very promising for the treatment of bacterial infection, but it was in scarce supply. He treated Kazu with as much sulfa as he would tolerate with morphine for the pain and hoped for the best.

After two fretful days and nights, his fever broke, and Dr. Laskin, wiping his own sweaty brow, pronounced that he thought Kazu would survive, but he wasn't going anywhere anytime soon.

"No way you're going to survive an ocean voyage. You need to build up your strength."

Kazu had no choice but to send a letter to Hoshi about his setback. He heard nothing back from her. He told himself that he couldn't blame her for being angry. By now he was supposed to be back in Seattle, helping with the store and with Ben. But as Hoshi would say, usually with a heavy impatient sigh, "*Shikata ga nai.*" *It can't be helped.*

With Adelaide's support, he could stand after a week, and limp around the clinic using a walking stick. The effort usually exhausted him, but as the days went on, he could go longer distances, clomping down the stairs to take in the briny Bering Sea air.

Both the doctor and Adelaide were expert foragers, and often brought him interesting pieces of driftwood, or weathered cedar from some old shipwreck. As long as his energy held out, he sat huddled in a fur-lined parka on the front step of the clinic and honed and whittled these pieces of wood into toys for his son—first a puffin, then a fur seal, then an otter—animals he had seen from the deck of the *Lisa Jo.* As he got better, he carved a standing bear, and an intricate little Native man whom he thought looked a lot like Otto Laskin. The last thing he carved was three-quarter sized wooden pistol. Each he would inscribe with the letters "BY" somewhere on the carving.

During the school year, Adelaide was the island's only teacher, and had access to the few books and supplies at her disposal. She brought him worn, dog-eared copies of classics *The Swiss Family Robinson*, *Adventures of Huckleberry Finn*, and *Treasure Island.* He read these in the evening, in the endless light from the windows.

Better yet, she brought him lined composition books and pencils, colored ones when she could find them. With them, he kept a record of his recovery, what he did and how far he walked each day. And he drew the birds. When the weather permitted, Adelaide packed him into her father's ancient truck with an even older pair of binoculars and drove him to the end of the road, where he could witness the endless variety and cacophony of sea-birds and sketch them on his schoolboy's lined tablets.

One warm day, they packed a picnic lunch and spread it out on an old quilted blanket on the spongy tundra. As they ate their Spam sandwiches and bread-and-butter pickles, he told her about his little boy, Ben, his wife, Hoshi, the dry goods store, and the life in Seattle, seeming so far away now, to which he needed to return. Addy told him she enjoyed teaching much more than nursing. Her students ranged in age from six to sixteen, and she taught them everything from cursive to geometry. Her mother had been Dr. Laskin's nurse until she died of pneumonia, and by necessity, Addy had taken over some of those duties.

She frowned and wrinkled her nose. "I'm not very good at it. Nursing, I mean."

He smiled and said, "You were good enough to save my life." He asked if she would sit for a sketch and with a dimpled smile, she agreed. He drew her as a falconer on a windswept cliff, her long hair flowing, a gyrfalcon perched on her arm, its wings outstretched.

Blushing, she said she loved it. "You drew me like a Greek goddess, Artemis, the huntress!" She burst into a giggle. "Way too fanciful for the likes of me."

The next warm day, they went out with their picnic lunch, and he sketched her again, this time as the little mermaid from Hans Christian Andersen, alone and pensive, perched on a rock. He thought she might like this better than the earlier sketch, but when he looked for her reaction, her eyes were wet with tears.

"I'm sorry. Don't you like it?" Kazu was horror-stricken. The last thing he wanted to do was to offend her. "I'll draw something else."

"She's waiting. Always waiting." Smiling, she took his hand. "You see me like no one else does." When she kissed him, he tasted the sweetness of the pickles and the salt of her tears.

* * *

For the rest of those warm days, picnic lunches took on a whole different meaning. After the Spam and the pickles and apples slices, she pressed herself to him under the seal skin throw, careful not to hurt his leg, and amid the sandwich wrappings and colored pencils they made sweet, gentle love while mosquitos hovered and whined. Afterward, they lay on their backs, her long black hair feathering her bare shoulders, looking at the sky overhead. Addy, like the schoolteacher she was, pointed out the shearwater, or the swift peregrine falcon, or the cormorants in formation, heading out to sea, or to the cliffs to roost.

Only sometimes lying next to her warm body, feeling her fingers in his hair, joining in her generous laugh did he feel a prick of guilt, a tiny poisonous sting, when he thought about Hoshi's silent reproachful frown and Ben's voice, small and demanding, like a hatchling's piercing cry.

He knew he had to go home, and that day would come sooner rather than later. He had been here two months, and the summer was beginning to wane. The birds would leave. The wind and snow would swirl and shriek like relentless banshees. This untamed island was worlds away from his responsibilities in Seattle, from being the dutiful husband, the diligent father. He told himself, as a half-hearted way of absolving himself of guilt, that he could never have a time like this again. He would treasure every moment of it, every second with Adelaide, the woman as free and wild as the island she sprang from, the woman who saved him.

* * *

He had just finished shading in the onion dome on the church when Addy drove up in her father's rattling pickup truck. She ground the gears, mouthed "Oh shit," then yanked on the handbrake. He rose to his feet, leaning on his cane, smiling at her. Driving was not one of her better skills. She stomped on the clutch like she was putting out a campfire. He noticed, through the dusty driver's window, that she had been crying.

He limped to the truck door and pulled it open, peering at her. "Cheer up, my girl, your driving's not that bad."

Blinking away tears, Addy continued gazing through the windshield. "Urgent call for you on the radio. Hoshi Yamane. Your wife."

13

Kazuhiro Yamane

September 1942

Kazu didn't think that Hoshi was that disturbed about her father's death. At least it didn't sound that way when her voice crackled from the St. Paul dockmaster's radio. *Father has died*, she said. *Stroke. You have to come home.*

He did go home, but not before Addy clung to him like a life preserver, her tears beading on his oilskin jacket. He would never forget her, he said, believing at the time that it was the truth, and pressed a small wooden carving of a heart into her hand.

He hugged Otto Laskin too, and shook his hand. He thanked the doctor for saving perhaps his life and certainly his leg—the damaged leg that would keep him out of the war, the injury that would painfully throb for most of his life.

The journey home took three weeks—from the tramper to the steamship, to the Seattle dock. His son, Ben, was delighted to see him, exclaiming over the carved wooden figures and the pencil drawings of exotic birds. Hoshi gave him a quick peck on the cheek and asked about his leg. He said it wouldn't keep him from helping out at the store. She nodded and said, "Good," and went back to her books.

Like cogs in the same wheel, they spun in the same slow orbit, day after day. Kazu dealt with the customers and worked the register, while Hoshi did the books and placed orders with the vendors. After closing, they assessed the inventory and restocked as needed. Then they returned to the small attached apartment, had a simple meal while Ben chatted happily, and fell into bed. The memory of Addy, the tufted puffin, the peregrine falcon, began to fade like historic photographs. The composition books of drawings sat on a shelf, gathering dust. For the next few months, life settled into a kind of numbing but comfortable sameness.

Until the Japanese attacked Pearl Harbor. *The Day That Would Live in Infamy.* Truer words were never spoken. For Kazu, his family and his community, it was a bitter awakening. It would shatter their sense of trust and security and destroy the lives they had built as surely and completely as if a bomb had been dropped directly on them.

In the end, being forced from their home and giving up most of her possessions didn't upset Hoshi much. When the soldiers came, their eyes downcast and embarrassed, Hoshi only had one suitcase and a bundle of bedding swaddling her precious *haribako*, her sewing box. Most of their things were sold for five cents on the dollar, when they could get it, to their *hakujin* neighbors. Or given away for free, like Ben's kitten, Panko, handed over to kindly old Mrs. Finch, who said she'd take good care of him until Ben "got back." Ben wept bitterly and clung to the tiny ginger cat until Hoshi freed it from the boy's desperate grasp. Even at his age, Ben somehow understood that they might never return.

What devastated Hoshi, after Executive Order 9066 was enacted and they were herded, numbered paper tags dangling from their coats, onto dusty coal trains with blackened windows—was leaving the store. The bolts of cloth, spools of thread, various and sundry items that made up the inventory of her family's Sawada Dry Goods Store—the inanimate things she counted and catalogued and recorded in columns every day—that was what broke her heart to leave.

They arrived at the Minidoka Relocation Camp in the middle of a dust storm. The half-finished barracks, covered with flapping sheets of tar paper, looked like derelict ships plying through an endless sea of grit.

* * *

This would be their prison for the foreseeable future, contained in barbed wire, watched over by armed guards in towers. Though he hadn't thought it possible when they first arrived, camp life settled into a different kind of numbing sameness. Queuing for rationed food, the toilet, the bath. Bitter cold and snow, followed by torrential rain and flooding, followed by Saharan heat, repeat.

They each tried to recapture part of the lives they had left behind. Hoshi used her shopkeeping skills to help run one of the camp stores. Since his leg prevented him from performing harder labor, Kazu taught camp middle and high-schoolers, among other things, art and drawing. Ben made the fastest and most complete adjustment. At five years old, he made friends quickly with the other children and didn't seem to be fazed at all by the questionable sanitation, communal living, and lack of privacy that aggrieved the adults.

When a few internees from Alaska arrived at camp, Kazu found himself wondering about Addy and Otto, and how they were faring. He had heard about the Japanese bombing of Dutch Harbor, and the invasion of Attu and Kiska. Several times he had thought of writing Addy, but then stopped himself. He was a married man. He had no business rekindling a relationship with a young woman, one to whom he could make no promises, offer no prospects. He convinced himself that her untamed world should never trespass on his—this seemingly endless cycle of barbed wire and armed guards, hand-dug latrines and ration tickets. He decided that for him, Adelaide Laskin should remain only as a sweet, dimming memory of that one, unrepeatable summer.

August 15, 1944
Kazuhiro Yamane
Minidoka War Relocation Center
Hunt, Idaho

Dear Kazuhiro;

I hope this letter finds you and your family well. The earlier letter that I wrote you came back with the last mail boat, so I'm trying a different internment camp. I learned that Camp Harmony (such a euphemism!) is just a temporary holding facility and detainees are usually sent onward to different camps. I never thought I'd see the day when this country would do this to their own citizens, but I guess after what happened to us, I shouldn't be surprised.

So much to tell you—I'll start at the beginning. In May of 1942, Addy gave birth to a little boy. Kazu, he's your son—she named him George Hiro Laskin. Please don't be upset with Addy—she didn't want to tell you because she knew you already had a family and didn't want you to feel guilty about George. It's OK, really—the three of us made a nice little family ourselves. More about George later.

Shortly after George was born, as you know, the Japanese bombed the military base at Dutch Harbor, then invaded Attu and Kiska. You may or may not know that we on St. Paul and St. George have been under the auspices of the U.S. Fish and Wildlife Service for decades. This has given the federal government exclusive right to harvest pelts from our northern fur seals—but that's another atrocity I'll bend your ear about if and when I ever see you.

So, the USFWS, in their infinite wisdom, decided to evacuate the ENTIRE populations of St. Paul and St. George, "for our own safety." They did this on June 16, 1942, when George was just three weeks old. We could only bring one suitcase per person, and had no idea at the time where we were going. As you can imagine, moving with no warning and very little luggage was an ordeal with a newborn baby!

An old transport ship called the Delarof picked us up—those of us from St. George and St. Paul, with our one suitcase each. Then we stopped in Dutch Harbor to pick up some villagers from Atka and we were all jammed in the hold, must have been more than five hundred of us. Eight days later, we arrived at Funter Bay on Admiralty Island in Southeast Alaska. They let everybody but the Atka folks off here. I was told that the Atka people were offloaded at an old herring plant at Killisnoo, near Angoon. The next day they moved the St. George folks to the Funter Bay mine site a mile away. I can only imagine what the mine site is like, since our location is no picnic—but here at our location, we at least have a post office and a store.

So that's where we are. I know that St. Paul is a remote place, but Funter Bay is much more primitive. It's the site of an old cannery that had fallen into disrepair. When we first got here, drinkable water was hard to come by, pipes freezing and all, and washing clothes was difficult as well. We had to thaw quite a few of little George's frozen diapers in front of the fire before pinning them on him! For the first few months, some of us lived in tents until we could build some rudimentary housing or repair the buildings already here. Last year, the military put up a few Quonset huts that at least appear to be somewhat wind and watertight.

Through it all, George was a trooper. He is two now, a strong, fine-looking young boy, Kazu—looks a lot like you. I've enclosed a photo of George and Addy. Addy carried on teaching some of the youngsters, and I helped out with my doctoring skills. The poor housing and water situations caused serious influenza and pneumonia problems over the winter. There was a tuberculosis outbreak as well, and we lost a few people.

I am sorry to have to tell you that Addy was one of those we lost. She died two weeks ago while we were waiting for transport to take her to Juneau for treatment. She's buried in the little cemetery behind the caretaker's house. I'd like to take her back home to rest next to her mother, but who knows how long it'll be before we're allowed to leave?

I'm writing now because I think you have a right to know—both about George and about Addy's passing. She made me promise not to burden you with the knowledge of your son, but now that she's gone, well, she doesn't have a lot to say about it. What the heck, she and her mother can give me disapproving looks from heaven.

She never told me in so many words, but I think she loved you, Kazu. Enough to have your son, and to give him part of your name, anyway. I hope you still think of her fondly. I miss her every day. Thank God I can still see my girl every time I look at George.

I hope I haven't overwhelmed you too much with all this. Please write back when you get this letter.

Yours truly,
Otto and George Laskin

14

Kazuhiro Yamane

Christmas 1944

Winter arrived, like the two winters before it, a howling demon across the flat arid Idaho plains. Coarse meal-like snow infiltrated the barracks, puffing through the flapping seams where the tar paper failed to meet the wooden studs, no matter how often it was repaired. Each weekday morning, Kazu trudged past the snow-smothered vegetable fields to Block 23—the high school, where his bleary-eyed teenage students huddled around the wood stove and pretended to absorb his lecture on American History, too polite to yawn or complain.

He couldn't blame them. Truthfully, he found it hard to care about the history of the country that had imprisoned them, its own citizens, and he found his own mind drifting. He got much livelier responses during art class, when his students were encouraged to actively create a more beautiful reality.

The pupils were less attentive than usual because it was the final school day before the Christmas break, and everyone, himself included, fidgeted in their seats. There would be no presents, of course, but the decorating of the dining halls had become a festive and competitive affair. Kazu's block had raised enough money to buy a small Christmas tree and hoped to outdo their neighboring blocks this year.

When the school day finally ended, and his students shot out the door, calling out, "Merry Christmas!" or "See you next year," Kazu breathed a sigh of relief and reversed his journey back to his barracks, noting how the temperature had dropped in the last few hours.

Clapping his hands together to try to warm them, he entered the dining hall for Block 41. He was greeted by Ben, breathless, who pulled at his father's gloved hand.

"See the tree, Papa!"

A scraggly evergreen of some kind was propped between two cafeteria-style tables. Someone had found a string of white lights that glowed feebly from between the branches. The smiling, round-faced woman who taught at the elementary school somehow had corralled Ben and his classmates into decorating the small tree with crinkled tinsel and crepe paper. The noise of the children shrieking with either delight or irritation was deafening.

Somewhere, Bing Crosby's "White Christmas" played, barely audible, on a record player. Kazu sat at one of the cafeteria tables and set his book bag at his feet. His leg throbbed from the cold and the walk through the snow. That and the music made him feel oddly nostalgic, made him think of the warm kisses, the dimpled smile of Adelaide Laskin.

The door to the dining hall blew open then, admitting Hoshi, stamping her feet free of the kernel-like snow. "I thought I'd find you here."

Hoshi had walked all the way in the snow from the store on Block 14, and cold seem to emanate from her like a block of ice. Snow clung to her knit cap and eyelashes, giving her an almost endearing child-like quality. She blew into her hands, covered with gloves except for the fingertips. "Crazy day in the store today."

"It's Christmas, Hoshi-chan." He rarely used the "chan" with her, an endearment usually used with children, and she gave him a quizzical glance.

Her furrowed brow returned. "We got some mail today from Mrs. Finch. It's addressed to all of us." Hoshi usually stopped by the post office on the way back to the barracks, but they almost never received any mail. "I hope the house hasn't burned down or anything."

Kazu called Ben to sit beside him. "A letter from Mrs. Finch, Ben."

Ben's face brightened. "Maybe she has news about Panko!" Ben spoke often of the little ginger cat, Panko, that had to be left behind with Mrs. Finch when the family was interned.

Hoshi opened the envelope, addressed to "The Yamanes" in Mrs. Finch's spidery penmanship. Inside was a Christmas card picturing a jovial Santa standing beside a roaring fireplace, stockings hung from the mantle, a fully decorated Christmas tree in the background. When Hoshi opened the card, a black and white photo fell to the floor.

The photo was of an older, well-dressed Caucasian woman sitting in a wing-backed chair beside a glittering Christmas tree. Several wrapped presents surrounded the tree, including what looked like a huge fruitcake wrapped in cellophane. In the woman's lap was a large striped cat, looking very content, with a garland of tinsel around its neck.

"It's Panko," Ben whispered, running his index finger on the cat's image.

Kazu read aloud what the woman had written in the card:

Merry Christmas, Yamane family!

I hope you are all well. I thought you might enjoy a picture of your boy Panko. You can hardly recognize him, can you? He's grown quite a bit, and hasn't missed too many meals—can't you tell? He's a good boy, and very good company for this old lady. I hope that you're all doing as well as can be expected. My deepest wish is that we can meet again when all this unpleasantness is over.

Merry Christmas, my dear friends.

With warmest regards,
Eunice Finch and Panko

"This unpleasantness?" Kazu almost laughed out loud at the well-intended old woman's euphemism for imprisonment and war.

Hoshi frowned to silence him. "There now. Isn't it nice that Panko is doing so well?" Hoshi asked her son.

To Kazu's surprise, Ben's eyes filled with tears, and he flung the photo back at his mother. He ran out the dining hall doors into the snow, an eddy of flakes swirling in his wake.

Kazu found the little boy in their barracks, sobbing inconsolably into his pillow. Kazu lay beside him and rubbed his back until the sobs subsided into sniffles.

"Panko has forgotten me while I'm in this stupid place. He has another life with Mrs. Finch. Even when we get out, he won't know me."

"Of course he'll remember you."

"No, he won't! I don't have a cat anymore!"

Kazu had an idea. From his book bag, he pulled out his sketchpad and pencil. "Of course you do. You have . . . Panko the Camp Cat."

Sniffing, Ben swiped at his eyes and watched as Kazu's pencil moved swiftly across the page. Soon, a line-drawn, cartoon version of Panko emerged. This version of Panko stood on his hind legs, had wide expressive eyes and smiled.

Ben snuggled up to his father as he drew. "Well, but he's not a real cat . . ."

"As real as you want him to be. He can have real adventures. And friends." He quickly sketched a small canine figure. "This could be his buddy—uh, Kayo Coyote!"

Ben chuckled. "Kayo Coyote. What kind of adventures?"

Kazu kept it simple, quickly sketching the whimsical line art figures of Panko. "In his first adventure, Panko the Camp Cat, who hates white bread and potatoes, dives into the canal to chase a floating fish head and almost drowns, but just in time, is saved by the camp fire brigade."

Ben pointed at the fire brigade. "They all look the same. And they all kind of look like Mr. Yanagihara."

Mr. Yanagihara was in the fire brigade, a jovial round-headed, round-bodied man, a living caricature. Kazu gave his son a sidelong glance. "Do you want speed, or accuracy?"

Ben clapped his hands. "Do another one!"

"In Panko the Camp Cat's next adventure, he slips past the barbed wire and escapes into the desert. Here he meets Kayo Coyote, who becomes his companion and ally in all of his adventures . . ."

As Kazu sketched a wide smile on Kayo Coyote's face, he found himself smiling as well. He could sketch these out into comic strips and put them together into a book for Ben for

Christmas. He already had ideas for more Panko the Camp Cat adventures, where he wandered far and wide into the Idaho desert, but always returned home to his boy, Ben.

Kazu realized that Ben had fallen asleep beside him, breathing deeply, his lips slightly parted. He closed his sketch pad and slowly rose. He stretched, feeling his leg twinge. He had the Christmas break to create the world of Panko the Camp Cat, where a daruma-shaped man can save you from drowning, where you can slip under the barbed wire and escape.

January 5, 1945
Kazuhiro Yamane
Minidoka War Relocation Center
Hunt, Idaho

Dear Kazu,

I hope the new year finds you and your family well. Except for the first letter I wrote, the others haven't been coming back, so I hope you're receiving them. I've got good news and bad news, and I hate opening with bad news, so . . .

First the good news: George and I have moved from the old cannery bunkhouse to one of the newer Quonset huts. We share it with two nice Aleut families with five children between them, one about George's age. It doesn't leak as badly as the bunkhouse and is up on some piling, so it doesn't flood when it rains. We've been lucky so far this winter—it hasn't been nearly as cold as 1942, when it was 10 degrees above zero that Christmas Eve.

This year, Christmas dinner was a real treat. Several of the men shot a couple of deer so we had quite a feast. The Fish and Wildlife folks complained about the illegal hunting at first, then just threw up their hands and issued them licenses. I mean, where's their Christmas spirit, right? I wrapped up the little wooden heart you carved for Addy and gave it to George for Christmas, saying it was from his mother. I didn't think you'd mind.

Now the not-so-good news: I'm very ill, Kazu. I'm a good enough doctor to know that my kidneys are failing. When (if!) this "internment" is over, I will not—I cannot—return to St. Paul. I have a very good doctor at St. Ann's in Juneau who is doing the best he can for me, and he will see me through to the end of this process, however long it takes.

This process will take a matter of months, if I'm lucky, but definitely not years. I'm afraid that there will be no one to care for George after I die. I have no other family, in St. Paul or elsewhere.

George is a good boy, a kind, sensitive boy. The foster care system is not the ideal situation for any child, but it would be especially detrimental for a boy like George. He's only three years old.

Please, Kazu, can you find it in your heart to take him into your family? I'm so sorry to spring this on you, this is not what Addy or I would have wanted at all, but George has no one else.

I suppose this is an exercise in futility, since you haven't answered any of my earlier letters, but I am desperate, and am hoping you are getting them. Please write when you receive this, whatever you decide. I don't know how much more time I have and I need to find a place for George.

I keep hearing that the end of the war is near. I hope they're right.

Sincerely,
Otto and George Laskin

15

Kazuhiro Yamane

January 1945

This New Year's at Minidoka was the most festive since the beginning of internment. More men than ever turned up to pound mochi for *mochitsuki*, and the dining hall workers did their best to replicate some of the *Shogatsu* delicacies.

More than ever, Kazu found himself restless. Part of this unsettled feeling was due to his injured leg that often ached, but most of the time just made him acutely aware of its weakness. For months now, more able-bodied adults with proper clearance had been leaving camp to work as hired labor for the local farmers and were able to buy extra Christmas treats for their families. Young men with two strong legs had signed up in the all-Nisei 442nd Regimental Combat Team and performed admirably.

There was an uneasy feeling too, of the end of things. They would be released from Minidoka, but what did they have to return to? There was no store, no home; little Ben didn't even have his cat. Many fellow internees mumbled about settling elsewhere, maybe the Midwest, anywhere but the West Coast, where history could easily repeat itself.

This life would end, and they would need to restart another. He and Hoshi had discussed this recently after Ben had gone to bed.

"We should be near Setsuo and his family." Hoshi carefully sewed a button onto one of Ben's shirts. Setsuo was Hoshi's older brother, her only sibling, currently incarcerated at Heart Mountain with his wife and two daughters.

Kazu had taken out his sketch pad and started sharpening his pencil. He was about to start a new Panko the Camp Cat comic for Ben. Surprisingly, these little comics had become quite popular among both adults and children, and one had run in an issue of the camp paper, *The Minidoka Irrigator.* "Sure, they're the only family we have."

Hoshi nodded. "He has a friend, a Chinese guy, who would let him buy his business. Then he could hire us."

"What kind of business?"

"A store, of course. What other kind of business do we know?" Hoshi chewed off the end of the thread, inspected her work, then folded the little shirt carefully. She poked the needle into the pincushion that looked like a tomato and closed the drawer to the little *haribako.*

"Where is this business?"

"California. The San Francisco area. Where the weather's warmer." She pulled her worn sweater around her and shivered.

"You mean, where they have earthquakes? And that huge fire?"

"That was ages ago, silly." Hoshi waved a hand at him dismissively. "Don't stay up too late. School starts tomorrow, remember."

He mumbled something that sounded like, "Yeah, yeah." He hated that she treated him like Ben sometimes, but he bit his tongue and tempered his responses, since very little separated their living quarters from their neighbors, the chatty Ishikawas.

He picked up his pencil and began drawing:

The Adventures of Panko the Camp Cat

In this story, the evil rat Klaus Ratzenburger infiltrates the camp. Ratzenburger wears a swastika on his arm and has long claws and sharp teeth. He invades the food stores and steals sweet mochi rice and Vienna sausages, leaving the camp residents nothing to eat but stale white bread and moldy potatoes. The boy Ben, who is the camp leader, deputizes Panko the Camp Cat, giving him a vest with a silver star.

Panko escapes under the barbed wire and challenges Ratzenburger to a duel in the Idaho desert, with Kayo the Coyote officiating. Panko has a gleaming *katana*, while Ratzenburger brandishes a rapier. A fierce battle ensues until sunset when finally, Panko lops off one of Ratzenburger's clawed hands and the rapier falls to the ground. Shrieking with pain and anger, Ratzenburger retreats into the loneliness of the desert. Panko and Kayo hear Ratzenburger screaming, "Ach, you haven't seen the last of me yet, Panko!"

Panko returns to camp where he is paraded through the streets on the fire truck driven by one of the daruma-looking firemen. "You've saved us, Panko!" "You're our hero!" The boy Ben gives him the Key to the Camp that looks like a fishbone. Camp residents line the street, tossing long strands of cooked *udon* like tickertape and dry bonito flakes like confetti.

March 30, 1945
Mr. Kazuhiro Yamane
Minidoka Relocation Camp
Hunt, Idaho

Dear Mr. Yamane;

I am not sure that you will receive this letter, but I am hoping that it will make its way to you.

It is with great sorrow that I inform you that our friend, Dr. Otto Laskin, passed away on March 19, 1945. As you may know, Dr. Laskin suffered from end-stage renal disease. We tried to keep him as comfortable as possible and he passed on quietly here at our facility. Dr. Laskin's wish was to be interred in the cemetery at Funter Bay beside his daughter Adelaide. He has already made arrangements in this regard.

I enclose this photo of his grandson, George Laskin, as Dr. Laskin requested. In his last days, he told me that he was hoping to live long enough to hear from you, and that you would be able to accommodate young George, as he has no other family. Unfortunately, since there has been no communication from you, it is inevitable that George enters the foster care system.

I am sorry to be the bearer of such sad news. Please don't hesitate to contact me if I can be of any assistance. I remain,

Yours truly,
Dr. Jonathan Copeland

Internal Medicine
St. Ann's Hospital
Juneau, Alaska

16

Kazuhiro Yamane

July 1945

Raucous teenagers pedaled second-hand bicycles toward the ball fields, raising dust like swarms of insects as they passed Kazu on the road. "Hey, Mr. Yamane," they called out, waving baseball gloved-hands. Kazu raised a hand in greeting, ducking away from the dust as he trudged from the school to the barracks through the relentless afternoon heat.

The inside of the barracks was only marginally cooler, but at least it was in the shade. This time of the afternoon, it was quiet. The men were either working in the camp fields or as hired labor on someone else's farms. The women were working in the laundry or mess halls, or like Hoshi, in one of the camp stores. Ben was usually playing cowboys outdoors with his friend, Billy Ishikawa, the youngest of their neighbors three children.

But today, Ben was sitting on his bed surrounded by scraps of cloth, scissors, and other sewing supplies. Hoshi's *haribako* gaped open beside Ben, every drawer and small cabinet door open, its contents strewn across the rough blanket. Kazu felt his temper rise. Ben knew better than to snoop in his mother's things. They all lived in such close quarters; there were unwritten rules of etiquette when it came to other people's property.

"Ben!" He said, and the little boy jumped.

"I was just looking . . ." Ben's eyes were downcast.

"You know better than this, Ben. How would you like it if she rummaged through your things?"

"I was just looking for something to make a star, you know? Some bright-colored material, maybe, that Mom could sew onto my vest, like Panko's?" Ben's face was red, his lower lip beginning to quiver.

Kazu realized that he was in some ways responsible for Ben's lapse in judgment. His latest story of Panko had deputized the cat with a silver star, and Hoshi had just recently sewn Ben a patchwork vest with various fabric scraps.

He sighed. "OK, but let's put everything away first, just the way you found it. Then let's *ask* Mom about the material, and she can take a look to see if she has it. She would really be upset if she knew you were rifling through her things."

Sniffling a little, Ben began gathering up the tins of needles and pins, pincushions, fabric samples, and embroidery threads.

"Try to put them back where you found them. You know Mom will know if anything's out of place." Kazu felt sorry for the little boy and bent to help him.

That's when he saw the envelopes. Six of them, all addressed to "Kazuhiro Yamane," and all torn open across the top. Five of them were from "O. Laskin." His stomach dropped.

"Ben, where did you get these envelopes?" Kazu tried to keep his voice even.

"Oh, those were in the secret spot, under here." Ben pointed to a drawer bottom. "You slide this back, and look, a secret spot!" He was triumphant, pointing out the shallow compartment.

"Did you open these envelopes, Ben?"

The little boy shook his head.

"I won't be mad, I just need to know for sure."

"No, Papa. I didn't open them. They were just like that."

Kazu nodded. "OK, let's leave these out for now. But put the rest away."

He wanted to be alone while he read these letters, so he sent Ben out to find his friend Billy. After the boy scampered out with his miniature holster and wooden gun, Kazu sat down on the edge of a bunk to read in the stifling heat of the barracks.

He had read them all and returned them to their envelopes by the time Hoshi returned to the barracks, blowing tendrils of hair off her sweaty forehead.

"We sold out of all the Nehi. You know, Ben and Billy could make some money with a lemonade stand . . . what?" She noticed Kazu, elbows on his knees, staring at her. Then a glimmer of recognition as her eyes found the stack of envelopes beside him on the bunk.

Kazu's voice was barely above a whisper. "When were you going to tell me about these?"

She ran her hand across her damp forehead. "Me? Tell you? When were you going to tell me? About the girl? About the child?"

"If you read these, then you've figured out that I didn't know about the child!"

"Well, about the girl, then!"

"Listen, I'm not denying that we were . . . together. And I'm sorry that you found out like this. I never meant to hurt you or Ben."

Hoshi snorted. "I can't believe you. You can't do any real work—but you're feeling strong enough to screw some seal-hunting savage on some God-forsaken rock!"

"Hey!" Kazu was stunned. He had never heard Hoshi swear, and frankly had never heard her string so many words together at a time. "You can cuss me out as much as you want, but she's not to blame."

Hoshi opened and closed the haribako doors with fierce energy. "How did you find them? Do you look through my things when I'm not here?"

"Oh, Hoshi." Kazu was suddenly exhausted. "Ben found them looking for some fabric for a deputy badge for his vest. He came across them by accident. I never look through your stuff, you know I don't."

"I don't know anything for sure any more."

"When, Hoshi? When were you going to tell me about those letters?"

Hoshi slumped onto the bunk across from him. "I don't know. Maybe never. I opened the first one because I thought Dr. Laskin was sending us a bill for his services. He took care of you for a few months, after all. I was trying to figure out how we would pay him. Then when I read it, and about his daughter, and the baby . . ." For the first time in a long time, Kazu saw Hoshi's eyes tearing. "I thought I would ignore it. They were put in a place worse than here. And the girl died, right?"

Kazu rubbed his thigh, trying to knead out its ever-present ache.

"Several others came, some with pictures of the boy. He was being cared for by his grandfather, and they seemed to be doing OK. Then the one came telling you he was dying. And he begged you to take the boy. And I knew that could never happen, Kazu."

"But why?" Even to himself, he sounded faraway and querulous, like a crow cawing.

She glared at him. "You would have me raise this boy alongside Ben? This boy who is the product of your—temporary insanity? How long before everyone would know? How long before everyone would know that this half-savage boy is your son?"

Kazu stood suddenly and Hoshi cringed reflexively. "The boy's mother is Aleut. Do not call her a savage."

Hoshi waved her hand as if batting at a fly. "Oh, so gallant."

"So, over all these months, you kept these letters from me? What a burden it must have been to bear." He tried unsuccessfully to keep the sarcasm from his voice.

"I bore it in silence, like I always do. Then the letter from the doctor came, saying Otto Laskin had died. Then I knew it could end there. He had no other family. The boy was only three and wouldn't know about you. It could end, and we would have our lives back." She looked hopeful.

Kazu found himself looking at a photo of a smiling three-year-old George, bundled in a heavy wool coat, leaning against the door to a Quonset hut. He had Addy's dimples, and something about Kazu through the eyes and the shape of his face. "He has no one, Hoshi."

"*Baka*!" Hoshi spat out the word for "stupid," and stomped her foot. Dust rose into the stifling heat. "Don't you get it? I'm trying to make this go away."

"He's a three-year-old child, Hoshi. He's alone."

"God damn it, Kazu! This is your mistake, not mine. I'm not going to pay for it, and neither is Ben."

As if on cue, Ben appeared in the doorway, he eyes round as saucers. His parents never argued—he probably wondered if he'd entered the wrong barracks. Kazu wondered how much the boy had heard.

He was about to call Ben to him to comfort and reassure him, when Hoshi said, “Ben, go wash up. It’s almost time for dinner.”

The little boy obeyed, after some backward glances. Hoshi tucked the haribako under the bunk. She patted her hair in place, refastening a few bobby pins. She turned to Kazu, her face set as if in cement. “It ends. Either way, it ends.”

The Last Adventure of Panko the Camp Cat

The war is over, and Klaus Ratzenburger, the evil rodent, has been vanquished. The gates to the camp are opened, the barbed wire cut down, and everyone is leaving for faraway places—some for home, some just for somewhere else. Panko says goodbye to his good friend Kayo Coyote. Kayo tries to understand why they just can't keep having adventures in the desert, but Panko says it's not possible. Panko says goodbye to the boy Ben, who is brave but tearful.

"You have a family, people who love you. But there's another boy in Alaska who is alone and needs me, a small boy I didn't even know existed," Panko tells Ben. "I know it's hard to understand."

In the last frame, Panko walks off into a dust storm with his suitcase full of fish heads.

17

Mari

Summer 2024

By noon the next day, Mari found out almost all a librarian could know about Kazuhiro Yamane and George Laskin. Her grandfather left his wife, Hoshi, and his son when Ben was eight years old. One of his letters to Ben said he had found a job at a newspaper, so Mari contacted the Juneau Empire, the regional paper there. A bored human resources person was only too glad to go through their personnel archives and come up with Kazuhiro Yamane's file. He had worked there at the Empire in typesetting and production from 1948 through 1953. George Laskin was in the Juneau public school system from 1948 through 1953; then there were no records of his schooling.

A one-column inch obituary of Kazuhiro Yamane stated that he died on June 15, 1955, at forty-one years of age of a "sudden illness." At the time of his death, he was employed by a fish processing plant in Hoonah. He was survived by his son, George, age fourteen.

His obituary did not mention a wife and son in California. Kazuhiro Yamane owned no real estate, nor did he have a police record of any kind. His Alaska state driver's license had expired in 1953.

Mari found a record of George Laskin being adopted in 1955 and his name changed. From there, Kazuhiro Yamane's minimal footprint on earth seemed to have all but disappeared.

18

Beans

Summer 2024

When Beans FaceTimed his mother, Mari's brow was furrowed, the way it got when she was embroiled in a complicated research project.

"What's going on, Mom? Grandma giving you a headache?"

From the next room, Beans could hear his grandmother calling out, "I heard that."

"The news on Lloyd Paul is we can't prove that Lloyd's death was a homicide. Hell, we can't even prove he's dead, really. Most likely an accident, or at worst, undetermined."

Mari sighed. "That's good, I guess."

"So, what's new down your way?"

Mari shook her head. "You wouldn't believe this, Havi."

"Believe what?"

"I went through one of your grandfather's old trunks up in the attic? There's all kinds of beautiful sketches and some journals. Even some comic strips that it looks like your great-grandfather drew for your grandfather. In all this stuff, is a letter from a man, a doctor in St. Paul—Alaska, not Minnesota—who says that your grandfather has a half-brother. A half-Aleut boy—well, I guess he'd be an old man if he's still alive—about five years younger than him."

"Shit, you're kidding."

"Do I look like I'm kidding?" Mari peered over the top of her reading glasses.

"Who is this guy? Where is he?" Beans pulled out a pad and pen.

"Not really sure at this point. His name is—was—George Laskin; his mother died when he was very young. It looks like his father—your great-grandfather—died in Southeast Alaska somewhere. But George was adopted at some point when he was a teenager and his name changed and records sealed, looks like. There's no further trace of him, at least not that I can access."

"Dinner's ready, Mari." His grandmother's voice from off-screen. "Tell Havi he should be here. I made way too much sukiyaki."

Mari rolled her eyes. "Coming, Mom. Sheesh, she still thinks she needs to cook for a family of five."

"I'll see what I can find out from my end." He tucked the piece of paper in a pocket. He was stunned—*his grandfather had had a half-brother.* He knew very little about his Grandpa Ben's childhood—only that after the war, his mother had raised him alone in an apartment above her brother's store. That explained why his great-grandfather had left Ben and his mother, to be with his motherless son.

"And don't forget to check the mail," she reminded him before she signed off.

Of course, he had already forgotten about the mail. Beans made the short drive to the post office and unlocked one of the small mail boxes recessed into the far wall. He waved at Bernie, who was busy arguing foreign postal rates with a customer—amazingly, someone Beans didn't recognize.

Mari got very little snail mail, but Beans had promised to check her post office box regularly. Among the ad circulars and catalogs he liberated from the small PO box, he was surprised to see a post card addressed to him plastered with way too many stamps. It pictured the iconic view of the Golden Gate Bridge from the air. He smiled.

Amy. He and Amy Chandler had been dating only a few months before she was called for a guest dancing gig with the Oakland Ballet. He had met Amy under less-than-ideal circumstances—her roommate, another ballet dancer, had been one of the victims of the barista serial killer. It was a few weeks after the perpetrator was apprehended and the case closed before Beans wandered back into the coffee shop where she worked and summoned up the nerve to ask her out. After that, they had settled into what could only be described as an easiness that usually comes with knowing someone a long time. He had called her on the way to the Anchorage airport about his change in plans. Only Amy would think of sending him something as old-fashioned as a postcard, and then sending it by some kind of express service.

> *Hey copper; wish you were here. ☺ A couple of us got tired of the Residence Inn and rented this SICK Airbnb. View of the water. Killer Thai food down the street. Opening night coming up. Merde! Miss Arch and El. And you. XO, Amy*

He stared at the artificially colorized photo and Amy's increasingly cramped handwriting as she tried to cram all the words on the card. Another reason to go down to California. The Lloyd Paul case was a nonstarter. He could help his mother and grandmother with the heavy lifting. And he could see Amy, maybe even watch her perform with a big city ballet. The thought of seeing Amy again gave him a small frisson of pleasure.

His phone buzzed with a text. Fee. *Get down to the dock.*

He texted back. *On my way.*

The town seemed almost deserted. Even the YC store looked strangely abandoned, with Janelle looking out glumly from behind the cash register. It was still too early in the summer for the whole town to be out berry picking, he thought. Where was everyone?

He called Fee. "Everything OK? What's happening?"

Fee was obviously outdoors somewhere, with men's voices calling out in the background. "You won't believe this, Havi. Remember how Victor insisted that we needed to find Lloyd's head? Well, the divers are here and they're in the river now."

Most of the village had decided watching divers search for Lloyd's head was more entertaining than berry picking. Victor Paul had hired a salvage outfit out of Anchorage to scour the riverbed near the dock and the barge landing to look for his son's skull. Two divers moved back and forth across the river with poles and metal detectors, occasionally popping up like wet seals to report a broken propeller, ancient winch, snarls of fishing gear or whatever else had survived freezing and breakup over many years. Andreas K had driven his Greek/Mexican/Japanese food truck to the dock to serve the dietary needs of the spectators and was doing a fair business. Victor stood in gumboots at water's edge, his arms crossed, watching each bobbing head in the water.

Beans spotted Fee trying to keep kids in waders from joining in. "This isn't an Easter egg hunt, kids," she told them. "It's a police investigation."

"He talked about it, but I didn't think he'd actually do it." Beans shook his head.

"I think he's lost his fucking mind," Fee muttered. "But it's his money. They didn't find anything but some old chain and some scrap steel off the barge landing."

A sleek black head popped above the water. "We got something here."

A murmur rippled through the crowd.

The second black head emerged from the water and raised his mask. "Jesus. Coins. Quarters. Lots of quarters."

An uneasy chuckle from the spectators. Beans remembered that last night, the coins jingling in Lloyd's pockets after he cleaned out the machines at the washeteria. This is definitely where Lloyd went into the water, though not where he ended up.

"We got something else," the first diver said.

When he raised it up out of the water, Beans could hardly recognize it. Blackened with rust and silt, it looked vaguely like a chunk of metal debris that they had hauled out earlier. But after they had brought it to the dock and set it on a tarp with dozens of slimy quarters, he could see it for what it was—a gun.

Beans found himself holding his breath. *Was this Jimmy Beans's revolver, the one with the serial number filed off? Had his mother ditched it here that night?*

Fee retrieved a roll of paper towels from her truck and dabbed the mud and slime from the gun. What emerged was not Jimmy Beans's Colt, but a Heritage Rough Rider with the mother of pearl grips—Zachariah Green's gun. The gun that anybody who had ever bought weed in this town could recognize. A collective gasp rose from the crowd so no one could hear Beans exhale in relief.

"Jesus," Beans said so only Fee could hear him. "Zach Green's Wild West revolver."

"What the hell's it doing there?" Fee asked, her eyes wide.

"Must have dumped it before he skipped town."

During Zach Green's employment at the washeteria, he had a side gig selling weed and coke that paid way better than the Pauls did. He left for greener pastures, according to local gossip, shortly after Lloyd disappeared.

Janelle came to the dock after closing the store and watched impassively with Junior at her side as Victor commanded the divers he had commissioned. They continued until well past ten when they started losing light. Andreas K packed up his colorful koi-patterned awning and drove his food truck back to town. The crowd, slapping at mosquitos and subdued over the lack of any further discoveries, dissipated.

Victor shook the hands of the divers and loaded them in the back of his pickup truck to take them on their short ride to their bed-and-breakfast. Fee dropped the evidence bag containing Zach's gun and the quarters in the bed of her truck with a loud clang.

"I gotta say, the last thing I expected those guys to find was Zach's revolver," Fee said.

"No, the last thing would have been Lloyd's skull. This is the second to the last thing." Beans said. "But weird, isn't it, that we should find Zach's gun within days of Lloyd's leg washing up?"

"You think maybe Zach got tired of Lloyd's management style and offed him?" Fee winced as if her head hurt. "Then disposed of the gun? Jesus, why is there so much shit in the river?"

She followed him back to the Beans bungalow and sat on the sofa with one of Mari's Japanese lagers while they contemplated what would have possessed Zach to dispose of his gun that way.

"Seriously, you don't suppose he was responsible for Lloyd's disappearance, do you?" Fee asked.

"Who knows? He was a weed and coke dealer, but I never heard of him shooting anybody."

Beans grabbed a Diet Coke and opened a bag of pretzels while he told her about his grandfather's suddenly discovered half-Aleut half-brother.

Fee chewed on her thumbnail. "Wow. How sad. What a sacrifice your great-grandfather made—and your grandfather too, although it obviously wasn't his choice."

They were lost in their thoughts for a few seconds until a loud rap on the front door made them both jump. They glanced at each other, momentarily embarrassed at their unease. Fee shrugged and unsnapped her holster, while Beans peered through the peephole.

He sighed with relief. "It's your mother."

Gloria Gunnerson was wearing only a thin cotton nightgown and scuffed bedroom slippers, her hair standing in gray tufts from her head. She smiled and offered Beans two eggs cupped in her hands.

"Mom, what are you doing here? And where's Anita?" Fee's expression was pained as she looked past her mother into the darkness.

Gloria looked affronted. "I was bringing eggs. I saw your truck out front."

"Jesus, I'd better get you home." Fee draped her jacket over her mother's shoulders.

More loud rapping at the door. This time it was Anita, Gloria's caregiver, still in her nurse's scrubs, frantic and breathless.

"Oh crap, is your mother here? Thank God! I went to the bathroom for a second—"

"It was longer than that. You were doing Number Two." Gloria offered helpfully.

"TMI, Gloria. Anyway, when I got out, she was gone. I thought she might come in this direction, she usually, does, and I saw your truck here . . . Oh, thank God." Anita bent from her waist, catching her breath. Beans caught her familiar smell of stale cigarettes and a faint whiff of alcohol on her breath, but the woman didn't seem drunk.

"Go on home, Anita. It's been a long night for all of us. I got it from here." Fee picked up her keys from the coffee table.

"I'm really sorry." Anita seemed to be on the verge of tears. "She's just so fast sometimes . . ."

Fee smiled kindly. "Oh, don't I know it. No harm done. Go home and get some rest. I'll see you tomorrow."

After Anita left, the rumbling of her ancient Jeep fading into the night, Fee downed the rest of her beer. "Let's get you home, Mom." She herded her mother toward the door, then turned toward Beans. "Oh, don't forget Lloydie's service. Ten o'clock at the cemetery. Come by the shop first, though."

"Did they find Lloydie?" Gloria asked, wide-eyed.

19

Beans

Summer 2007

Kobayashi's Teriyaki was one of the few take out/dine in eateries in town, a popular restaurant serving tasty chicken and beef entrees as long as you didn't mind Styrofoam containers. For a few dollars more, they would also deliver anywhere within the Galena city limits.

As soon as he acquired his driver's license, this was Beans's job, and he was glad to have it—part-time jobs for teenagers were scarce in their village. Byron and Consuela Kobayashi's son, Andreas, was too young to drive, and his sister even younger. Four or five evenings out of the week, Beans delivered Styrofoamed and plastic-bagged dinners to Kobayashi Teriyaki customers. His clientele usually consisted of home and visiting sports teams, catered events at the GILA school or Fish and Wildlife, the seasonal Iditarod crowd, or hunting or ecotourist groups. He did, however, have a few regulars, and one was Zachariah Green, who never seemed to cook or pick up food for himself.

Zach Green usually stayed late at the washeteria, not so much for the laundromat business that he managed for Lloyd Paul, but to see to his far more lucrative enterprise of selling marijuana. At least once a week, Beans brought a Combo Special with extra sauce to the washeteria as his last delivery of the day.

The bell on the door emitted a soft tinkle as Beans entered the laundromat. The flickering fluorescent lighting illuminated a row of silent coin-operated washers and dryers, some with doors gaping open. Zach and his buddy, Caleb, had obviously returned recently from a hunting trip. Their huge grease-stained duffels, crammed with dirty laundry and gear, lay like corpses in the aisle. The room reeked of dryer sheets and steam, body odor, and weed.

Loud music and laughter burst from the back room. At least it sounds like he's with a guy friend, Beans thought. More than once he had walked in on Zach with a much younger woman—and while not in exactly prosecutable situations, made Beans want to unsee it.

Aerosmith's "Walk This Way" blared from Zach's tinny ghetto blaster, and the men were practically screaming to be heard above it.

Beans stood at the open doorway, waving away the drifts of skunky smoke wafting from the back room. "Hello? Delivery."

Zach Green spun in his tattered office chair and stared at him, bleary-eyed. Zach was thin and reedy, with stringy brown hair and a single gold-capped incisor. "Oh, right. Almost forgot. Thanks, Havi. Oh, and here you go, kid." He handed Beans a bottle in a paper bag. He'd already paid for the food on a credit card when he'd called in the order. This was a different transaction entirely. Beans pressed a wad of bills into Zach's hand.

The other man in the room was another of Lindbergh's classmates, one he didn't know as well, Caleb Redfern. Caleb quickly turned and hid his spliff behind his back, as if Beans didn't already know they were getting stoned in the back room.

Admittedly, Caleb had more to lose, like maybe his newly-acquired pilot's license and his reputation as a guide, if it got around that he was getting high on a regular basis with Zach Green. Unlike Zach, Caleb was sturdily built, blond, and most of the girls at school thought him handsome. It didn't hurt that he was old enough to buy liquor and had a plane. Caleb nodded genially at Beans. "Hey, how ya doin', Havi? What do you hear from Herc?"

"He's fishing Prince William Sound with Ingmar, on the *Elsinore*."

"Good for him. A hard-working guy, your brother."

Beans handed the bag of teriyaki to Zach and thanked him for the tip. Zach always tipped him generously, at least fifty percent of the food bill. "Here, kid, this isn't drinking money. Put this away for school," he'd say with what looked to Beans like a kind smile. Beans was grateful—he would be going to college in a couple of years, and he could definitely use the cash. Since his dad died, his mother was the family's breadwinner—so the more he could fend for himself, the better. At Christmas, prom, or other special occasion, Zach would fold a couple of twenty-dollar bills into his hand with a wink.

It was a firm unwritten rule that Zach dealt only in weed and cocaine—and only weed if his customer was a high schooler. No speed, no meth, no heroine or opioids, no date rape drugs. A charter customer or Iditarod spectator might want a little weed or blow to party with after a day of hunting or watching the race. These customers were referred to Zach—but if they wanted anything more exotic than that, they were on their own.

Beans had smoked marijuana for the first time when he was twelve, indoctrinated by Herc. Not his favorite. It stank, made him cough, and caused him to eat large volumes of weird food, like pork rinds and half-and-half. As a teenager, alcohol was his drug of choice.

Mari never kept alcohol in the house, and for good reason. Jimmy had crashed his floatplane while drunk. Her eldest son, Lindbergh, had rolled the pickup truck with Beans in it while hardly able to see straight. Herc, now living in Southeast Alaska, had taken spectacular falls off the wagon and only by the grace of his God managed to stay alive.

So Beans had to resort to subterfuge to get his alcohol. On the evenings he wasn't making deliveries, he would take the family Malamute-mix Muktuk on a long walk around town. Muktuk happily trotted along, knowing that the route would end up at the Gunnersons' and their seemingly endless supply of Milk Bones. Doc and Gloria Gunnerson were not big drinkers, but occasionally entertained, so kept a supply of liquor in the house. Conrad had managed to abscond with a bottle of vodka and stashed it in his room. While Beans and Conrad played video games and Muktuk snored on the bed, they nipped at and sometimes chugged (depending on whether it was a school night or not) the bottle of vodka. Before he left, Beans would pop a stick of sugar-free gum in his mouth, then stagger home with his dog, well after Mari and the rest of the family were in bed.

Every month or so, Beans and Conrad would pool their money and have Zach buy them a fifth of vodka to replenish their dwindling supply. Zach was only too glad to do it, "priming the pump" as he liked to say—getting the local kids to depend on him for their drugs and alcohol.

It was a symbiotic relationship, and one that worked. At least for a while.

* * *

It couldn't last, of course. After Lloyd disappeared, Victor, who hated Zach anyway, had a good excuse to fire him. He put Janelle in charge of the washeteria, along with just about everything else in the Pauls' vast business empire. Zach was said to have caught a plane south and like his former supervisor and champion Lloyd Paul, was never heard from again.

The washeteria ceased to be the hub of weed and alcohol sales to the underaged in town. Janelle restored it to a gleaming, legitimate laundromat with a clean, efficient office space in back. No dime bags. No bottles in brown paper sacks. No Wild West .22 revolver with pearl grips that Zach kept in a drawer, just in case.

The drug business didn't disappear, however. Caleb took over Zach's job selling weed and cocaine to the locals out of a hazmat storage locker in one of the warehouses at the airport. He also grudgingly bought alcohol for Beans and Conrad now and then until they reached legal age, but added a huge markup, knowing that he couldn't incentivize the boys to be weed customers.

Now, with the reappearance of Lloyd's leg and Zach's gun, Beans wondered half-seriously if parts of Zach Green might start washing up as well. And who was to say that Lloyd was really dead? For all of his bluster, Victor had a point—skull or no skull, there was no definitive proof that Lloyd wasn't somewhere living a new life, with a new leg, maybe. It was unlikely that he would or could go anywhere without his prosthesis, but if a guy wanted to fake his own death, wouldn't this be a great way to do it?

But why would he? By everyone's account, including his own and Mari's, Lloyd was in a great mood, euphoric about getting out of town. He shipped his skiff, pickup, and belongings to Nenana, where they awaited his retrieval—until they were destroyed in the fire that put Tundra Moving and Storage out of business. These were not the actions of a man who wanted to disappear. Unless he had secrets none of them knew about.

And Zach? Beans would bet he could find witnesses who saw Zach get on a plane to Anchorage, supposedly heading for the Lower Forty-Eight. Granted, no one kept in touch with him, but that didn't mean he never left town.

Beans rolled out of the narrow bunk bed, restless and unable to sleep. His childhood bedroom seemed stuffy and airless, even with the windows wide open. The appearance of Zach's .22 revolver had unsettled him. Was there a connection between Zach's gun and Lloyd's leg? He had half-expected to see Jimmy Beans's gun, but not Zach's. He shuffled into the kitchen and pulled a bottle of water from the refrigerator. Leaning into the coolness from the open refrigerator door, he downed half the bottle in one gulp and wiped his mouth with the back of his hand.

Through the open windows, across the tundra came the machine gun popping of firecrackers and the maniacal cackle of a fox.

20

Beans

Summer 2024

The next morning, Beans, bleary-eyed, stopped by Charbucks for a cup of drip coffee. He figured even Charlene couldn't screw that up, but he was wrong. It was only marginally better than the Americano he had earlier. He poured in another healthy dollop of half and half to mask the bitter burnt taste. Not surprisingly, there was no one else in the coffee shop, and Charlene acted busy wiping down the glass display cases. She already had on the too-tight black sheath in preparation for attending her Uncle Lloyd's graveside service later that day, and she tugged at it self-consciously.

"Want a pastry?" she asked hopefully.

Beans declined the stale-looking sugar-free Danishes and headed for the Public Safety Building. Fee winced when he entered with the cardboard cup printed with the Charbucks logo.

"Just in case drinking Charlene's coffee wasn't living dangerously enough for you." She handed him a bulging manila envelope.

"What's this?" He opened it to find a Glock 19 handgun and several magazines of ammunition.

"If we're going to hang out together, you're going to need a firearm," Fee said

He hefted it in his hand. It was very much like his own weapon, only a little lighter. "You just had a spare one lying around?"

"It was Arvid's." She rummaged around in the credenza behind her desk and pulled out a holster, tossing it across her desk to him. "This was his, too. He doesn't need either anymore, may he rest in peace. You should get some use out of them while you're here."

Galena's former police chief Arvid Streeter had died from Parkinson's disease five years ago and was buried in the same hillside cemetery where Lloyd Paul's leg was to be interred later this morning. Sure that it wasn't exactly legal, but telling himself that he was more or less deputized, and that he might need the gun in self-defense, he adjusted the holster so it would fit comfortably under his jacket.

"Thanks." As much as Beans's pacifist Buddhist soul hated violence, he had to admit that the weight of the gun made him feel more secure, especially now that Lloyd Paul's case might be evolving into a homicide—and his killer could still be among them.

Fee and Beans rode out to the cemetery together in her pickup. "You can expect the whole town to show up. Nobody wants to get on the bad side of Victor."

"Even though Victor's, well, Victor—I still feel kind of bad for him. He now has to face the almost certainty that his son is never coming home."

"He never left, did he?"

They had to park downhill from the cemetery and hike across uneven terrain to the small hillside burial ground. Beans passed the graves of his paternal grandparents, Harold and Daisy Beans, and his brother, Lindbergh. Near the top of the knoll, next to the grave of Victor's wife, Dolores, and several other Paul relatives, a small deep hole was dug. It was much too small to inter the remains of a full-grown man, but then again, they didn't have the remains of an entire man to bury.

The artificial limb that had been pulled from the beach was now encased in what looked like a hardwood pet casket. A ribboned spray of fireweed and lupine had been placed over the gleaming cedar. Already around the grave were Victor's brother Milton, a minister from the Lutheran Church in Ruby, Victor, Junior and Janelle, all dressed in black. Janelle's eyes were red-rimmed from crying, and she dabbed at her face with a damp tissue. Charlene stood next to her mother, stolid and pale, in her tight dress and black pumps.

A dozen Paul relatives from up and down the Yukon and several employees of the YC store trudged up the hill, as did Andreas K., followed by Caleb Redfern, the pilot who ran most of the floatplane passenger and cargo charters in and out of Galena. Most of the crowd who had been dockside at the skull-diving exercise were present at the graveyard as well. At the end of the line of mourners, dressed in a dark suit and tie and carrying carnations, was Bernie Waterman.

The service was too long, with Lloyd's Uncle Milton waxing poetic about his nephew's numerous and mostly fictitious accomplishments. Everyone fidgeted, shifting from foot to foot on the rocky scree. Finally, the small coffin was lowered into the grave. Bernie Waterman passed a red carnation to each of the family members to toss in after it. Reverend Milton mumbled a few more words of Christian piety and it was finally over. "Amen," the crowd intoned.

"Sorta wordy for an appendage burial," Fee said under her breath to Beans.

"Imagine if there was a skull in there too," Beans added, trying hard not to smile.

"Shit, you're awful," Fee said, barely moving her lips.

"You started it."

Fee smiled suddenly, and it was like old times, skinny Fee with her scabby knees, following her brother and him on her oversized bike.

Janelle, Junior, and Charlene hurried down the hillside in front of the other mourners. They needed to finish setting up for the informal beer and brat reception that was to be held on Victor's back lawn. Fee realized that she'd blocked their vehicle in with her pickup and scurried down the incline to move it out of the way.

Beans hung back to talk to Victor, although he wasn't quite sure why. The old man stood staring down at the beagle-sized coffin.

"I'm sorry, Victor."

He looked up, startled. "Oh, yeah. Well. I used to blame your mother, you know. I blamed her for breaking his heart, running him off."

"Maybe it's better this way, finally. At least you know now, and you can move on."

"I used to blame her for running him off," he repeated. "And he was here the whole time. Him and those fucking quarters." His voice broke, and he looked away. "You'll come, won't you? You and the Gunnerson girl? Come and have a brat. I got a keg and everything. Tell a few Lloydie stories."

He was sure Victor didn't want to hear his Lloydie experiences, but he said, "Sure, Victor. We'll be there." For the first time in his life, Beans patted the old man on the shoulder and turned to join Fee at the truck.

* * *

Victor Paul's house, the largest in town, sat on a small rise with a sprawling backyard that rolled down to the river. Because of its relative elevation, and unlike most of the riverside houses, it had only flooded twice in the many years he'd owned it. Long picnic tables covered with red and white checked tablecloths had been set up in the bright summer sunshine. Junior and Andreas K manned the fifty-five-gallon drums that had been reconditioned into barbecues and flipped dozens of sausages and marinated moose ribs on the grills. Janelle and Charlene brought out tray after tray of salads, side dishes, and desserts.

"These are not bad," Fee said, taking another bite from her sandwich. "The old man may be in mourning, but he still knows a bargain. I bet he bought these sausages on some kind of Fourth of July special."

True to his word, Victor had tapped a keg in a corner of the yard and red Solo cups began appearing everywhere. Now that he was on administrative leave, Beans considered having a swig or two of beer. Every now and then, he got nostalgic for the taste and familiar buzz of alcohol but then decided against it. Like his father and older brothers before him, he'd gone down that road before, and it was best not to take that detour again. He sipped on a can of Diet Coke instead, and agreed with Fee that the bratwursts were pretty tasty.

Most of the village was there, eating Victor's food and drinking his beer, but not saying much about his son. Beans mingled through the food line, exchanging greetings with old neighbors and classmates. Halfway through a serving of excellent wild rhubarb pie, he looked up to see Anita leading Gloria Gunnerson by the hand down the lawn. Beaming, Gloria was decked out in a red, white, and blue outfit and was carrying a small American flag.

"For crying out—Anita, why is she here?" Fee, annoyed, asked her mother's caretaker.

Anita looked frazzled. "She's convinced it's the Fourth of July and everybody is at the parade. I had to bring her. She wouldn't take no for an answer. I'll get her something to eat, and we'll leave right away."

Janelle came by with a cup of punch and offered it to Fee's mother. "Oh, it's no problem, Fee. Gloria, would you like some punch?"

"Oh yes, thank you, it's my favorite." Gloria took it gratefully. "When does the parade start?"

"Mom," Fee said, her patience strained. "This isn't a parade. This is a service for Lloyd Paul."

"I'll fix her a plate, why don't I? I'll be right back." Anita beelined for the keg.

"Oh yes, Lloydie is dead, isn't he?" Gloria looked thoughtful. "I remember the night he died."

Fee rolled her eyes. "No, you don't, Mom."

"Oh yes I do, girlie!" Gloria's voice carried across the lawn. "I never slept well after the Change, you know that. So I was awake late that night, and I took Conrad's old bike, the one he was always tinkering with. And I rode this way, and that, and went to the fuel dock. It was dark, and cold, not long after breakup. And then I saw Lloydie die."

Beans was conscious of a sudden hush that fell over Victor's backyard. The only sound was the sizzling of the brats and ribs on the grill and Anita priming the keg.

"All those coins. He was very heavy." Gloria said wisely.

"OK, that's enough." Fee's face was flushed. "I'll get Anita to bring you home."

"Let me fix a plate for her, Fee," Janelle's kind face was worried.

"I'll bring her a brat later. She needs to go home." Fee sighed. "I'm so sorry, Janelle."

Janelle took Fee's hand. "It's fine, really, Fee."

"When's the parade?" Gloria waved her miniature flag.

21

Beans

Summer 2024

Even after the hearty fare at Victor's, Beans was hungry again by early evening. He grabbed a spoon out of the kitchen drawer and opened the freezer. Since he had given up drinking years ago, he had taken up various dietary vices including Nacho Doritos and pistachio nuts (not at the same time), but his latest high-calorie habit was ice cream. He could have sworn he bought a quart of chocolate ice cream at YC just the other day. Now there was a scant cup left. He shuffled to the living room and turned on the TV. Some outfit out of the Pacific Northwest was building treehouses in Sweden or someplace like that, and he let his mind wander on and off the screen while he spooned up what was left of his Häagen-Dazs.

His cell phone barked. Half-watching a construction worker rappel down the side of a tree, he answered it.

"So, when were you going to tell me?" It was Piper, and she was not pleased.

He turned the volume down on the television. "Tell you what?" He really did have trouble sometimes keeping up with the runaway train of her thoughts.

"That our great-grandfather had a wartime love child!"

"Oh, right, did Mom tell you about George Whatsit?"

"Laskin! George Hiro Laskin! And if he's still alive, he would be some kind of great uncle or whatever."

"So, you obviously know all about—"

"No thanks to you! You had this whole conversation with our mother and never bothered to share any of it with me."

Off your high horse, Piper. Cut me some slack, Beans thought. What he said was, "My apologies, Ms. Beans, your FOMO was eclipsed by the discovery of long-missing Lloydie's poor sad leg."

"Oh. Right. Sorry." Piper really did sound contrite. "But you see what this means, don't you? Now Grandpa Ben's attitude toward us—well, I can kind of understand it. His own father abandoned him to raise his half-Aleut child. I mean, he wasn't left any other option, but he *chose* a part-Native bastard child *over* his legitimate son! Grandpa Ben must have seen George Laskin in every one of our faces, and if not hated, resented us for it."

"Maybe I can understand it, but I can't condone it. We were kids, Piper. What did we ever do to deserve the cold shoulder? How he treated Mom was bad enough, but he wouldn't even speak to Dad."

"Yeah, but—" Beans recognized this as one of Piper's favorite transitional phrases, one commonly used when she realized she was losing an argument. "You see what this also means?"

"I'm sure you'll tell me."

"We could have some part-Aleut relatives somewhere!"

"From what Mom says, George Laskin was adopted after his—and Grandpa Ben's—father died. His trail goes kind of cold after that."

"You are going to look into it, though, aren't you? I mean, you ham-fisted five-o types can go places we mere mortals can't."

Beans chuckled, all irritation with her dissipated. Only Piper could insult and compliment him in the same sentence. "I'll see what I can do. No promises, though. Adoption records are normally private."

"I know you'll do your best, Havi. So, how was Lloydie's leg funeral?"

He filled her in on the service and reception afterward.

"Nothing says sympathy like brats and beer, does it?" She gave him a quick report on the eating and eliminating habits of his cat and dog and signed off.

Beans turned the volume up on the TV again. Now it was a house-flipping show taking place in Miami. *The other end of the world. Sweden is closer.* His ice cream had melted, so he tipped up the container and drank it down like a shake.

He picked up his phone and tapped in a number, even though he knew the recipient would be behind the wheel of a bus right now. "Hello, Cam? This is Beans. I know you're driving the Thirty Route now, but when you get this message, can you give me a call please on my cell phone? Thanks, buddy." He hoped that was literal and precise enough for Cameron Kristovich's sensibilities.

Then he selected Amy Chandler's number, just to hear her voice on her message. He was pretty sure that she'd be in rehearsals, especially since the ballet's premiere was imminent. Instead, he heard a click, the discordant sounds of an orchestra tuning up, and her warm, laughing voice saying, "Hey, copper."

The second violin, first flute, and one of the percussionists were stuck in a traffic snarl on the bridge so the entire company and orchestra were awaiting their arrival, Amy said. Beans imagined her, agile and graceful, in a frothy pink tutu and toe shoes, flexing and pliéing in the wings.

"So, I've got time to talk. Did you get my postcard? I hope so, I spent a small fortune on postage."

Yes, he did, he said. And before he knew it, he had filled her in on Mari's discovery of her father's half-brother, Lloyd Paul's brat-and-beer funeral reception, and ended with the finding of Zach Green's gun. He didn't know what it was about this young woman that made him so willing to divulge rarely shared parts of his life and work.

"Wow, you've been so busy! And me only in final rehearsals for a world premiere of a major ballet."

He knew she was jittery about the opening, a rare occurrence for Amy. She had been dancing in the corps at the Anchorage Ballet for several years now, and a featured role in this new ballet could be a springboard in her career. She chattered on about petty disturbances within the company, new restaurants in the area, how the conductor could use a haircut, and other trivialities, a sure sign that Amy was a bundle of nerves.

After he hung up with her, he texted his mother: *How would you and Grandma like to go to the ballet? Details to follow.*

22

Beans

Summer 2024

Beans's sleep had been haunted by nightmares of Zach Green's body parts washing up on the beach—his old dog Muktuk digging up a foot encased in an XtraTuf boot, a crow flying off with a pale severed finger, an ear and a gold incisor churned up by the tide like flotsam. He rolled out of bed and stumbled into the kitchen to fire up the Black & Decker coffeemaker just as the morning dawned, dusty and cloudless.

He yawned as he stirred a healthy pour of nondairy creamer into his coffee, and his eyes fell on Amy's postcard on the kitchen counter. Although he'd just talked to her, he decided to reciprocate her postcard with a rambling snail mail letter on Captain Cook Hotel stationery. After he sealed and addressed it, he searched through the rolltop desk and realized that neither he nor Mari had any stamps. He stopped just as he was about to walk out the door to the post office. After a moment's hesitation, he took the Glock in its holster with him. *Funny how the gun had become a part of him again so quickly. Like a phantom appendage. Not so much funny as unsettling, maybe.*

Only one other vehicle was parked in front of the post office, a newer model Dodge pickup. Bernie Waterman was behind the counter as usual, sorting mail and stacking boxes. He looked up and slipped his reading glasses to the top of his head when Beans walked through the door.

"What brings you here, Havi?"

"I'd like a book of stamps, please." Way more stamps than he needed, but somehow just buying one seemed weirdly cheap.

Bernie handed him his stamps just as Caleb Redfern came out of the back room, hauling a mail bag stenciled with OUTPORTS over his shoulder. His smile was warm as he shook Beans's hand in his crushing grip. "Saw you at Lloydie's service. I bet the family's glad that's behind them." He nodded to Bernie. "Going downriver as far as St. Mary's this time. See you in a couple of days." Caleb clomped through the door, and Beans watched through a haze of dust as he loaded the mail bag into the bed of the Dodge pickup.

"Strange about that gun showing up, isn't it?" Bernie asked.

"Sure is," Beans said, browsing through the greeting cards.

"Zach Green's, I assume."

"Sure looked like it." Everybody in town knew it was Zach Green's revolver, and he didn't feel like giving Bernie any gossip fodder.

"Why do you suppose it was in the river?" Beans felt Bernie's sharp, intelligent eyes search his face.

Beans shrugged. "Your guess is as good as mine. Probably didn't feel like putting it in his checked luggage."

Beans flipped through a rack of postcards picturing various Yukon River scenes, including the iconic Nenana Ice Classic shot of the tripod on the frozen river and action shots of Iditarod dog teams. He picked one out randomly, thinking he might send it to Amy if he stayed in Galena much longer, and took it to the counter to pay for along with the stamps.

"You ever hear from Zach?" Bernie asked, handing him his change.

"Me? No, he was quite a bit older than me, in Lindbergh and Caleb's class." Beans pocketed his change.

"You know, I'd see him all the time, when he was working right next door, of course. I didn't expect him to be a Facebook friend or anything, but I expected him to keep in touch with somebody in town. Young people." Bernie tsk-tsked. "Always looking for something better."

* * *

Next door at the washeteria, Janelle was sweeping the floors and dusting the tops of the machines. He still wasn't really sure what Janelle's job was—it seemed like she was involved in every aspect of the Pauls' various businesses. He waved at her through the plate glass window, and she came out, broom in hand.

"Thanks for the reception yesterday, Janelle. I think everyone enjoyed it."

"I think Lloyd would have enjoyed it too, having everyone come out like that."

"How's your dad doing?"

She pushed a strand of curly hair from her damp forehead. "You know, I think he's OK with it now. I think he has a sense of an . . . ending."

Beans was glad she didn't say "closure." To him that word better described the buttoning of a fly on a pair of jeans than any stage of bereavement.

Janelle asked after Mari and when she might be returning home.

"I'm not sure exactly, but she'll be back in time for the start of the school year."

"Tell her please, that I hope all is well with her mother. I miss my mom every day. Having her mother for as long as she has is a blessing." She gave him a sad smile and turned to sweep the laundromat's entryway.

* * *

He wondered if Fee shared the same sentiment. When he arrived at the station, she was already on the phone with Anita or one of the other caregivers, her patience clearly held together with the finest of threads. "Tell her that everyone has enough eggs. She needs to sit her butt in her chair and watch *General Hospital*."

She hung up and sighed. "Thank God for soap operas. Otherwise, what would people with dementia watch?"

Beans wondered how much longer Fee would be able to continue caring for her mother at home and working a full-time job—it was clear that keeping Gloria out of harm's way was taking its toll on her daughter.

Fee stood and grabbed her keys. "You're just in time to help me teach bicycle safety to third graders. Come on, it's a blast, and you got nothing else to do."

He declined, saying he needed to make a few phone calls, but he conceded that she had a point. It wouldn't take long for the locals to wonder what he was doing there, since there was no evidence that Lloyd's disappearance was a homicide, and he clearly was not visiting his mother.

His phone barked. *Cam Kristovich.*

"Hey, hi, Cam. How are you?"

A tentative voice. "Hello, Detective Beans. I am fine. I am returning your call of yesterday at 17:35."

It took a while for Beans and Heller to get used to Cam's flat affect and literal interpretation of everything they said. But it was a small price to pay to have their own "My Little Robot" as Heller liked to call him fondly behind his back. Cam's eidetic memory was nothing short of incredible—he remembered photos, faces, patterns, and written and spoken language. If Cam hadn't been able to remember and recognize a detail in endless hours of security video, it's unlikely they would have been able to solve the barista killings case. Business software was like child's play to him. Best of all, he was like a walking, talking, search engine and benevolent hacker. Any topic that required deep and sometimes dark web research was handed over to Cam.

"Cam, I would like you to research something for me. This is a Priority Five." On a scale from one to five, five was lowest priority—it was important to Cam to qualify tasks assigned to him.

"OK, I have one Priority One that should be finished within thirty minutes. After that I have two Priority Threes that should be finished by eleven today. I can do this task for you after that."

"Perfect. Write this name down. George Laskin. L-A-S-K-I-N. He was born sometime in 1942 in St. Paul, Alaska, I think, to Adelaide Laskin. Not sure if his father's name was recorded or not. In 1955, he was adopted and his name changed. I think the adoption occurred in Southeast Alaska somewhere, but this is an assumption only. I'd like to know what his name is now, and where he is now, if he's still alive. And I'd like to know if he has descendants."

"Adoption records are often difficult to access."

"Yes, Cam. That's why I'm asking you."

"I will try my best." Beans could tell that the young man was pleased and intrigued by the challenge.

"I know you will. And this is a personal request," Beans continued, "so if Detective Heller or anyone else in in the department asks you to work on anything, please put their requests ahead of this one."

"Yes. That is the purpose of the Priority Ranking System we devised." Cam didn't add, *You dumbshit*, but he might as well have.

Beans thanked Cam and hung up. Something in his back pocket crunched as he sat down, and he realized he had the small paper bag with the book of stamps and the postcard he had purchased at the post office. Pulling the creased postcard out, he noted that it depicted a dimpled apple-cheeked Native Alaskan toddler wearing a parka with a fur-lined hood, his arms around a huge blue-eyed Malamute.

23

Beans

Summer 2024

Fourth of July was forecast to be the hottest day of the year so far, well into the eighties. The dust-suppression truck had already been out at dawn, spraying palliative to keep parade-goers from choking on street dust. Beans ventured out early as well, helping Fee cordon off cross streets in preparation for the parade.

The Fourth of July in Galena was always a festive affair, with family-friendly races along the dike by the airport, ending with a community dance. This year, in honor of the new fire truck (purchased after the old one mysteriously burned), the city fathers agreed to start the celebration with a parade down the main street of Old Town. The gleaming new fire truck, loaded with the town's youngsters throwing out candy to spectators, would figure prominently.

Food booths lined the side streets, selling fry bread, corn on the cob, snow cones, deep fried pike, hot dogs, and moose burgers. Andreas K's Greek/Mexican/Japanese food truck advertised his spicy miso tacos and picadillo gyros with sesame slaw—a new item that Beans planned to sample before the day was out.

The high school marching band, already sweating in their blue and yellow uniforms, gathered near the parade start. The cheerleaders and drum majorette took turns drinking from a huge to-go cup. He suspected there was more in there than lemonade, but things might have changed since his days in high school.

Fee whooped her truck's siren and flashed its lights, and the parade began. Beans elected to walk alongside the fire truck, in case some of the smaller kids leaned too far out to pelt the crowd with peppermints. After the fire truck came a fleet of bigger kids on their bikes, most wisely wearing helmets, useful to protect themselves from the hail of hard candy more than anything else. The cheerleaders and majorette, a little unsteady on their feet, came next, then the marching band with their spirited rendition of *Tequila*, *Roam*, and something by KC and the Sunshine Band. The local Boy and Girl Scout troops came next, giving away small American flags to the spectators. A trio of aged veterans in a convertible waved heartily to great applause from the crowd. The town fuel delivery truck, honking loudly, was followed by a gleaming pickup truck advertising the local marine supply store. The septic tank pumper truck rumbled down the street, and everyone's favorite, the dust-suppressant tanker truck, was met with even greater applause and whistles than the veterans. Tribal leaders, the mayor, and city council members followed, waving sparklers while perched in the beds of red, white, and blue pickup trucks, Sousa marches blaring from loud speakers.

The whole parade probably took no longer than an hour. By the end of that time, Beans's white polo shirt was soaked through with sweat and mosquitos were setting up camp in his ears. He could almost taste a fruit-punch-flavored snow cone melting down his throat. The crowd began milling about, moving across the parade route to the food booths. Beans was handing children down from the bed of the fire truck to a waiting fireman when a woman's sharp scream split the heavy afternoon air.

"Gloria!"

A small woman in baggy khaki shorts and an oversized T-shirt pushed her way through groups of people, calling "Gloria!" over and over. Beans's stomach lurched when he recognized Anita, frantic, pushing through the crowd.

Beans leaped down from the fire truck and caught up with Anita. "What's happened?"

"She's gone, Havi!" Anita's eyes were wide. "We were back there, watching the kids on their bikes. I turned to bum a smoke, just for a second, and when I looked back, she was gone! I asked everybody around us, but nobody noticed where she went. Just for a second! I took her eyes off her for a second. Oh, God. *Gloria*!"

A small crowd had gathered around them, several neighbors offering to search for her, just as Fee caught up with them. Anita, distraught, wrung the front of her Iditarod T-shirt.

"What is it, Anita? Where's Mom?" Fee's sharp eyes scanned the crowd.

"She's gone, Fee! I turned my back for no longer than a second, I swear. And when I turned back to see if she wanted a snow cone, she was gone."

Fee took a deep breath. "We'll talk about this later, Anita."

Beans was surprised by how calm Fee was. She organized Anita and three of the firemen to fan out from the center of town to look for Gloria. "She's wearing a red, white, and blue pantsuit, the one she wore to Victor's the other day. I'll stay here and see if she circles back. Call if you spot her."

Beans offered to take his truck and drive around the perimeter of town. He drove by the fuel dock first and saw Junior there, manning the pumps. His young cousin, Drew, had tied his aluminum skiff to the dock and fiddled with the outboard while he drank a beer. No, he hadn't seen Gloria at all, but would let Fee know if he did. "How was the parade?" he called after Beans as he drove off.

No sighting of Gloria at the YC. Victor said, frowning, "What does Fee pay that woman to watch her, anyway?"

Beans pulled out his cell phone and called Fee. "I'm going to swing by the school, then your house and Mom's, just in case. Don't give up. We haven't looked everywhere yet."

Except for a security guard, who promised to keep an eye out for Gloria, the school was deserted. It was so warm now that his shirt was sticking to the torn vinyl seat of the old pickup. He drove down the road to the Gunnersons' house.

The house looked quiet and deserted except for a single white hen strutting in the groundcover. Beans parked the truck and got out. *Is this one of Gloria's brood?* She always kept them in their pen because they could easily fall prey to foxes. But then, she could have forgotten, like she had forgotten so many other things.

"Mrs. G?" Beans knocked on the front door. He shielded his eyes from the bright afternoon glare and peered in the window. Tidy but apparently vacant. He knocked again. "Gloria?"

He went around the side of the house to the backyard, where he could hear the squawking and clucking of more chickens. A bright burst of sunshine temporarily blinded him as he rounded the corner. He shaded his eyes and the prone figure of Gloria came into focus, sprawled in front of the open door to the chicken coop. Her arms were extended in front of her, as if she were leading a cheer. A half dozen cracked eggs oozed on the pavers. She was unconscious, bleeding from a wound to her right temple.

"Gloria!" Beans rushed to her side. Her pulse was erratic, her breathing shallow, but she was alive.

He called 911 and Fee in quick succession. The paramedics, who were on high alert for the Fourth of July, arrived at the house in minutes and already had Gloria on a gurney when Fee screeched to a stop and leaped out of her pickup, wide-eyed and breathless.

"I found her on the ground right outside the chicken coop," Beans said. "I don't know how long she's been there. She might have lost consciousness, then hit her head as she fell."

"Is she—" Fee's lower lip trembled.

"No," one of the young paramedics said. "She's very much alive. Coming with us, Fee?"

Fee nodded and stepped into the back of the ambulance with Gloria's gurney. The young paramedic placed an oxygen mask over Gloria's nose and mouth and secured it with an elastic band. Fee gripped Gloria's hand and looked out at Beans with dark liquid eyes. Beans extended his thumb and pinkie in a "call me" gesture as the ambulance doors closed. The siren wailed through the streets toward the Edgar Noller Health Clinic.

The Gunnerson house seemed lonely and especially quiet after the departure of the ambulance. Beans picked up the eggshells and cleaned up as much of the raw egg as he could, while the chickens clucked and pecked around him. He located the bloodied corner of a potting bench where Gloria probably hit her head as she fell.

Heart attack or stroke? He knew that Alzheimer's patients were predisposed toward stroke—did she walk all the way from the parade route home, then suffer a stroke while gathering eggs? A wave of sadness washed over him, envisioning Gloria Gunnerson in her backyard, alone and fearful while a dark curtain fell over her vision and her world slipped away.

One of Gloria's white chickens pecked at his shoelaces, reminding him that they needed to be rounded up and tended to. This took a little longer than anticipated. He had forgotten in the year since his episode with last year's barista serial killer, how quick chickens can be who don't want to be caught. By the time he got them all in their coop, fed and watered, it was nearly dusk and finally cooling down, with firecrackers echoing like gunfire in the distance

Fee called from the clinic, her voice reedy with stress and exhaustion, as he arrived back at Mari's house. "The good news is, they don't think it's a stroke or a heart attack."

"Some kind of seizure, then?" Beans opened the refrigerator, looking for something to eat but seeing only Gloria's eggs, shut the door again. "Is she conscious?"

"No, not yet. She took a pretty nasty knock on the head, poor thing. They're infusing her with all kinds of IV dextrose or glucose or whatever. She's showing signs of improvement, but still unconscious."

"Wait, they're giving her sugar?"

"Yeah, get this. Mom is suffering from severe hypoglycemia. She's not diabetic—but she ODed on insulin."

"What? Did your dad keep any insulin around the house?"

"No! After he died, we cleaned all of his medical stuff out."

"Then where did she get the insulin?"

She sighed. "I wish I knew, Havi." She yawned. "I just talked with the doc. They said I might as well go home. She's got a concussion, but they've stabilized her blood sugar. They'll call me when she wakes up. Oh God, I need to call Conrad. Tomorrow. It's the middle of the night there. I might as well wait and give him bad news in the light of day."

24

Beans

Summer 2024

The next morning was cooler, with mist lying like a pale carpet over the river. Beans had a scheduled Zoom meeting with his boss, Lieutenant Nelson DuBois that morning, so he made it a point to straighten up the living room, and especially to put away the Glock that was on loan to him from the Galena Police Department. Beans put on a crisp short-sleeved shirt, but elected to remain in running shorts for the half of his body that would remain off camera. He was already sweating, and it wasn't all from the humid weather. He hoped that DuBois had some good news about the Helms shooting investigation.

DuBois's smiling face filled the screen. He was an elegant Black man with short graying hair and striking green eyes. "How are you doing, Detective? I understand you're helping your mom out during this little hiatus?"

"Well, it started out that way, sir, but I'm now in Galena, helping out an old friend."

They small-talked about the heat in the Interior for a few minutes, then DuBois got down to business. "The Committee has wound up their investigation into the Willis Helms officer-involved shooting, Beans. I don't have to tell you that there's been lots of controversy on this. I, for one, don't see why, but that's the climate we're working in. At any rate, the Committee has concluded that your shooting of Willis Helms, while perhaps a little unorthodox, was justified. There will be no further disciplinary action."

Beans breathed a sigh of relief. "Thank you, sir."

DuBois continued, "However—you will be required to complete the mandatory psych sessions, of course. Most officers have found these to be very helpful."

"Yes, sir." Beans didn't mind these, and as long as he could return to work, he would be more than willing to talk to a shrink.

"And toxicology reports are back on Helms. He was a walking cocktail of drugs—meth, booze, some cocaine—he was higher than a kite. It's no wonder that he was acting erratically," DuBois said.

Beans shook his head. "I don't feel good about any of this, as you know, sir."

"Well, I'm sorry for Willis, but I'm happy that this was resolved satisfactorily for us, anyway," DuBois said. "You have at least a week and a half left of paid leave, right? Go ahead and take it—help your friend and your mom, take a little vacation. Let's round it up. I don't want to see you back in the office before the first of August."

"Sounds good, thank you, sir."

* * *

Beans was surprised to see Fee behind her desk at the Public Safety Building. She looked tired, her eyes red rimmed, her normally neatly ironed khaki uniform rumpled.

"What are you doing here? Get to the hospital. I can cover."

"It's OK. I got up early to call Conrad, so I figured I might as well come in. I already talked to the clinic, and Mom's still drifting in and out, though they say her vital signs are good. She's probably just settling in for a nap. I'll go over there later."

"Did you talk to Conrad? How is he?"

"About as well as can be expected. He can't figure out how Mom got insulin either. I told him she wasn't awake yet, but he wants to be here. He'll get here as soon as he can make all the connections from Naha." Conrad was a helicopter mechanic for the US Army stationed in Okinawa. "Yuki will stay home with the kids."

Beans told her about his Zoom conversation with Lieutenant DuBois, and that he was cleared to return to duty.

"That's great of course, but—" She frowned, until he told her that he wasn't expected back to work until the first of August.

"Well, we'll be a two-cop department for a few more days, anyway." She gave him a sad half-smile.

Overnight, most of Galena had heard that Gloria was in the hospital. Neighbors dropped by the Public Safety Building all morning with food, flowers, and get-well messages. Jeannie, one of Gloria's caregivers, dropped off a chicken casserole and gave Fee a long, tearful hug. Geno brought by one of Andreas' moussakas ("It's actually a 'moose-saka'," he said with a dazzling smile) and a bottle of ouzo. Victor Paul surprised both Fee and Beans by offering a frozen Marie Callender cheesecake and some pepperoni sticks. By noon, they could barely get the small lunchroom refrigerator door closed.

While Fee spent the afternoon sitting at Gloria's bedside and consulting with her doctors, Beans took calls about stolen bikes, missing dogs, and noisy neighbors. By the end of the afternoon, he had put a few dozen miles on Mari's truck and given everyone an update on Gloria's condition—stable, but no change.

Fee arrived back at the Public Safety Building, dead on her feet, but smiling. "Mom is back among us! She opened her eyes, smiled, even asked about her chickens. She doesn't know what happened to her, or how she got the insulin—but I guess that wouldn't be unusual for her. She might be discharged tomorrow."

They loaded both their vehicles with the Tupperware containers of food and flowers and drove to the Gunnerson house. Fee insisted that Beans take at least two casseroles home; she managed to get the rest in either her refrigerator or freezer. She put Victor's Marie Callender cheesecake on the counter to thaw. "I'm eating this one tonight."

Beans fed and watered Gloria's chickens—what is it with him and chickens?—and returned to the Beans family bungalow. He heated a casserole and ate in front of the TV, then half-dozed and half-watched a Mariners game until it went into extra innings and he crawled into his old bunk bed.

He was exhausted but again, sleep still didn't come easily. Even now, his thoughts returned to Willis Helms, as they often did when he was tired enough to let them. Why had Willis been dealt such a cruel hand in this life? He had lived in a drug-addled, alcoholic haze and had died in a slurry of blood and root beer. Had he done something in a past life to deserve this one? Why did he have to die so violently? Then he thought, selfishly—*And why did I have to be the one to kill him?*

25

Beans

Summer 2024

The next morning, Beans showered, tossed down a cup of Black & Decker coffee, and arrived at the Public Safety Building just as Fee did. She rushed into the office, carrying half a cheesecake covered with plastic wrap. "I can't eat any more of this. I'm putting it in the break room. Our resident locusts should take care of it in no time."

The endless stream of neighbors and well-wishers continued until it was time to meet Conrad's plane. The Galena airport that day was humming with activity. A cargo plane had just landed with a bypass mail load, and dozens of shrink-wrapped thousand-pound pallets of groceries and supplies were being staged on the tarmac. One of the young cargo handlers at the airport honked and whistled at Fee as he zipped by on a forklift, grinning from behind his Maui Jim sunglasses.

"Not so secret admirer?" Beans asked, grinning.

Fee grimaced. "He's very pretty, but the elevator doesn't go all the way to the top with that one. Plus his wife would murder me for sure."

Beans watched as the cargo handler drove a pallet of goods into a nearby warehouse. "Is it my imagination, or is there a lot more bypass mail coming in than there used to be?"

"Not your imagination. The volume's been steadily increasing for years. Such a deal for us Alaskans, right?" This was a system exclusive to Alaska whereby shippers could bypass the traditional Postal Service infrastructure, and send goods directly to the airline, with groceries and everything else reaching remote locations in Alaska for a highly subsidized rate. "We're talking millions and millions of pounds these days, and steadily growing." Fee added. "We still get seasonal barge shipments, of course, but bypass mail is year-round. Galena's become quite the hub, too—lots of bigger shipments get broken down, then sent out from here."

Conrad's plane coasted to a stop on the tarmac. Fee's brother was the first to deplane, and Beans recognized him immediately—tall and fit, with a broad familiar smile. He shared Fee's dark hair and eyes, and there was something of Doc Gunnerson's Nordic heritage in his slender, long-limbed grace. He drew Beans and his sister into a crushing embrace. Fee clung to him, dampening the front of his jacket with her tears.

The three of them drove together to the clinic, Fee telling Conrad not to get his hopes up. Their mom was pretty good yesterday, but that could turn on a dime. When they walked into her room, Beans was pleasantly surprised and relieved to see Gloria sitting up in bed beaming at them, surrounded by flowers and cards. She had a black eye, probably from her fall, and her bandaged head made her look like one of the war wounded, but she was alert and in fine spirits.

"Conrad! When did you get here? Where are Yuki and my grandchildren?"

Conrad explained that he was there to see her, specifically, and that his family couldn't make the trip this time. "What happened, Mom? Do you remember?"

Gloria frowned. "I remember Trev driving the septic truck in the parade, then I woke up here. I feel very well-rested, though. But the food is crap. Is somebody feeding the chickens?"

Beans assured her that the chickens hadn't missed a single meal, were well-watered, and he was collecting the eggs too.

She patted his cheek fondly. "You're such a good boy, Havi."

"Mom, do you remember if somebody gave you a shot, or something to eat or drink on the day of the parade?" Fee asked.

Gloria's brow furrowed in thought. "Anita gave me a Dr Pepper," she volunteered.

* * *

The doctors decided they wanted Gloria to stay in the hospital another day to monitor her concussion, a development she was not happy about. "Somebody bring me one of Andreas' tacos," she commanded. Fee promised she would stop by with one on her way home.

Beans brought Conrad back to the Gunnerson house while Fee returned to work because, as she said, "somebody has to." He filled Conrad in on what happened on the Fourth of July.

"At first, I thought your mom had some kind of heart attack or stroke. I'm glad it turned out to be something less . . . permanent." Just like the old days, Beans opened the Gunnersons' refrigerator and helped himself and Conrad to glasses of Gloria's lemonade.

Conrad sat back on the sofa and looked around, running a hand through his dark hair. "Jesus, lots of memories in this old place."

"No kidding." Just seeing Conrad again brought them flooding back.

Conrad sighed. "I'll be honest with you, Havi. I wasn't sure it was a good idea when Fee came back here to take care of Mom. She's young. I didn't want her tied here, to this town, watching Mom deteriorate. Yuki and I were prepared to move Mom closer to us, but Fee wouldn't hear of it. She wanted Mom to stay in her own house. She sacrificed so much to do this, and I don't think Mom's even aware of it."

Beans felt a weight on his chest, a vicarious burden. "I think your mom appreciates Fee."

"Does she? I hope so." Conrad swiped a hand across his eyes. "Well, I hope Fee knows that she doesn't need to stay if she doesn't want to. Mom has resources. Between the house and what Dad left her, she should be set. We could arrange something." He sniffed, stared up at the ceiling for a second, then pulled out his phone. "Hey, let me show you the wife and kids."

They spent the rest of the afternoon looking at photos, going through yearbooks, and driving through town, reliving past triumphs and tragedies. The high school gym where Conrad sank the three-point shot at the buzzer that won the Eagles a seed in the state semi-finals. The ditch where Lindbergh had rolled the truck with Beans in it. The bare patch of tundra where Beans's father Jimmy died in a fiery crash. Again, it all played back like a flickering sepia newsreel in his memory.

They sat in the truck, staring at the barren expanse, when Conrad said, "Don't you ever wonder, Havi, how the whole thing happened?"

"What?"

"The crash. Your dad's plane. Your dad was a gearhead, like me. He was crazy meticulous about that plane, man. It was his baby. I used to watch, remember, when he'd go through his, I don't know, two-hundred-point checklist. He would check *everything.* His preflight inspection went on for-fucking-ever. I remember the couple of times he took me up, I wondered if we'd ever leave the ground before dark. It was even worse if he was taking a charter group."

"Dad was drunk, Conrad. That's how it happened." It wasn't a secret that Jimmy Beans was an alcoholic. He loved his buddy Conrad, but he didn't want to relive his dad's death again.

"Maybe so, but he could pilot that plane drunk and blindfolded, practically. No, I just wonder what really happened. I mean, he was drunk, so they never investigated further, did they? And then the fire—" Conrad shuddered. "Sorry, I shouldn't have brought this up."

"It's OK, buddy." Beans put the truck into drive. His memories of the day of the crash were still vivid, and he'd since wondered what had actually gone wrong with the plane—but without any evidence, it was just idle speculation. "You hungry? As your mom would testify, Andreas makes killer tacos."

Beans and Conrad decided instead to shoot a few baskets at the high school gym. The security guard remembered the epic three-pointer that Conrad sank that year to get them into the semi-finals and let them in. Conrad still played in a league on base so was in much better basketball shape than Beans, but sharing the court with his high-school friend was still a fond muscle memory.

They stopped off at the YC for a couple of Gatorades before heading back to the house. Victor nodded to Beans, then did a double-take when he saw Conrad. He went to the freezer case and pulled out a Sara Lee poundcake. "Here. For you and your sister. Take some to Gloria too."

Conrad thanked him, stunned. "Who is he, and what have they done with Victor?" he asked Beans, when they were in the truck.

"He's been different since the Lloydie leg thing. Fee's still eating the pepperoni sticks he brought earlier."

They drove for a while in silence. Then Conrad turned to Beans, a puzzled look on his face. "I don't get it. Where did Mom get insulin? Nobody's diabetic in our family. There's no insulin in the house."

"A guess only, but maybe Anita?"

"She's a nurse, right? She works at a clinic where there's drugs and probably knows how to administer them."

"But I can't figure out why. Why would Anita—or anybody—give your mom insulin that she doesn't need?"

Conrad shook his head, then started tapping on his phone. "Hey, remember that movie with—" he snapped his fingers, trying to remember, "oh, you know, the hot redhead—Jessica Chastain? Where she's a nurse, and her good friend is another nurse, played by Eddie Redmayne, I think?" Conrad was a huge movie buff with an encyclopedic knowledge of old and recent films.

"Um—" It sounded familiar to Beans. "It was based on a true story, right?"

"Yeah, yeah. OK, here it is." Conrad read from his phone. "It's called 'The Good Nurse', and in it, Eddie Redmayne is a serial killer who poisons his patients, most of them elderly, with insulin. He puts it in their IV bags." Conrad looked triumphant. "Hell of a good flick."

"So you're suggesting that Anita tried to *kill* your mom?" Beans took his eyes off the road to stare at Conrad. "But why?"

Conrad shrugged. "How the hell should I know? Maybe she's a nutjob, like Eddie Redmayne. Maybe she's tired of caregiving."

The dusty road ahead of him seemed to loom endlessly. Was it possible that Gloria's insulin poisoning was attempted murder? *No way. This is Galena.*

* * *

That evening, over not-so-shitty pizza, Fee wasn't as ready to embrace the possibility that someone had tried to poison Gloria as her brother was. "Why would anybody want to kill Mom? She's a sweet, harmless, demented old lady."

"There's the Eddie Redmayne-nutjob factor," Conrad said.

Fee rolled her eyes. "Too many movies, Conrad."

"But that was a true story," her brother protested.

Beans had a sudden memory—Gloria blurting out that she had ridden her son's bike to the dock that night, and had seen Lloyd die all those years ago. "Remember what your mom said at Victor's after Lloyd's funeral. Most of the town heard Gloria say that she witnessed Lloyd's death," Beans said, as he sprinkled parmesan onto his slice of pepperoni pizza.

"But she didn't say she saw someone *kill* Lloyd, did she?" Conrad asked.

"No, but she said he was very heavy, with all those quarters in his pockets," Fee said. "It sounded like she saw him go in, whether he fell in himself or not. We don't know if she saw anyone else there."

"And the question still remains—where did the insulin come from that poisoned your mother?" Beans chewed thoughtfully.

"She either took it herself, if she found a syringe lying in the street while wandering around during the parade, which is unlikely. Or someone gave it to her. We can work on the 'why' part of it later. Right now, the most likely suspect—"

"Is Anita." Fee sighed.

26

Beans

Summer 2024

Beans wished it would rain. With this run of warm, humid weather, the Yukon River seemed to drift listlessly, a light morning mist loitering on its surface. After another sticky, biting fly-accompanied run along its banks, he peeled off his sweat-soaked running gear and stepped into a lukewarm shower. His cell phone was barking as he turned off the faucet. Toweling his head dry, he put it on hands free. *Heller.*

"Yo, Hellboy."

"Morning, sunshine. Find any more appendages today?"

"Not yet, but it's early." Beans told Heller about Gloria's recovery from an overdose of insulin. "We can't figure out where she got it. We're talking today to her caregiver and the last to see her before I found her. Nobody in the immediate family or associates are insulin-dependent, though."

"But even in a town Galena's size, there has to be more than one diabetic, right?"

Beans stopped toweling his hair for a minute. Every now and then Heller said something significant, and he usually tossed it out like an offhand comment. He wasn't quite sure why such a general statement somehow seemed important, but his instinct said it was. He made a mental note.

"Hey, I'm glad that everything worked out with the IA investigation," Heller continued. "I mean, of course you were going to be reinstated, that's a no-brainer, but still—it'll be good to have your ugly Buddhist mug back down here again."

"Thanks, I love you too, Heller."

"DuBois said he was giving you until the end of the month, so I say milk it for all it's worth."

"I intend to."

"Really. I mean, I've been there. Take all the time you're given. And don't blow off talking to the shrink."

Beans was taken aback. "When did you—"

"Years ago, when I was on patrol. We'll talk about it over a beer. Or a Coke, whatever." More shuffling of papers over the phone line and Beans resigned himself to the fact that this topic was closed, at least for now.

At the Public Safety Building, Fee chewed thoughtfully on her thumbnail, a childhood habit she apparently hadn't outgrown. "I really don't think Anita's how Mom got the insulin. She's a CNA, and they usually aren't licensed to administer meds themselves without additional training. I checked with the clinic where she worked, and there's no insulin that's unaccounted for. I mean, it's not like anybody can just get on Amazon and order it without a prescription."

There's got to be more than one diabetic in town. Heller's offhand words came back to Beans like a vicious earworm.

"I wonder—does it make sense to get a subpoena for a list of diabetics in town? But first," Fee said, strapping on her holster, "let's talk to Anita."

* * *

They found Anita Belknap sitting on the front steps of the travel trailer she rented from her brother, Curtis, smoking a cigarette. Her Hello Kitty scrubs seemed to hang off of her thin frame, and she twitched ash nervously onto the gravel in front of her. She looked haggard and sleep-deprived, and the sour smell of stale alcohol hovered around her like an aura.

Her eyes welled with tears as soon as she saw Fee. "Are you here to fire me?"

Fee's voice was kind. "No, Anita, but we'd like to talk to you for a minute. We won't take too much of your time."

Anita nodded, stubbed out her cigarette, and showed them into the trailer. The travel trailer was cramped and cluttered with dirty dishes, unfolded laundry, and overflowing ashtrays. A small electric fan rotated in jerky spasms from a stack of dog-eared tabloids. Anita pushed aside a pile of sticky dishes and gestured for Fee to sit on one side of a narrow dining table. Beans stood, leaning against the kitchen counter. "Get you some coffee?" she asked.

Both Beans and Fee declined. He was sure that Fee had just had a cup of Nespresso before she left her house, and Beans thought that even his Black & Decker brew was better than anything Anita could offer. She sighed as she sank into a chair opposite Fee.

"I'm sorry I didn't come by, Fee. But I thought you wouldn't want to see me, at least not for a while." Anita brought a fresh cigarette to her lips to light, but Beans was relieved that she thought better of it and set both cigarette and lighter on the table.

"It's OK, Anita." Fee said. "We know now that my mom suffered from an overdose of insulin. We're trying to find out how that happened."

"Insulin? But your mom's not diabetic! There's no way I would hurt Gloria, ever!" Anita's eyes were wide. "And I can't administer meds without a doc or RN supervising."

"Why don't you just tell us what happened that day, the Fourth of July, to help us figure things out?" Beans asked. "Start from what you did in the morning."

Anita's fingers drummed on the tabletop. "Let's see, I got up just before seven and showered. I was at your place just before eight, I remember, since you needed to get going early to block off streets for the parade."

Fee nodded.

"I fixed Gloria some breakfast but she hardly ate anything. She was so excited for the parade, since we almost never have them around here. She wanted to see the parade first, then go out to the airport for the races." Anita sniffed and blotted her eyes with a tissue. "I helped her get dressed, we watched an episode of *General Hospital*, then I packed up a couple of folding chairs into my car. I found her hat that she sometimes puts under the couch cushions. I packed the small cooler with drinks and a few snacks that she likes—you know, string cheese and Fig Newtons."

"So, by about ten o'clock we were setting up our chairs on the parade route. I wanted to get there plenty early so we'd have good seats, and we did." Anita smiled sadly. "Gloria was very pleased that there was no one blocking her view."

"Do you know who was sitting or standing around you?" Beans asked.

"Not that I remember. Most of the folks I know were in the parade or working at the food booths," Anita said.

"OK, then what?"

"I got Gloria a Dr Pepper from the cooler. And then the parade started. The new fire truck, the kids on the bikes . . . Gloria was having the best time! Just about when Trev was going by with the septic truck, I realized I left my smokes at the house. I told Gloria to stay put, and I turned away, for just a minute, I swear, to bum a smoke from a guy on the other side of me. He gave me a ciggy and a light, and when I turned back, she was gone."

"Did anyone around you see her leave?"

"No! I asked everybody around, but nobody saw anything! I thought maybe she went to the food booths, but nobody saw her—how far could she have gone, right?" Anita broke into a sob. "And that's when I saw you, Havi, and we all split up to look for her."

"So where did you go?" Beans asked.

Anita rotated the coffee cup between her fingers. "I retraced the parade route first. I asked everybody if they'd seen Gloria. Then I went up around the washeteria and the post office. The washeteria was all locked up for the holiday." She furrowed her brow. "Not the post office, though."

"The post office was open? Not on a federal holiday." Fee looked incredulous.

"No, not the post office lobby—the office in the back. The window was open, so I could hear voices."

"Gloria's?" Beans asked.

"No, not Gloria's. I recognized Bernie Waterman, of course. He was chewing somebody's ass out, but I couldn't make out what they were saying." She paused for a moment, her fingers twitching near the unlit cigarette, then went on. "I didn't want them to think I'd been eavesdropping, so I knocked on the door real loud and I heard somebody say, 'Fuck!Who's that?' Bernie opened the door just a little bit, so I couldn't see all the way in. He says, all friendly-like, "Well, hello, Anita. Post office is closed today.' I was almost insane with worry by then, and told him about Gloria being missing. He said he hadn't seen Gloria all day, wished me a Happy Fourth of July, and couldn't get the door closed fast enough.'" Anita sniffed.

Beans glanced at Fee, who shrugged. "OK, you left the post office. Then where did you go?"

Anita rubbed her eyes. "After that I went to the Yukon Inn. There was nowhere else I could think to look. I got wasted. Ask Max, the bartender. I was there until the dance started." She sighed. "I'm sorry, Fee. I just couldn't face you."

27

Mari

Summer 2024

"So, what's this about a ballet?" Mari asked her son. She was driving to the Goodwill with the first of many donation runs. There was barely enough room in the garage to walk through it now, and Mari decided she couldn't wait until her brother returned from his overseas trip to start hauling the junk out of their parents' house. The RAV4 was so packed with boxes of old mismatched dishes and frayed linen that she couldn't see out the back of the car. She hoped that wasn't some kind of moving violation here in California.

"Mom, are you driving and talking on the phone at the same time?" Beans asked, sounding like he was about to start a lecture.

"Don't worry, Havi. I'm on one of those Bluetooth thingies. My hands are on the wheel, I promise." Behind her, a car horn blared. She waved, although she remembered that nobody could see her anyway behind all those boxes.

"Just pay attention, will you? You're not in Galena, you know."

Mari rolled her eyes. "You can't see me, but I'm rolling my eyes right now. You texted something about a ballet, so now I'm curious. Is this Amy's ballet?"

Beans said yes, that the ballet opened in a couple of weeks, and would she and Grandma like to go?

"Of course, Havi! But are you going to be able to get away?"

He told her he was going to be fully reinstated, but his boss had extended his leave to the end of the month. "So, I should be able to go down, help you and Grandma out, and we can all get our dose of culture. I mean, there's nothing like this in Galena."

"That's for sure. That's one thing I miss." *Also Trader Joe's. Olive Garden. Chipotle. Wal-Mart. Sushi. Ramen. Wine bars.*

"That's if I can get out of here by then. God, so much has been going on, I'm sorry I haven't been in touch. You know, Victor hired a salvage crew to look for Lloyd's skull in the river."

"Oh my Lord. Any sense that man ever had went out the window when it came to his Lloydie."

"Yeah, well, no skull. But they did find lots of quarters."

Mari's foot jerked on the brake pedal and a car, maybe the same one, honked. "Did they find anything else?"

"A gun, Mom."

She glanced in the rearview mirror while she took a deep breath. "A gun?"

"Not Dad's, if that's what you're worried about. It was Zach Green's revolver."

"Oh." She exhaled, relieved.

"That's what you did that night, right? You went to the fuel dock to dispose of Dad's gun."

"Well, now, I should think that would be obvious." She looked in the rearview mirror at the cubist tilt of her right cheek.

He told his mother about finding Gloria unconscious on the Fourth of July.

"Oh my God, did she have a heart attack? That's what took Doc, you know."

"No, she overdosed on insulin. And nobody in the family is diabetic. We're trying to figure out where she got it and how it was administered to her." Beans took a deep breath. "She's OK now, resting in the hospital. But it's looking like someone tried to kill her, Mom."

A blare of horns behind her as Mari swerved across two lanes of traffic to pull into a Dollar Store parking lot. "What? Why would anybody want to kill Gloria? And who?" She took deep breaths, trying to get her heart rate to return to normal. "Jesus, don't tell me this while I'm driving in this God-awful traffic! Mom would never forgive me if I wrecked her car!"

"We're trying to figure that out now."

Mari put the car in Park and turned off the engine. "What's happening, Havi? It started with Lloyd's leg, and now . . ." She put her forehead against the steering wheel. It was starting to get hot in the car with the A/C off.

"I have to ask you, Mom, did you see anything that night, the night Lloyd disappeared? When you went to dump the gun?"

She was glad they were on a phone call and he couldn't see her face. "No, of course not."

"Did you see Gloria at all that night?"

"Just when we went to have Doc stitch you up. I didn't see her after that."

"Did you see Lloyd again that night?" She heard him take a deep breath. "Did you shoot him? Nobody would blame you if you did. There's no evidence to prove you did, hell, there's not even a body. You'd never be tried for it. But did you?" Beans's voice sounded almost tender.

"No! How can you even ask me that?" She started the car, and yanked it into gear.

"It's the same question Fee asked me, Mom! She saw us that night, how badly we were injured. She was a kid, but no fool. I think she still half thinks that I did it."

Mari let herself calm down as she changed lanes and subjects. "Well, now I've got to hustle over to Goodwill if I'm going get Grandma to the pool in time for Water Aerobics. Be sure and let me know how Gloria's doing."

She hung up, mildly irritated and so done with this phone conversation. *How did it go from ballet to murder so quickly? The downside of having a cop for a son.* She could count on the fingers of one hand the number of violent deaths there had been in Galena in the last thirty years. But now, just in the last few days—Lloyd Paul's leg. *And Gloria. Poor Gloria. What exactly did she see?* She took a deep breath, and felt guilty and embarrassed at the relief that washed over her.

But she's fine. It doesn't matter now.

Even more so than the tragic demarcation of time around Jimmy Beans's death, Mari felt time divided into the periods "before Lloyd's disappearance" and "after Lloyd's disappearance." She often thought about Lloyd's last night in a dreamlike sequence. The truck sputtering through the empty streets, the early breakup that caused the river to swell, the chunks of ice like broken concrete drifting downstream, the hollow splash.

Enough about Lloyd Paul. The leg on the beach. The guns in the river. She would go to Goodwill, take her mother to Water Aerobics, then immerse herself again in curating her father's history. She would lose herself in Ben Yamane's hidden world of carved wooden animals, whimsical cat cartoons, and unanswered letters.

October 12, 1945
Mr. Setsuo Sawada
45 11th St.
San Francisco, California

Dear brother-in-law;

I'm sure this letter comes as a surprise to you. I hope that you and your family are well, and Hoshi and Ben as well. I also hope that your relatives in Japan were spared the devastation from the atomic bombs that were dropped a few months ago. Such cruelty we humans inflict on each other, one way or another.

I'm not sure how much your sister has told you about why I left, but you deserve to hear it from me. While I was fishing in Alaska, I was seriously injured—the same leg injury that still plagues me. A kind doctor in St. Paul, Otto Laskin, saved my life. His nurse, also his daughter, was a young woman named Adelaide. During my long recovery, Addy and I became good friends, and then much more. I'm not proud of my actions, but I will not apologize for them either, other than to say I'm sorry for the hurt it caused Hoshi and Ben.

When it was time for me to leave St. Paul, I had no idea that Addy was pregnant. She made her father promise not to tell me—she knew that I was married and had a son. She had her baby, George Hiro Laskin, weeks before she and everyone else in St. Paul and St. George were relocated and interned at Funter Bay.

I didn't hear any more from either Otto or Addy. Then Ben found a stash of letters that Hoshi had hidden in her sewing box. She had saved letters sent to me from Otto over the course of several years. She said she had opened the first one thinking it was a bill for Dr. Laskin's services, then realized he had written that Addy had died, and that she had left a son, my son. I'm sure Hoshi was horrified, as you can expect, but kept this news from me. Several other letters came—one informing me that Otto was gravely ill, dying, begging me to take three-year-old George.

The last letter came from a doctor at the hospital in Juneau, informing me that Otto Laskin had passed away and George was in foster care. I would have known none of this if Ben hadn't found the letters—Hoshi had no plans to tell me of their existence.

Hoshi absolutely refused to let George come to us, to become part of our family. You know what she's like once she's made up her mind. What's sad is that I think she would have liked George, and George and Ben could have been raised as brothers.

Ben has his mother, and you and your family, people to love him and look out after him. I felt I was left with no choice but to find George and fulfill my responsibility to him. It was the most difficult thing I've ever done, to leave Ben. I thought more than once about taking him with me, but knew I couldn't do that to Hoshi, not after what I've put her through.

I found George in a foster home with four other children, all older. The foster parents were well-meaning, I think, but had few resources, and the accommodations were almost as bad as Minidoka.

For now, we are living in a boarding house a few blocks off of Franklin Street in Juneau. It's clean, has decent meals, and the nice woman who runs it dotes on George, happily watching him while I'm at work. I found a decent-paying job with the local newspaper, and I'm saving money to be able to rent our own place. George is bright and energetic, a joyful child. I think you and your girls would like him.

I've always considered you more "brother" than "brother-in-law" so I'm writing because I have a favor to ask. Please forward the enclosed letter on to Ben. I know that any letter I send directly to him would probably be confiscated and destroyed by Hoshi—I have no illusions about how much she hates me, and I know I am not blameless.

Thank you, Setsuo.

Your brother,
Kazuhiro Yamane
125B Spring St.
Juneau, AK

* * *

Dear Ben;

I know it's hard for you to understand why I left, but I'll try to explain. You have a younger brother named George, who lives in Alaska. His mother is not your mother, but a nice lady named Addy who got very ill and died. Then his grandfather died too, and George was left all alone. He doesn't have an uncle and aunt or cousins, like you do.

George is my son the same way you are my son. The only difference is that you have a family—your mom, Uncle Setsuo, Aunty Misako, Eiko and Sachi—where George has only me. So I had to come here to take care of him.

We live in Juneau, Alaska, and I work for a newspaper in town. A few days ago, it snowed for the first time this year. I took a picture of George in front of the house where we're living, trying to build a snowman. He's a very busy boy, likes to run and play. You would like him, I think. I hope you'll get to meet him one day.

Please write to me when you have a chance and give the letter to Uncle Setsuo. He knows how to reach me. Please don't tell your mother about our writing to each other—let it be our secret. I think your mother would be angry, both with me and with Uncle Setsuo, and we don't want that.

I'm sorry, son. I think about you and miss you every day.

Love,
Papa

28

Beans

Summer 2024

The next morning, Fee rushed in late, her face flushed, her ponytail untidy. "I got into a long discussion with Anita's nursing supervisor about what a fine CNA she is, a regular Florence Nightingale. Then she told me that Type 2 diabetes is practically an epidemic among the Native population. That's all she could tell me. HIPAA regulations, you know." She collapsed into her wheeled office chair, folded her arms on her desk and lay her head down, a childlike gesture of exhausted futility. Her shoulders began to shake.

"Hey, you OK?" Beans crossed the room and sat on a corner of her desk. He was sure that worry, frustration, and lack of sleep had worn her to a frazzle.

"Just peachy." She looked up, her eyes red and teary. She rubbed at them with the heels of her hand. "After I got here, it wasn't long before I realized how much work Mom was. And the life I gave up to be here." She frowned, fresh tears running down her face. "And Jesus, Havi, I started to resent her for it! What kind of selfish, shitty daughter is that? And what kind of shitty daughter is not even able to keep her own mom safe?" She lay her head back on her folded arms. "And I'm an even shittier cop, crying on duty."

"You're a good cop and an even better daughter," Beans said, handing her a box of tissues. "Buck up, and blow your nose, Gunnerson."

"Way to sugar coat it, Havi," Fee sniffed, but she was smiling now.

He sank onto his creaking office chair and spun in short arcs while Fee dried her eyes and brushed her ponytail back into a gleaming cascade down her back. His eyes fell on the small American flag that had been given out by the Boy and Girl Scouts during the parade and now sat in the cracked Iditarod mug he used as a pencil holder.

"Hey, what do you think Bernie was up to on the Fourth of July? I mean, it's a federal holiday. What's he doing at the post office having some kind of argument?"

"Yeah." Fee looked pensive. "Who do you think Bernie was chewing out? Other than Caleb flying the village deliveries, he's got no staff there at the post office. Did it seem like Anita overheard a performance review to you?"

"Not really."

"And the other guy seemed kind of startled and fearful when Anita interrupted them, didn't you think?"

"Yeah, like they were caught in the act. Of what, I don't know." Beans was glad that Bernie's involvement in just about every aspect of life in Galena activated Fee's suspicious cop instincts as well.

An internet search yielded several Bernard Watermans, only one of them in Alaska. He had a LinkedIn account with sparse information, and a basic Facebook profile, listing his marital status as single, that he worked as the postmaster in Galena, Alaska, and that he had grown up in Racine, Wisconsin. No other social media accounts, a minimal online presence. He could be a very private individual—or just have a lot to hide. It might go nowhere, Beans thought, but it might be the thread that when pulled, unraveled the whole deal.

Beans called Heller's cell. "Can you have Cam do a deep dive on a Bernard Waterman of Galena?"

"Sure, what's up?"

"Maybe nothing. I just got a feeling about this guy."

"Yeah, you and your feelings. OK, I'll get him on it." Beans thanked him and signed off.

* * *

Heller rang him first thing in the morning, sounding triumphant. "Your buddy the simple civil servant Bernie Waterman—not. He's one of the partners of Outport Enterprises, LLC. Other partners are a Taiwanese guy and a food distribution bigwig in Anchorage. They own a float plane, a DeHavilland Otter, tail number N899JB. They also own—get this—a hunting lodge on the Yukon River, not too far from Galena—White Rock Lodge."

Beans paused with his coffee cup halfway to his lips. He remembered that as a kid, the well-appointed White Rock Lodge was a going concern, with his dad flying hunting and fishing charters in and out throughout the season. He had heard that its owners at the time, an investment group out of California, had gone bankrupt with the dot com crash and that the bank had taken it over.

"Since when have they owned the lodge?" he asked. "And where does a postal worker like Waterman get the money to buy in on a lodge, not to mention a float plane? Did somebody die and leave him a fortune?"

Rustle of papers and mouse clicking. "Looks like they got it from the bank in 2005, so they got a hell of a deal. Even filed for permits to repair the dock the same year. Looks like Waterman's dad was a commercial pilot for United back in Wisconsin; mom was a homemaker. Both parents are deceased, strictly middle-class folks. My guess is his partners are the money guys."

So why do they need mail-sorting, stamp-selling Bernie?

Beans thought on this until Fee arrived at the Public Safety Building, looking hot and bothered, her normally crisply pressed khaki uniform looking crushed and wilted.

"They discharged Mom from the clinic this morning. Conrad is convinced an Eddy Redmayne killer nurse is still after her, so he's not letting her out of his sight."

"That's probably not a bad idea." If someone was indeed after Gloria, they might not stop after one attempt. "Does she remember anything more?"

Fee shook her head. "Not a thing. Trev driving the septic truck, then nothing until she regained consciousness. The hit on the head doesn't help her memory issues any."

Beans filled Fee in on what Heller had dug up on Bernie Waterman and Outport Enterprises, and their purchase of White Rock Lodge.

"I haven't heard anything about White Rock Lodge in years. You'd think we'd know if it was still operating, the way news travels through town like wildfire," Fee said. "And supplies, employees, everything would need to come through Galena, wouldn't you think?

"Outport filed for a permit for dock repairs years ago, but there's no indication that the work was ever done." He had an idea. "How about a boat trip?"

As he slipped the borrowed Glock into its holster, Beans felt for the first time since he shot Willis Helms that life might be returning to normal for him. The burden of Willis' death would be constant, but the remorse had begun to dull. Here, in the hometown he hadn't seen in the summer for years, with the weight of a dead cop's gun across his shoulder, with a new partner, a young woman from his past—he felt the familiar gears of police work fall into place and grind into motion. *I'm back.* He smiled to himself as he followed Fee out the door.

29

Beans

Summer 2024

The skiff they borrowed from Fish & Wildlife had a flat-bottomed hull and what the F&W officer called a "peppy" seventy-five-horsepower outboard motor. They loaded a cooler of water, first aid supplies, bullet-proof vests and other police paraphernalia. In addition to their handguns, Fee included a pump action Remington shotgun—"Bears," she noted.

Like most of his friends raised on the Yukon River, Fee was an expert boat handler. She started the outboard and steered them out of the fuel dock heading downriver. Mallards and goldeneyes squawked and flapped in front of the skiff's bow. The boat skimmed smoothly across the silty brown surface of the river, leaving a frothy wake.

The air had a slightly funky smell of something decomposing, but it made Beans strangely nostalgic. His best family memories, especially those of his father, were on this river. The Beans family's favorite patch for picking berries was just around the bend, up a muddy slough. They trolled for kings back when they ran thick up here, his father sitting in the stern of the boat with a can of Rainier steadied between his knees. Herc had pulled a record-setting pike from a mile downriver, breaking a finger in the process. Piper proudly claimed that she learned to pee into a coffee can on this river, since being part of a Beans family fishing excursion meant coming ashore only when you were done for the day. One fall day, Jimmy and Lindbergh, giddy on Jack and Coke, were charged by an enraged moose cow and barely escaped by swimming out into the freezing water farther than the cow would go. It was only fitting that Jimmy Beans's final resting place was this river.

Fee pointed out the landing where Lloyd's leg had been found. "Lloydie's last known position."

Another final resting place.

At the Innoko National Wildlife Refuge, the riverside landscape grew marshier and greener with sedge and grasses. They followed the gentle, wide curves of the river, accompanied by the cackling calls of the marsh birds, listening for the rumble of a floatplane engine.

The river arced northward near the junction with the Koyukuk when they saw it. Almost hidden behind a stand of scraggly black spruce, a red and white floatplane with the tail number N899JB, tied up to a small half-rotted dock. On the shore was a large log building in a similar state of disrepair, its roof partially collapsed, its windows broken.

Fee killed the motor and coasted the skiff to a stop on a gravel bank, not visible from the log building.

"Welcome to White Rock Lodge," Beans said quietly, as he tossed a bullet-proof vest to Fee. Despite the heat and humidity, he strapped one on himself.

Fee had managed to bring the skiff to shore before it passed in front of the lodge, so Beans was hoping they were as yet undetected. He slung the Remington shotgun over his shoulder and unsnapped his holster. Sweating in their bullet-proof vests, they slogged through the swampy shoreline, fanning the mosquito-riddled air in front of them and trying to move as silently as possible.

The scrub opened up onto a narrow gravel-covered area on the east side of the log building. From here, they had a good view of the dock and the plane. Through a broken window, they heard movement and a hushed voice coming from the front of the house.

Beans pointed to himself, then the open back doorway, indicating the route he would take. He gestured to the wrap-around porch and Fee nodded, understanding that they would split up, and she would move around to the side of the building. Although they could only hear one voice, there was no way to tell if there were more occupants. Beans wanted to make sure they were covered from several vantage points.

The back doorway opened into a large enclosed sunroom that was probably used in the summer months as a screened-in outdoor kitchen. The stone floor was soundless under his feet and did not betray his position. To his left, Fee moved stealthily across the porch.

He passed through another doorway that led to a cavernous great room with a huge river rock fireplace, choked with ash and debris. On the other side of the room was a sleeping bag, a lantern, an insulated cooler, a pair of hiking boots and a rucksack, clearly where someone had set up camp. An empty bottle of tequila and five empty cans of Budweiser were lined up near the rucksack like sentinels. Propped against the wall were three large canvas mail bags, brimming with shrink-wrapped parcels, stenciled with the word OUTPORTS. Beans was sure that these three bags did not contain either mail or groceries. He glimpsed Fee's dark head as she peered through the window.

The hushed conversation was coming from the left of the large double doors, where Caleb Redfern gazed out the broken windows, a can of Budweiser in his hand, talking on his cell phone in his stocking feet. He seemed to be unaware of Beans and Fee's presence. Stuck into his belt at the small of his back was a nine-millimeter revolver.

"So, I'll need to lay low, maybe hole up in one of those upriver cabins until we figure something out. Hard to hide the fucking plane, though. Hey, where are you, anyway? You better not have left me here holding my dick. Call me back." Caleb turned slowly, idly scratching his chest until he caught sight of Beans. His eyes grew wide.

"Hands up, Caleb," Beans said, his Glock drawn. "We have some questions."

Caleb's eyes darted to the canvas bags against the wall, then back to Beans. "What's this all about, Havi? What are you doing here?"

"I could ask the same of you."

"Taking a break from deliveries, you know—"

"Come on, you're just a few minutes from Galena. What's in the bags, Caleb?" Beans asked.

Caleb shrugged. "What do you think? Mail."

Beans sidled over to the bags. "This is a shit ton of mail going to the 'outports.'"

Caleb slowly began raising his hands, then suddenly hurled the can of beer at Beans's face. He deflected it with his elbow, but that split second was all Caleb needed to pull the nine-mil from his belt and fire. The shot went wide and splintered through one of the few remaining windows in the sunroom.

As glass from the window tinkled to the floor, Fee burst through the front double doors, her gun drawn.

"Police, Caleb! Drop your weapon!"

Caleb was quicker than a cat. One of the double doors had crashed against the wall and bounced back toward Fee. In the time it took for her to get clear of the door, Caleb had spun and fired. Fee fell backward to the floor with a loud grunt and was still.

Oh Jesus. Conrad's sister.

"Caleb! Drop the gun!" Beans took careful aim, not to kill. *Not again.*

"What are you doing with a gun, Havi? Aren't you on, like, detention because you killed a guy?" Caleb had his gun trained on Beans, and probably not to wing him.

Beans tried to keep his voice calm. "This doesn't have to get ugly, Caleb. Just drop the weapon."

"That's where we disagree, Havi. I think it does have to get ugly. I'm not going to drop my gun. Are you?"

"Not likely."

Caleb shook his head. "See? Stubborn. Just like your old man."

"What do you mean?" This conversation had suddenly taken an unexpected turn.

"Your old man, Jimmy Beans. Never was a more bullheaded guy."

"Leave my dad out of this."

"Jimmy—he had a chance to make a bunch of dough—you and your sister could have gone to fucking Harvard—but no, he couldn't be talked into it." Caleb's voice had a boozy drawl to it.

"Talked into what?"

"The drugs, man!" Caleb swept his hand toward the mail bags. "He could have made a bundle flying shit up and down the river, but no, not holier-than-thou Jimmy Beans. Too bad. Then he knew too much."

Beans's blood seemed to run cold. "My dad died in a plane crash."

Caleb sighed impatiently. "But it wasn't an accident, man."

Beans felt his stomach freefall, but kept his gun trained on Caleb. His index finger danced lightly on the Glock's trigger. "Tell me, or so help me, I'll drop you now."

"Then you'll never know, will you?" Caleb smiled briefly, then his face grew serious. "I took Jimmy to the Yukon Inn."

"Then you rigged his plane to crash?" Beans whispered, his blood running cold.

Caleb shook his head. "No, not me. My job was to get him toasted." He shrugged. "Jimmy didn't deserve it. But he would have fucked the whole operation."

"What operation?"

"Shit, I've said too much already." He aimed the nine-millimeter at Beans's chest.

Beans fired without hesitating. *Not this time.* It felt almost exactly like his own weapon back in Anchorage and he half-expected to see Willis Helms staring at him in surprise, trying to hold his blood in his body. Instead, Caleb's right arm flew back, his revolver momentarily airborne. Shrieking, he grabbed his shoulder and loped out the door, tripping down the front steps in his stocking feet. Beans followed his trail of blood across the porch and the steps and ran through the knee-high grass and young spruce toward the dock and the floatplane.

"Stop, Caleb! Police!" Fee screamed. Holding her side and limping painfully, she stumbled across the overgrown lawn toward Beans and the fleeing man. "Don't let him get to the plane!"

Caleb thudded onto the decrepit dock, turned, and smiling as if he just remembered something, reached down to his right ankle. He came up with a small pistol in his bloody hands. He took aim, then with a loud crack, disappeared.

Beans jogged over to the spot where Caleb had vanished. The rotted wood of the dock had given way, and Caleb had fallen into the river below. Sputtering and bleeding, he waded to shore and collapsed on the muddy bank. Beans had shot him in the arm, a through-and-through, painful but not life-threatening. He said a silent sutra. Beans didn't want another soul on his karmic tally.

Fee caught up to him and collapsed in the tall grass, wincing. "Wow, that packed a wallop." She rubbed her right ribcage, protected by the Kevlar vest. "That'll leave a mark."

Beans photographed the three mail bags before loading them into the skiff. There was little doubt in his mind about what they contained, especially from what Caleb had said, but they would be fully inspected back in town. Fee did what little she could to patch Caleb up as she Mirandized him. Caleb was mostly silent, only grunting when asked if he understood his rights. They cuffed him and sat him up in the skiff so everyone in town could get a good look at him as they pulled into the fuel dock.

Junior Mangold almost swallowed a wad of chew in surprise when he saw Caleb, bleeding and restrained in the boat. "Holy Jesus! What happened to you?"

Caleb was silent. Beans drove Caleb and Fee to the clinic to have their injuries tended to, ironically in adjoining beds, with

Caleb cuffed to his. After his wound was dressed, he was dosed with painkillers, remanded back into Beans's and Fee's custody, and put into the holding cell. Fee had a couple of bruised ribs that she said only hurt when she laughed, and she returned to duty immediately.

Conrad rushed in just as Fee was settling herself very slowly behind her desk. "I heard you were shot!" His eyes were wide with concern.

"I'm fine, Conrad. Just don't try to hug me." She winced.

"And you?" Conrad asked Beans. "Are you OK?"

"Just dandy." It suddenly occurred to Beans that he might need to face another internal inquiry regarding an officer-involved shooting—this time not with his own gun—and he cringed inwardly.

His cell phone barked. *Heller.*

"I heard you were shot!" Heller screamed into the phone, echoing Conrad.

"No, I'm not shot, calm down," Beans said. "I shot someone."

A pause. "What? Again?

Beans winced at the *again*, but he spoke calmly. "I shot Caleb Redfern after he fired at Fee. Fee's fine; she had on a vest. Redfern has a minor through-and-through; he's sleeping off the anesthesia in the cell." Beans surprised himself by how calm he was.

"Oh." Heller sounded relieved. "So, you're OK?"

"Fine. How did you hear I was shot?"

"Just some chatter on the radio. Obviously not a reliable source. So hey, good job getting Redfern. He shows up in our research as one of Outport's minor partners."

"He was hiding out at, guess where—the old White Rock Lodge, with a load of drugs he was hauling downriver."

"Did you get the postman too?" Heller asked.

Beans had driven by the post office and Bernie's residence while Fee and Caleb were being tended to at the clinic. The post office was "Closed until further notice." Bernie's bungalow was locked up, the curtains drawn.

"I think he's long gone."

30

Beans

Summer 2024

The one phone call Caleb Redfern had wanted to make was to Bernie Waterman. It again went immediately to voicemail. Subsequent calls made to the post office rang with no answer. His vehicle, a blue Ford Ranger pickup, had been located at the airport.

"Your buddy Bernie has taken a runner, Caleb," Fee said.

"Son of a bitch," Caleb muttered, sullen and disheveled, wearing scrubs from the clinic, his arm in a sling. "So much for 'one for all and all for one.'"

"Looks like he flew out yesterday, while we were tracking you down," Beans said.

"He knew we were on your tail and wanted to put as much distance between you as possible," Fee said.

The three mail bags contained small reused Amazon boxes wrapped tightly with green shrink wrap and black Sharpie-marked with the names of various villages—Ruby, Holy Cross, Marshall, and more. As Beans suspected, the boxes contained quart Ziploc bags of pills, powder, and capsules, enough illegal substances to keep the entire Yukon–Kuskokwim Delta high until Labor Day.

"I want an attorney," Caleb said. "And a sandwich."

The sandwich was supplied quickly, but it would be the next day before an attorney from the Anchorage public defender's office was able to fly up. Louise Goldsmith, serious, bespectacled, with a curly blond bob and perfect skin, got off the plane the next day hefting a heavy briefcase in one hand and a pair of gumboots in the other. Beans's partner Ed Heller followed her off the plane, mopping sweat off his brow.

After a long, hushed private conversation with her client, Louise Goldsmith gathered Caleb, Beans, Fee, and Heller in the room and said, "He will give you Waterman and his colleagues for consideration on the homicide."

"The disappearance of Lloyd Paul is at best an undetermined manner of death," Beans said.

"Not Lloyd Paul." Goldsmith trained her gaze on Beans. "The twenty-year-old murder of your father, Jimmy Beans."

All the air in the room seemed to have been sucked down an elevator shaft, taking Beans free-falling with it. Fee's mouth dropped open. Heller was frozen in place, staring at Beans. Only Caleb and Goldsmith were mobile—Caleb's eyes darted between Beans and his attorney, and Goldsmith scribbled on a legal pad.

Beans tried to keep his voice level. "Caleb told me that my dad's plane was sabotaged."

"It was Bernie's idea. I didn't touch the plane." Caleb held up his hands.

"OK, so maybe you're an accessory. How did my dad get involved in the first place?" Beans asked.

"Back when you were a kid, remember, Zach used to sell weed and a little coke out the washeteria? He bought you some booze in the day too, as I recall."

Beans nodded. "Yeah, sure."

Caleb went on—apparently now that the jig was up, he wanted to tell all. "All the drugs were controlled by Bernie. His contact in Anchorage would send pallets of groceries via bypass mail to YC, some packed with weed and coke. My contact at the airport would flag the pallets and break out the drug shipments. Because my guy is such an epic fuckwit, Lloyd Paul found out about it, and we had to cut him in. Strictly small potatoes, just neighborhood dealing at that point."

Beans thought this story was going on far too long and his head was starting to spin. "So you and Zach and Bernie were the drug kingpins of Galena. What does this have to do with my dad?"

"Well, it had nothing to do with Jimmy until the Taiwanese dude came to town."

"Who?" Goldsmith asked.

"Donovan Ching. Big real estate guy, based in Las Vegas. Also likes to hunt and fish. He came up late one summer on a junket and stayed at the White Rock Lodge when it was still a pretty happenin' spot. Jimmy flew him in and took him hunting and fishing. He was looking for some blow, and Jimmy hooked him up with Bernie. Before you know it, everyone's thick as thieves—staying at the White Rock and living the lifestyles of the rich and famous."

The incongruous image of middle-aged Bernie Waterman came to Beans's mind, the mild-mannered postmaster stamping mail behind the counter in his Dockers and argyle vest, while secretly ruling as the drug czar of the Middle Yukon.

Caleb fidgeted in his chair. "So, pretty soon, Donovan wants in as well. Talks them into a much more sophisticated operation. The basic premise of bypass mail, using Galena as a distribution hub to other locations up and down the Yukon. And anything within range—the Kuskokwim, even the coastal villages. He was talking about expanding the product line, too—not just weed and blow, but opioids, meth, date rape stuff."

Beans felt in his pocket for a stick of sugar-free gum but didn't find any. He would have to live with the nausea.

"Of course, key to this expansion is a way to get the product from Galena to the 'outports.'"

"A plane," Beans said, acid roiling in his stomach.

"Right. I mean, a skiff would do in a pinch, but ideally, you'd want a plane. Bernie told the other two what a great guy Jimmy Beans was, and how he had young kids who probably wanted to go to college. So he'd probably be up for earning a few extra bucks."

Beans flashed on the caribou hunts on the tundra, the Yukon River kings, snowmachine rides, his father's belly laugh, the gun in the piano.

"They invited Jimmy up for a big meeting at the lodge and presented this proposal to him—how he was going to be a vital part of this operation, Outport Enterprises. And Jimmy surprised the shit out of everybody when he said 'no.' Not just 'no,' but '*hell no*, no way am I bringing this shit to kids on the river.' Everybody was disappointed, of course, but they couldn't talk Jimmy into it."

"Is that when they decided to kill him?" It took an effort to get the words out, and his voice didn't sound like his own, but someone else's, far away. Heller shook his head sadly.

Caleb nodded. "Jimmy flew Zach and me back to Galena. The others stayed at the lodge to party some more, but before we left, Bernie gave Zach and me specific instructions. Like I told Havi, I took Jimmy to the Yukon for a few pops. While I was getting him wasted, Zach's job was to take a Snoopy tool and get into Jimmy's tail cone. He was to remove the lock ring on the horizontal stabilizer trim tab actuator. Bernie's dad was a pilot so he knew what to do, and Zach used to be a helluva mechanic before he started dealing weed. Bernie told Zach to make sure to put the tail cone back good and tight, because drunk or sober, Jimmy Beans sure as hell would notice if it wasn't. They felt bad about it, but he knows too much, Bernie said. Jimmy should have come aboard with us, he said. He had to make it look like an accident, he said."

They felt bad about it. Bernie the postman who said Jimmy Beans was "one of the best." Beans took a deep breath. "How did you know my father wouldn't have a charter that day? That other people wouldn't die as well?"

"I guess we didn't. Probably a stroke of luck that he didn't have anybody else on board. After Jimmy went down, they got their own plane and paid to get me licensed, since Zach wanted no part of it." Caleb pressed his eyes shut. "Fuck. For what it's worth, I'm sorry, Havi."

Beans felt for a moment that he had left his body, that he was floating above the table, above this village scumbag casually discussing Jimmy Beans's murder. He imagined his father, getting piss-eyed drunk that day because his conscience wouldn't let him join an operation that would give his family the best things in life. Then getting in his plane and having the one thing that he knew would always respond to his commands, as faithful as a mechanical dog, suddenly plunge to the ground, while he was helpless, strapped in the cockpit.

Like it was yesterday, Beans's fourteen-year-old self gripped Otter under his arm, trying to keep up with Piper as she raced to the site of the huge explosive booms and the dark clouds of smoke. He could almost reach out and touch her dark hair streaming behind her, hear her hiccupping sobs in her wake, smell Otter's chocolate bars melting from his hands and onto Beans's hand-me-down T-shirt.

He pressed his fingers to his temples. "Why tell us now? My mom, my siblings—we could have all gone to our graves thinking my dad's plane crash was a horrible accident. Why after all these years are you telling me this now?"

Caleb's face twisted. "I want that fucker Bernie to pay! Bernie was afraid Jimmy would torpedo the whole operation. Bernie is the one who convinced the others that Jimmy needed to be silenced. Bernie is the one who got out of Dodge and left me holding the bag. Or bags. Literally. Yeah, me and Zach were part of it, and I gotta live with that. But Bernie was the one turning the screws. Bernie is the reason that Jimmy was killed."

Beans looked across the table and saw Fee's eyes welling with tears.

* * *

In a flash, Beans heard his chair crash to the floor behind him and loud scrapes and shuffles and cries of surprise as everyone leapt to their feet. Without knowing he was going to do it, he had lunged across the conference table, and had Caleb's collar and his sling gripped in his fists. Caleb's face with two days' worth of stubble, eyes wide and terrified, was inches from Beans's own. Caleb whimpered as his cuffed hands pushed against Beans's chest.

Louise Goldsmith yelped and sprang away from the table. Fee tried to loosen Beans's grip on Caleb's sling, pleading with him. Beans felt Heller pull at the back of his sweaty shirt.

"Hey, hey, come on, take it easy." Heller's deep voice commanded.

"Havi! Havi! Let go!" It was Fee's plaintive voice that brought him back through that dark tunnel into the brightly lit conference room of the Public Safety Building. He released Caleb, staring at his hands as if they didn't belong to him.

Goldsmith straightened her glasses on her face. "I think we could all use a break."

Beans nodded. It was like he had awakened from a dream.

He felt Heller's meaty hand on his shoulder. "Come on, buddy, let's get some air."

Outside, Heller cracked open a bottle of water and handed it to Beans. Beans nodded gratefully and drank.

"Wow, didn't know you had those Jack Reacher moves," Heller said, admiration in his voice.

"Shit, I'll be lucky if he doesn't bring assault charges against me." Beans held the chilled water bottle against his face.

Heller snorted. "He's an accomplice to a murder and a drug trafficker. Hell, he's lucky we didn't let you kill him."

Fee joined them outside, her eyes wide and concerned. She laid her hand on Beans's arm. "You OK?"

He patted her hand. "Yeah, sorry about that."

"I think you showed remarkable restraint. I might have shot him. Again," Fee said, matter-of-factly.

* * *

Back inside, Beans shrugged and muttered, "Sorry."

"I deserved it," Caleb said, picking at a tear in his sling. "I'm just glad you didn't kill me at White Rock."

They all seated themselves, Caleb's attorney nodding her acquiescence, and Fee turned the recorder back on. Beans continued, "So you said that Lloyd Paul was cut in on this operation as well."

Caleb groaned, dropping his head against the back of his chair. "Lloyd Paul. Jesus Christ. Couldn't keep his mouth shut to save his life. He was a greedy fuck too, kept asking for a bigger piece. Bernie finally made up some bullshit story about a big signing bonus waiting for him in Anchorage and how they were going to make him an 'integral part of the supply chain,' was the way he put it. Lloyd took the bait. Shipped his truck, his boat, all his shit upriver and was moving out of town."

"But then he disappeared," Beans said.

Caleb leaned forward, his gaze intense. "Hey, Lloyd Paul is not on me. Yeah, I was supposed to pick him up that night. Zach and me were supposed to 'disappear' Lloyd Paul, right?" Caleb made air quotes with his cuffed hands.

"Only, when we came to pick him up, he wasn't there. Lloyd blew us off. We waited around for as long as we could. The upstream ice was moving in fast, so we had to take off or get stuck there. We figured he was sleeping it off somewhere."

"About what time was this?" Beans asked.

"We were supposed to meet at midnight. But no Lloydie."

"Did you or your 'colleagues' ever hear from Lloyd again?" Beans asked.

Caleb shook his head. "Nope. We didn't touch him, I swear. We thought he got wind of what was planned for him, and he got out of town on a skiff, but . . . he was gone. And then, what? Almost twenty years later, his leg shows up? That's wild."

* * *

A few hours later, Beans sat at his desk across from Fee's, trying to determine the best way to tell his mother that her husband had been murdered, and had not crashed his plane in a drunken accident twenty years ago. Louise Goldsmith had said, with a sad smile, that she would let him discuss the Caleb Redfern plea deal with his family. There was no statute of limitation on murder; if they wanted to go ahead and prosecute Caleb Redfern for his role in Jimmy Beans's death, that was their prerogative. She would await their decision.

Heller came through the office and dropped a cold Diet Coke on his desk. "Waterman got off a plane in Anchorage but there's no sign of him flying out. We've got APBs out on him. It's just a matter of time." Heller looked at him with concern. "You look like shit. Do you want a sandwich or something? A Spam musubi from Andreas K's?"

Beans shook his head. He was bone tired. His altercation with Caleb had left him exhausted, like he imagined recovering from a grand mal seizure must be like. He definitely did not want his mother to see him like this. No FaceTime this time. He picked up his cell phone to call her.

31

Mari

Summer 2024

Mari inhaled the summertime perfume of the ripe honeydew melon in her hands. It weighed as much as her head did, she knew, and it would take them a week to eat it, but hell, how often did she get melons this fresh in Galena? She placed it in her cart, where it rolled next to the bottle of French rosé and stopped.

She was like a kid in a candy store in Whole Foods. The sights, the smells, *the prepared food section, oh my!*—a garden of delights. She sampled the smoky baba ghanoush from a tiny paper cup with a tiny recyclable plastic spoon and knew she was not in Kansas anymore, or Galena for that matter. She told herself, for the umpteenth time, that she loved her life in Galena, but she did appreciate the amenities of northern California.

Her phone vibrated in her pocket. *Havi.*

"Hi, baby. What's up?" She licked the little plastic spoon and wondered if it was in poor taste to ask for another sample.

"Hi, Mom." He sounded hesitant, faraway, but then he was in Galena, she told herself. "Where are you?"

"Whole Foods. Or Whole Paycheck, as I've heard somebody say. Probably somebody who works at Safeway."

"I got so much to tell you. Is there someplace you can sit down?"

"I'm done here. Let me check out, and I'll go to one of those sidewalk tables. Is everything OK?" She was worried; Havi didn't sound like himself.

"Don't worry. Just call me back when you're done."

She paid for her purchases, found a table under a striped umbrella, her groceries in a green reusable tote on a chair next to her, and sipped at an iced caramel macchiato. *Way better than Charbucks.*

She dialed her son. "OK, I'm sitting down. You've got me worried now, Havi."

He took a deep breath and began. She gasped when he told her that they apprehended Caleb Redfern with mail bags full of drugs heading for the villages. At the part where he and Fee confronted Caleb at the old White Rock Lodge, she asked, "He shot at you?"

"And Fee. She was wearing a vest, so wasn't hurt, just a couple of bruised ribs. He missed me entirely. But I shot him."

"Where'd you get a gun?" Mari asked.

"It's Arvid's. I wounded Caleb, but he'll be OK."

"Are you OK?" she asked.

"I'm fine. It wasn't like Willis."

She slurped her iced drink through the straw. "Wow, Caleb Redfern? He was always such a polite boy."

She heard Beans take another deep breath. Then he began to tell a story that she wouldn't have believed possible. He told her about her husband flying Bernie and the other partners of Outport Enterprises to the White Rock Lodge. There they approached

Jimmy about being a part of a larger distribution network, flying drugs from Galena to villages all over the Yukon and Kuskokwim villages.

"Bernie Waterman? The mailman? Part of an international drug ring? Your father would have never been part of that!"

"You're right. He refused. They killed him for it, Mom." His voice faltered.

"What?" She was sure she hadn't heard him right.

He told her all of it, how Caleb confessed to distracting Jimmy while Zach tampered with Jimmy's plane. He didn't want any loose ends, according to Caleb. "It wasn't an accident, Mom. Under Bernie's instruction, Zach rigged the plane to crash."

It wasn't just the iced drink that made Mari suddenly grow cold. "But, but . . . Caleb and Zach—they were Lindbergh's friends. Bernie sold us stamps, for crying out loud."

"Caleb said Bernie gave them more money than they've ever seen. If it means anything, he says he's sorry—Dad didn't deserve it and neither did we."

Her voice was colder than the slushy ice in her drink. "They murdered your father. They can all go to hell."

Beans's voice was solemn. "They might already be there, Mom. Remember how Zach used to tip me a crazy amount of money for delivering teriyaki to him? He would say it's for school. And just before he left town, he gave me a hundred bucks. For graduation, he said. I think it was his way of trying to make amends. And no one has heard of him since Lloyd disappeared."

She was silent for so long that Beans said, "Mom?"

"I always wondered. Your dad was so careful about everything. Sure, he was drunk a lot of the time. And after the fire, it seemed hopeless to press for an investigation . . ."

He told her that Caleb was asking for leniency for his part in Jimmy's death in exchange for informing on Bernie and his partners. "Caleb came forward when he didn't need to, Mom. He has enough on Bernie to roll on him, even without Dad's murder. He could have let us continue thinking Dad's death was an accident."

That might have been a blessing. She held the cold drink cup against her forehead. "Are you getting soft on Caleb, the man who helped kill your father?"

"You know that's not what I mean, Mom. Caleb isn't pulling the strings."

Mari put on her sunglasses against the bright California sunshine. "Yeah, I know. Bernie's the one behind it all. He's the one who should pay. Caleb shouldn't go unpunished, but it's Bernie calling the shots."

"Should we call Piper? Or Herc or Otter?"

"Are you kidding? Piper would call for drawing and quartering!" She almost chuckled. "No, I think they trust us. I think they'd be OK with whatever the two of us decide."

They made a conference call to one of Beans's former classmates who was now an attorney in Anchorage. "You know, you could bring civil suit against . . . wrongful death . . ." the enthusiastic young man said. Mari had stopped listening at some point. She had no interest in going after a drug kingpin/postmaster for his money. It wouldn't bring Jimmy Beans back.

In the end, they agreed on leniency for Caleb, as long as he did not hold back on nailing Bernie Waterman. And Caleb would need to meet Mari, face to face, and apologize for his part in Jimmy's crash.

She and Havi hung up, promising to FaceTime soon. She tossed her now mostly flavorless iced drink into the trash and stood to leave. She shouldered the green reusable Whole Foods bag that now seemed impossibly heavy, and headed towards the RAV4. Just as she opened the back door, one of the handles of the bag broke. As she grappled for the bag, the flawless honeydew melon seemed to leap out and plunge to the pavement. Its cracked, pale green wreckage spilled seed and juice on the hot asphalt, its aroma now sickening sweet.

Perfect one moment, irreparably broken the next.

Sobs erupted from her, uncontrolled. She bent from her waist, trying to catch her breath, as salty tears mixed with the sweet juice at her feet. Shoppers carrying their own reusable totes gave her wide berth, probably thinking Whole Foods must be charging way too much for melons or she was having some kind of psychotic episode. But she didn't care. She leaned against the RAV4 with the door open, the entrails of the broken melon at her feet, until her sobs subsided to hiccups. Still sniffing, she picked up whatever larger detritus of melon she could and dropped them into the broken-handled bag. *Reusable, my ass.* At least the bottle of French rosé was unharmed.

"Do you need some help?" A young Black woman, a concerned look on her face, approached with a little girl in a stroller.

"Oh no, but thank you, thank you for asking. I'm OK. I'm OK now." Through her tears, she gave the kind young woman a fragile smile.

* * *

Her mother was upstairs taking her usual afternoon nap, so there was no blaring newsreel or Japanese travelogue filling the Fremont house with incessant chatter. She washed her face at the kitchen sink and dried it with paper towels. In the silence of the kitchen, Mari unscrewed the cap of the now-room temperature French rosé (*they're almost all screwcaps these days, thank you, Jesus*) and poured a glass. She raised it in a toast, said, "There you go, Jimmy," and sipped the dry, floral liquid.

At the dining room table, the carved wooden bear and the little Native Alaskan man lay across a stack of folded letters, more one-way correspondence to Ben from his father. Setting her glass on the sideboard, she smoothed the letters, yellowed and crackling with age, and set her reading glasses on her nose. She would slip again into the long-ago past, to another part of her family's history, uncharted territory until now.

July 7, 1947
Ben Yamane
c/o Setsuo Sawada
45 11th St.
San Francisco CA

Dear Ben;

I hope you've received my previous letters. I hope you and your mother are well.

Summer has come to Southeast Alaska now and the days are long and warm. George and I have moved into our new house—well, not brand new, just new to us. It's not far from the old place, and close enough for me to walk to work.

The best thing about having a house with a yard is that we now have a puppy! I have enclosed a photo of him with George. It's hard to tell from the photo, but he's all black with blue eyes and his name is Sumi. You remember that "Sumi" is the word for "black ink" in Japanese, so it suits him fine. He is a very active puppy and enjoys chewing on sticks and shoes. He has very big feet, so I think he'll be a large dog. He and George are best friends.

Hmm. Maybe I should draw a Sumi and Panko comic? What do you think?

George will start school in the fall. He already reads quite well (not as well as you, of course) and even knows a few Japanese words.

How are you? Are you playing baseball this summer? Uncle Setsuo wrote that you and Sachi are learning to play the piano. Are you enjoying that?

I have become a pretty good cook of a few dishes—but only a few. I make great scrambled eggs, and George loves hamburgers. He also likes onigiri with smoked salmon in the middle, and your mother's recipe for oyako donburi, which used to be your favorite. Is it still?

Please write, Ben. Again, give your letter to Uncle Setsuo and he'll get it to me. I think about you and miss you every day.

Love,
Papa

Enclosed with the letter, a comic strip titled: "Panko the Camp Cat Crosses the Taku"

* * *

In this comic strip, Panko the Camp Cat, with his suitcase full of fish heads, arrives at the bank of the mighty Taku River in Alaska. Across the river is the island where the small boy George is, the younger brother of the boy Ben. The river is wide, and too deep for Panko to wade across, (and everyone knows that Panko can't swim) but he can hear the small boy calling him from across the water. "Panko!"

Panko sits on his suitcase at the water's edge and tries to figure out how to get across to the small boy George. Then he hears a mighty roar!

A huge grizzly bear, smelling the fish heads in the suitcase, gallops up the beach at Panko. Terrified, Panko yells and throws rocks at the monstrous bear, but it still advances.

Then out of nowhere, a snarling dark blur speeds up the beach. It's a big black dog with icy blue eyes. It growls and barks and bares its long teeth, the hair on its back standing up like brush bristles. The bear and the black dog circle each other like boxers in a ring until the black dog lunges, and the bear backs down, huffing in disgust, and lumbers back into the woods without looking back.

Panko thanks the black dog for saving him, and finds out his name is Sumi. Panko tells Sumi that he is trying to get across the river to visit the small boy George. "But it's too far," he tells the black dog, "and it's too deep for me to cross."

"Nonsense," Sumi says. "Climb on my back and hang on."

Panko climbs on the black dog's back with his suitcase of fish heads. The dog jumps into the river and paddles with his huge feet. Before long, they are on the opposite shore, and Sumi shakes water off his coat, drenching Panko, who was wet enough already.

At the shore to meet them is the small boy George, who jumps up and down with excitement to see Panko and his new friend Sumi.

"You've come!" he says joyfully, and prepares them a feast of smoked salmon *onigiri* and cloudberry cobbler.

May 30, 1953
Ben Yamane
c/o Setsuo Sawada
45 11th St.
San Francisco, CA

Dear Ben;

I know that you are receiving my letters, as Uncle Setsuo says he is passing them on to you, so I can't blame the United States Postal Service for not delivering the mail. I'm sorry that you don't feel up to making contact yet. But I'll continue writing, hoping that someday soon you'll write back.

Our big news is that we've moved! George, Sumi and I are now living in Hoonah, on Chichagof Island. We're still in Southeast Alaska, but in a more remote location west of Juneau. I am now working as a watchman at a fish processing plant. We have our own house separate from the factory with a view of the water. There are a pair of eagles nesting in a nearby fir tree; I've already sketched them. I bought a new pair of binoculars so we can see when the eggs hatch.

It's beautiful here, and George and Sumi love it. There are rocky beaches to scramble across, and woods to hike through—although as you can expect, George and Sumi do a lot more scrambling and hiking than I do. The berries are plentiful, fishing is good, and some of the workers from the plant put up a little smoke house for us. I've added smoked salmon and berry cobbler to my list of recipes!

I've enclosed a photo of George and Sumi in our little skiff. We use it to get across the harbor from the plant, and to explore the nearby area. George has become an excellent boat handler, better than me, which isn't really saying much. I've enclosed another photo of our little house from the water.

Because it's such a remote location, there is no school here. George is enrolled in correspondence classes—he has daily lessons that I monitor (or he'd skip out on them for sure!). He is doing quite well—he reads above his grade level, I think, and especially enjoys science and adventure books. He's read pretty much everything that's available here on the island, so I'll need to think of something to keep him entertained during the long dark winter days to come.

I'm sure that you're making plans to attend university soon. You've always done so well in school. What field of study will you be pursuing? What university(ies) are you looking at?

Ben, George asks about you all the time. Having a brother is a dream come true for him. He's eleven now, and would love to write to you, but I've been encouraging him to wait until I hear from you. That way we'll know that you're ready to receive a letter from your little brother.

I hope that this letter is the one you answer. I'm sorry that my actions caused you and your mother so much pain, but I hope that now that you're older, you can understand why I had to do what I did.

Please write. I've included our mailing address in Hoonah, but Uncle Setsuo also knows how to reach me. Recently, he sent me a photo of Eiko, Sachi and you standing in front of the store. How you've grown! Practically a man.

I think about you and miss you every day, son.

Much love,
Papa

32

Beans

Summer 2024

Beans offered Heller the guest room—the room with the double bed that was Piper's until she left home for college. He didn't think that solidly built middle-aged Heller would appreciate climbing into one of the narrow bunk beds that Beans and his younger brother Otter used to share.

Heller said he could stay at one of the B&B's in town, but Beans insisted that he would welcome the company. After what he had learned today, he was grateful for the gruff, unexcitable presence of Heller, as large and unflappable as an Old English Sheepdog.

"I gotta say, that Mexican/Japanese/Greek place is pretty damn good," Heller said, a toothpick between his teeth.

They had met Fee, Conrad, and Gloria for dinner at Andreas K's. Heller had been an amicable dinner companion, sharing with the Gunnersons photos of his three daughters, comparing notes with Conrad on his time in the service in Japan, seriously interested in Fee's challenges as a cop in bush Alaska. Gloria had been very entertaining, fully recovered from her insulin overdose, telling stories about growing up in the little village of Koyukuk. They weren't sure which were part of her actual history and which were fabrications of her fragile memory, but they were amusing anyway.

"I think it's Greek/Mexican/Japanese, but—you're right—Andreas K is the best at Mediterranean/Latino/Asian fusion. In fact, he's probably the only one doing it. Maybe in the world."

"But it makes me thirsty," Heller opened the refrigerator. "Did you say your mom had some Japanese beer in here?"

"Yeah, help yourself." Beans tried to remember where Mari put the guest towels. There were the "extra" towels that were used for family and wiping down the dog, and then there were the guest towels, the ones that matched, that were only used for company.

"Wow, what's with all the eggs?"

"Those are from Gloria. She likes to bring them over. I guess I should make omelets tomorrow."

Heller pulled out a bottle of Asahi and shut the refrigerator door. "You know how to make omelets? You'll make someone a wonderful wife."

Beans flipped him off as he opened kitchen cabinets looking for towels. "We still haven't figured out how Gloria got that insulin."

"Do you think she might still be in danger?" Heller asked, as he rummaged through a drawer for a bottle opener. "She's a great old gal. I'd hate for something to happen to her."

Heller's offhand statement still echoed in Beans's memory. *Even a village as small as Galena has more than one diabetic.* Beans suddenly remembered that the good guest towels were in the rolltop desk drawer. He handed Heller a matched set of towels.

"Great! Do you mind if I take a quick shower? Been sweating like a pig all day."

"Sure, go ahead." He had just finished making up the bed in the guest room when his cell phone barked. *Cam Kristovich.*

"Hi, Cam. How are you?"

"Hello, Detective Beans. I am fine."

Beans could hear what he thought was the theme song to a Marvel movie in the background. "What can I do for you, Cam?"

"The Priority Five task you assigned me a few days ago—current name and location of George Laskin, who was adopted in 1955?"

He had almost forgotten about his great-grandfather's son. "Oh, right! Have you had any luck?"

"It was not a matter of luck. It was very difficult to access those adoption records. Yes, I have his adopted name. George Laskin was adopted by Ivan and Joan Lindeman in 1955. He is still alive, and last known address is Juneau, Alaska. George Lindeman was married in 1962 to Cynthia Morgan and had one child, Yvonne. That is as far as I've gotten."

"Great work, Cam! That's all I need for now." He jotted down the information. Mari, with her librarian skillset, could take it from there. "Thank you."

"You're welcome," Cam said with his flat delivery, then, "Goodbye."

"Was that My Little Robot?" Heller asked as he emerged from the bathroom, Dial soap-scented steam in his wake.

"I had him do a little digging into family history. He really is amazing."

"He can tell you what day of the week your birthday will fall on for any given year. It's a great party trick." Heller checked his phone. "No word yet about Donovan Ching or Waterman."

When did Bernie Waterman, Jovial Village Mailman, become Bernie Waterman, Evil Postmaster of Galena?, Beans wondered. He recalled Bernie giving a talk at the high school for Career Day—"Your Future in the US Postal Service." He remembered Bernie dressing up as Santa Claus for Christmas events and giving out candy to kids. At some point the candy had become weed and coke—and worse.

"You know, Mexico would be the most obvious option for Ching, but he has ties to the Far East. He could be heading in that direction instead of south."

"So far, it looks like he dropped off the face of the earth," Heller said. "Feds say there's no sign of him. They're watching the airports and border crossings, but no sightings yet."

They didn't have to wait very long to find Bernie Waterman. The next day, Heller got word that Alaska State Troopers pulled over a Chevy Blazer going ninety eastbound on the Alcan Highway just outside of Delta Junction. The driver was Bernie Waterman with a pretty convincing fake ID, although not good enough to fool the trooper, who had just seen the BOLO on Waterman that morning. The Blazer was packed with camping gear, supplies, a rifle, handgun, and lots of ammunition. It looked like Bernie was planning to live off the grid for a while. He would spend that time instead as a guest of the Alaska Department of Corrections.

Mari was elated that Jimmy's killer would be brought to justice. "I can't wait to look that bastard Waterman in the eye." She planned to be there in the courtroom and started writing a victim impact statement to deliver at his trial.

Beans shared with his mother the details that Cam had uncovered about her unknown uncle, George Laskin aka

Lindeman. "This is wonderful! I can work with this! Tell your friend Cam that he's a genius."

"I think he already knows this." Still, he would tell Cam anyway. Underneath that placid exterior, he knew it pleased the young man when his superior intellect was complimented.

He hung up with Mari, then changed into running gear. He had neglected his exercise routine in the last few days and was determined to get back into it, stifling humidity or not. He took off from the house, biting insects pacing him every step of the way. His shirt was already sticking to him by the time he passed the now closed and shuttered "Until Further Notice" post office.

There were still some details that needled at Beans about Outport Enterprises—how deeply had Lloyd Paul been involved, and had he been killed for it? Caleb claimed to know nothing of Lloyd's disappearance. And what was the White Rock Lodge's role in the Outport Enterprises operation? If Donovan Ching was such a high roller, why was the lodge allowed to fall into disrepair?

Heller was still en route to Anchorage, so Beans sent him a text: "Ask Caleb if he knows why White Rock wasn't maintained."

He waved at Janelle as he passed the washeteria, and she flagged him down.

"Do you know what's happened to Bernie? Why is the post office closed? What are we supposed to do about our mail?" She put her hands on her ample hips, her normally genial demeanor replaced by irritation.

Good questions, but ones he couldn't or didn't want to answer yet. Maybe it was time for him to leave Galena—the locals were beginning to think he was their neighborhood policeman. "Who normally takes over when Bernie goes on vacation? Maybe the best thing is to check with the main post office in Anchorage." She wasn't satisfied by his answer, but he waved at her again and picked up his pace, swatting at the swarming gnats.

* * *

On his way home, Beans ran by the Gunnersons'. Fee wasn't home, and Gloria was napping, but Conrad was out back, feeding the chickens.

"They're kind of a pain in the ass, but I gotta admit, they have a calming effect. And I like the fresh eggs. Need any?"

Beans declined, thinking of the several week's supply he already had in the refrigerator. Conrad offered him a glass of Gloria's lemonade, and they sat in the shade of the porch to drink it.

"I'm sorry, Conrad. With all the craziness with Waterman and all, we put Gloria's insulin overdose case on the back burner."

"Do you think it's someone who believes she knew something about Lloyd's disappearance?"

"Who else would want to kill your mother?"

Conrad chuckled. "Sometimes Fee. Just kidding, of course."

But that afternoon in Victor Paul's backyard, dozens of people heard Gloria say that she saw Lloyd die. Who thought Gloria needed to be silenced before she divulged this knowledge? *Someone who had something to do with Lloyd's death—or at least witnessed it.*

Fee's pickup truck stuttered to an idle alongside him as he was walking home. "What, did you run out of steam? Hop in, I'll give you a ride."

The heat and humidity had sapped him of all energy, and the sugar in the lemonade had given him a side ache when he tried to resume running. *What a wuss.* He got in with a grateful sigh.

"You know, I think we need to talk to everybody who was at Victor's the day of Lloyd's funeral and find out where they were during the parade. We've pretty much eliminated Anita in your mother's overdose, but not anybody else. At least we can see who is alibiing whom."

Fee nodded. "I'll start on the list of reception attendees."

* * *

His cell phone began barking as he entered the house. It was Heller. "Beans, we need you to secure the White Rock Lodge as a possible crime scene."

"You're kidding, right?" Was this another of Heller's practical jokes?

"No way. Like you asked, I questioned Caleb about why big swinging dicks like Ching and his cohorts allowed White Rock to fall into ruin. He said that back in 2009, he flew a young woman up there—one way."

"What? Who?" He thought there was a loose end with the White Rock Lodge, but this he hadn't figured on.

"He doesn't know. He flew a lot of women in there, but all came out, except for one. There's the body of a young woman somewhere at White Rock, and Ching didn't want to take the chance that she'd be found."

"What about Bernie? What does he say?"

"Nothing. He's lawyered up and is saying jack."

"Fee and I have already compromised the crime scene. Hell, Caleb was camping in the lobby."

"I'll be up there with a crime scene unit as soon as I can. But meanwhile . . ." Heller paused. "You still got a weapon, right?"

"Yeah, Fee insisted I carry it."

"Not just a pretty face, that Fee," Heller said appreciatively, then signed off.

* * *

For the second time they were in the borrowed Fish & Wildlife skiff, navigating the gently winding Yukon. This time Conrad was with them, refusing to be left behind, but complaining about wearing the bullet-proof vest.

"Why do we have to wear this? You caught all the bad guys, right?" Conrad whined.

"Just shut up! I can always leave you at home with Mom, you know," Fee said, sounding eerily like her mother in better days. Gloria was spending the day at a Conrad-vetted senior day care run by one of Mari's assistant librarians. "If your wife found out you were with me on a police action, I would never hear the end of it."

She gave Conrad the pump action Remington shotgun to carry, saying he could only hit a target as big as a bear anyway.

Seen from the water, even in disrepair, the White Rock Lodge was an impressive structure. The log building was two stories high, with a wrap-around porch on the lower floor. Off to one side of the dock was its namesake, a huge glacial erratic in an unusual pale sandstone color that must have arrived in the last Ice Age. Since there was no plane or boat in front of the lodge, they pulled up at the derelict dock rather than trudging through the brush. Beans jumped over the side and secured the boat while Fee and Conrad scrambled out.

They followed the trail of Caleb's blood up the front steps and onto the wraparound porch. Before long, they had walked through the entire lower floor, masked and gloved, with booties over their shoes this time. In their earlier hurried pursuit of Caleb, Beans and Fee hadn't appreciated the size and scale of the building. The lodge had a huge open plan living room with a large fireplace against one wall. Some kind of taxidermied head had adorned a discolored area of the wall above the mantle. The kitchen too, was huge, with an industrial ten-burner stove that now housed a large family of lemmings. Every window on the main level was broken, and the stone floor covered with broken glass, rodent droppings, and grit.

A creaking, rustic stairway led to six second-floor bedrooms. Any furnishings were long gone. Small creatures, deer mice or their relatives, scampered away at their footfalls. The bedroom farthest from the stairway was the largest and brightest, with tall, paneless windows letting in the light off the water. Covering most of the floor of this room was a filthy woven carpet, faded and chewed with numerous frayed holes.

Beans looked at Fee, who returned his stare. "Let's roll it up," he said, and she nodded.

With Conrad helping and careful not to stir up too much dust, they rolled the carpet against one wall. Under it, covering a four-by-four area of the floor, was what was once a large stain, faded with bleach and time.

33

Beans

Summer 2024

Beans and Fee ran crime scene tape across the doorway of the White Rock Lodge, while Conrad made disparaging remarks.

"Jesus, who's going to come all the way upriver and crawl around in there anyway? And you might as well tape up all the windows as well, since they're all broken. And the mudroom in back doesn't even have a door." He finally caught on that he was the object of Fee's silent fuming and said, "OK, then, didn't you say there was a horseshoe pit somewhere around the back? I'm going to check it out."

"You do that," Fee said between gritted teeth. "Should have left him at home."

They heard him crashing through the dry brush, calling out, "Shit, there's a big old stone barbecue here, and what is that, a pizza oven? How come Dad never brought us up here, Fee?"

"Probably because it was frequented by guys like Donovan Ching. Hey, be careful out there and don't touch anything, OK? And keep the booties on—I don't want you messing up the crime scene."

"Yeah, yeah, I know the drill. Whoa, what's that?"

"Did you find the horseshoe pit?" Beans asked.

"No, no." Conrad's voice was suddenly hesitant. "You guys better take a look at this."

They found Conrad behind the lodge, across an expanse of overgrown lawn and rotted wooden picnic tables. He was crouched next to a small rise in the earth, probably a result of the grading necessary to build the lodge. He prodded at something on the ground with a stick.

"Is this what I think it is?" Conrad asked.

It was a piece of a human jawbone, as weathered and gray as petrified wood.

"Oh, Jesus," Fee breathed. "This must be Caleb's one-way passenger.'"

It was Beans who finally found what once had been a shallow grave, on the other side of the earthen mound, the farthest point from the water. Over the course of years, the grave had been dug up by animals, the remains scattered and the disturbed earth once again overgrown with weeds. The only signs that this had been someone's final resting place were scraps of tattered fabric, a few small bones, and a pearl stud earring.

* * *

The next day brought Heller and a team of crime scene investigators who swarmed over the White Rock Lodge and its grounds. They determined that the stain on the floor in the upstairs bedroom, as they suspected, was blood that had been partially cleaned up. They did an archeological-grade excavation of the grave and uncovered more denim fabric, scraps of nylon, and a broken gold chain.

"Where is this woman missing from? Alaska? Vegas? Seattle? From how long ago? Caleb must have brought this person here, what, fifteen years ago?"

"I'll take the jawbone back so Chuckie can work his magic." Chuckie Hefner was the Anchorage medical examiner. "And I'll squeeze Caleb for more particulars."

Just in case, Beans had the techs examine the fireplace, the barbecue and the pizza oven for human remains.

Heller grimaced. "Seriously, Beans?" But he didn't argue.

* * *

Beans was reviewing a list of attendees at Lloyd Paul's reception when Heller called the next day from Anchorage.

"Chuckie confirmed that the jawbone belonged to a female. Preliminary phenotyping shows her as Northern European, Native Alaskan, and Asian, with brown hair and brown eyes. He could probably make a positive ID just with dental records if we could come up with a name. No fingerprints or genetic material on the fabric or jewelry."

"Has Caleb said anymore?"

Heller snorted. "He's like a freaking squeeze bottle of mayonnaise, just squirting information out every now and then when you press it. He's beginning to annoy the crap out of me. But he's pretty sure that Ching picked them up in Alaska somewhere—either Anchorage or Fairbanks."

"That narrows it down. Can you put Cam on it?"

"Priority One. Missing Alaskan women, ages, what—fifteen through thirty-five? Don't think he'd go for anybody older than that. Reported missing in 2008, 2009?"

"That's a good range. I'm sure it'll be a depressingly large number—especially among indigenous women. We'll need him to cull the women who were murdered or were eventually found."

In the meantime, they continued on Gloria Gunnerson's insulin overdose case. Beans and Fee decided to divide in half the list of attendees to Lloyd Paul's gathering. This was the grinding gumshoe type of police work that Beans didn't enjoy, but was a necessary part of the job. He took some comfort in knowing that his list was shorter by two—Caleb Redfern and Bernie Waterman were accounted for.

He started at the fuel dock, checking with Junior Mangold on his whereabouts during the Fourth of July parade.

Junior moved a wad of chew to the other cheek. "I was here working, Havi. Time and a half for the holiday. My cousin Drew was here working on his boat the whole time. You saw us here, remember?"

Next, he called on Janelle and Victor at the YC Store. Both said they were at the store, and alibied each other. Charlene Mangold was in the parade, driving the convertible the old veterans were perched in. Tammy Underwood, a part-time employee at the YC Store, said she was at the store first thing in the morning, then brought lunch to Junior well before the time Gloria was poisoned, then helped Andreas and Geno at their food truck. Trev the Septic Tank guy was, *duh*, driving the septic truck in the parade.

Fee didn't have any better luck. The only person on her list who was not either working at the parade or in the parade was Gus, the security guard at the school. Beans could alibi him at least for part of the time—he saw him there when he was driving around looking for Gloria, and the rest of the time he could be seen on the school's CCTV cameras.

"Well, maybe our assumption was wrong—maybe it wasn't somebody who was at Victor's that day." Fee threw up her hands in exasperation. "And really, anybody who had been at Victor's could have told someone what Mom said, and *that* person could have jabbed her."

"You know, there's another possibility."

Fee looked at him. "What's that?"

He shrugged. "Somebody's lying."

34

Beans

Summer 2024

As he expected, the list of missing women Beans had requested from Cam was hundreds of records long. And it was heartbreaking—young women who were last seen walking along a highway, sharing a drink with a stranger at a bar, or going to the store to buy milk for a toddler—all had simply vanished. He sent a precise email back to Cam, asking if he could sort the list by apparel and jewelry, if any. He was specifically looking for women who were last seen wearing any kind of denim, pearl earrings, and/or a gold necklace. It was a long shot, but one worth taking, he thought.

Heller called to check in. No more news on Donovan Ching, aka Ching Nanyou, his Chinese name. "He's got dual citizenship, so he could have fake passports for both the US and Taiwan—the possibilities are endless."

Frustrated by his lack of progress in identifying the White Rock Jane Doe, Beans stood, stretched, and decided some fresh air would do him some good. The day was cool and overcast, for a change, and he was glad that his jacket hid the Glock in its holster as he strolled by the post office.

The town was still reeling over the apprehension of long-time postmaster Bernie Waterman. No one could believe that their affable public servant had been organizing and shipping drugs in and out of Galena for decades.

Janelle wasn't at her usual post at the washeteria, so Beans assumed she was in the back room or at the YC Store. Beans wondered idly who was taking over the local drug business with Bernie and Caleb out of the picture. Maybe a vacuum was forming that would soon be filled, if it hadn't been already.

The YC Store was similarly unoccupied. Beans opened the ice cream freezer, taking his time picking out a Fudgsicle. Victor tromped through the back door, carrying a handful of packaged deli meat he brought in from the walk-in cooler behind the building.

"Shit, I almost got locked in again! Almost had to call the police—that would be you, I guess. That damn cooler door! I got a new handle coming from the manufacturer, but it's not here yet—God knows when it'll be here, the mail the way it is." He shook his shaggy head in disgust.

Those were as many words as Beans heard Victor utter in his life.

He put the Fudgsicle and a pack of sugar-free gum on the counter and reached into his pocket for his wallet.

Victor waved his hand for Beans to put his wallet away. He went around the counter to put the packaged meat into a refrigerated case.

"No, Victor, I should pay for this." Memories of Victor Paul chasing him into the street for a couple of pennies suddenly felt like yesterday.

Victor busied himself rearranging packs of bologna and salami on wire shelves in the cooler. "Nah, it's fine. And take a Drumstick for the Gunnerson girl. Used to be her favorite."

Fee was returning to the Public Safety Building just as Beans arrived with his half-eaten Fudgsicle and a partly melted Drumstick. She stared at him in surprise.

"Don't look at me. I think the real Victor has been abducted by aliens."

"Maybe this is his version of bribing the police," Fee said, licking the side of the cone to stop a drip.

She lapped at the Drumstick as she told Beans about the runaway dog she had just corralled. "Tattoo was by the river, rolling in something disgusting. He's home, safe and smelly. Had to hose down the back of my truck."

* * *

Conrad was leaving that day, returning to Okinawa. He needed to get back to work, he said, and trusted Fee would keep him in the loop on Gloria's case. "And who the poor girl at the White Rock Lodge is. Shit, who would've thought Galena would be a hotbed of crime?"

They drove him to the airport in Mari's truck, since Fee's still had a dead animal smell to it from whatever Tattoo the dog had rolled in. Conrad gave Beans a rib-cracking hug. "It's been too long, Havi. Keep in touch."

"I'm usually here at Christmas, if you'd ever show up then."

"Maybe, maybe. Alaska at Christmas. Kids might like that. And by then, you sleuths should have all these cases tied up." Conrad shot them both a dazzling smile.

Beans put an arm around Fee as they watched Conrad go through security. "God, he's a pain in the ass, but I'll miss him," Fee sniffed.

By the time they returned to the Public Safety Building, Cam had reduced the missing women's list to an almost manageable number. *Bless him, he took Priority One seriously.* Of course he did. Beans scanned it quickly, hoping something would jump out at him. Nothing really struck him except a profound sadness—young women who were last seen wearing jeans and a sequined hoodie, or a Seahawks jersey, with a silver locket, or a gold initial pendant around her neck. No pearl earrings. Piper or Fee could have been one of these women.

Piper. Beans was surprised that he hadn't heard from her. He and Mari had agreed that she would tell his siblings about how their father actually died. They had all loved Jimmy, but Piper was the closest to him, the only girl and their dad's favorite. If Beans had lunged across the table at Caleb, he could only imagine what Piper's reaction would have been. He decided he would give her time to digest this new reality.

He was sitting on the front porch after a sweaty run, hoping for a breeze to move the still air when Mari called.

"I've got more intel on our relative George Laskin/Lindeman," Mari said. She sounded upbeat, positive. She loved research projects, but Beans couldn't help but think that maybe the truth of how Jimmy Beans died might have freed something in her. Not just a happy-go-lucky drunk who had crashed his plane and left his children fatherless, like most of the village thought at the time, Jimmy had refused to run drugs on the river and had paid for it with his life. Beans always knew that Mari loved Jimmy unconditionally, but now he was sure she was proud of her husband as well.

"Oh yeah? Please don't say he's some kind of serial killer."

"Don't be silly. The Lindemans are bigtime Southeast fishermen. They own a couple of limit seiners—the *Vixen*, and the *Silver Dawn*."

"I think I've heard Herc talk about them."

"I'm sure you have. They're highliners! Looks like the daughter, Yvonne, married her high school sweetheart, William Olsen, right after graduation."

"Should I be writing this down so I can tell Piper, or will you?"

"It's up to you. Tell you what, I'll put it in an email to all of you. Anyway, Yvonne and William had a baby five months later—ha, I know what that's like—a little girl named Christine."

"Wow, good sleuthing, Mom!"

"So far, so good, but I don't have it all yet. Cynthia Lindeman passed away five years ago of a stroke. Yvonne divorced William back in the nineties and is single, still lives in Juneau and still fishes. She's well into her sixties, so good for her. George Lindeman is eighty-three and lives in Douglas, across the channel from Juneau. Just think, Havi—George and Yvonne could be Otter's neighbors!"

"Otter lives out in Auke Bay, Mom."

"You know what I mean! Even in Juneau, everybody knows everybody!"

There was some truth to that. "OK, what's next?"

"Well, courtesy of Facebook, I might try messaging Yvonne and see if she and her dad might be agreeable to—you know, talk on the phone, or FaceTime or whatever. It would be great to know what George remembers of his father—your great-grandfather."

"I don't want to discourage you, but don't be surprised if your welcome isn't a warm one. I mean, Grandpa Ben's family thought of George as the bastard child who broke up the family, right?"

"Your Grandpa Ben's mother didn't like anybody. She wasn't very nice to your grandmother either—called her *inaka kusai*, a country hick." Mari's mother had grown up in Hawaii, the Sansei child of sugar plantation workers.

He could tell that his mother was not to be dissuaded. "Well, good luck. Let me know how it goes. Oh, and Mom?"

"What is it, Havi? I've got to start dinner in a minute."

"Did you tell Piper about what really happened with Dad's plane?"

A long silence. "I did. And she didn't react the way I thought she would."

"What do you mean?"

"I thought she'd be livid. I thought she'd call for Caleb's head on a spike."

"So how did she react?"

"She was—well, triumphant! She started laughing, chortling even, if that's a word that's used anymore. 'I knew it!' she said. 'I knew Papa wouldn't crash the second most precious thing in the world to him!'"

35

Mari

Summer 2024

In the end, Mari gave up on her father's ancient Canon and bought a new HP printer/scanner to scan the smaller of Kazu's drawings in the composition books and sketch pads. The larger format drawings and comic strips she took to a nearby FedEx Office for scanning and digitizing. She was amazed that there were nearly fifty drawings of various sizes, and three dozen Panko the Camp Cat comic strips. She also took photos of all the wooden carvings Kazu did, all engraved with the letters "BY." She was excited by the prospect of assembling all of these images into a book to give to her children. They knew so little about her side of the family, and she was beginning to understand why.

Kazu's letters to Ben were heartfelt and beseeching, but obviously had done nothing to move him. It seemed that none of the letters Kazu sent were answered. While she was sure that Kazu meant to let Ben know as much about George and their life together as possible, she wondered if the happy account of their lives just served to fester more resentment in the son he left behind. His father abandoned him to be with another boy—one that he built snowmen with, went fishing and boating with, had adventures with. He got a dog for this boy. All the while Ben was forced to live with his bitter, unforgiving mother in a cramped apartment above a dry goods store. All the while, it seemed, he was the imprisoned boy Ben in Camp from the Panko comic strips.

Mari was impressed that in none of the letters to his son did Kazu say anything against Ben's mother, even though it was obvious that she had put Kazu in an untenable situation by refusing to take George in.

Mari wondered too, if her father felt guilty for the way things turned out. If Ben had not found the letters in his mother's sewing box, none of this would have happened. His mother would have kept them hidden, maybe eventually burned them. His father would not have known about George, he would have stayed, and their lives would have gone on the way they always had. Not for the first time, she felt sorry for Ben Yamane, her unbending, stoic father. Emotionally forsaken by a mother who refused to embrace an orphaned child, and abandoned by a father who left him for that child. Betrayed by his parents and betrayed by his own innocent actions.

And Ben, in turn, saved all of his father's correspondence rather than destroying them. Every revealing letter, every drawing and Panko comic strip was sequestered in a musty foot locker, hidden from his children and grandchildren like pornography, his own guilty secret. Refusing to forgive his father, but refusing to forget him.

* * *

She unfolded the last of the Panko the Camp Cat comic strips.

The Final Adventures of Panko the Camp Cat

Spring 1955

Panko the Camp Cat, Sumi the Black Dog, and the small boy George live on an island where berries almost burst from the bushes and the fish almost jump into their nets. They run through the woods and splash in the chilly surf. Life is almost perfect on their island.

Until one day Panko feels something in the air, something like a breeze, but more like a promise. He takes his suitcase with the fish heads to the beach because that's where it's coming from.

And there, in the distance, Panko sees a little boat with a fine, white sail. As it gets closer, he sees a small figure standing in the bow, waving. As it gets even closer, he recognizes the boy Ben from Camp, wearing his vest with a silver star. Panko is so happy to see him, he leaps for joy.

"Come with me," the boy Ben calls, laughing, and drops his anchor a way off shore.

"I can't," says Panko, "it's too deep to cross, and you know I don't swim at all well."

"No!" the small boy George and Sumi cry. "Stay here with us, Panko, with the berries and the fish, the beaver dams, and the roast ptarmigan."

"Come," the boy Ben says. "You can make it. You can swim. Use your suitcase."

"My suitcase?" Panko puts the suitcase with the fish heads in the water and is surprised to see that it floats! Holding it in front of him, he uses it to float on and kicks his legs through the cold clear water until he reaches the boy Ben's boat.

"You've come," Panko says, as the boy Ben reaches to pull him aboard.

"Of course," says the boy Ben. "I will always come, no matter how far away you are."

36

Beans

Summer 2024

Beans fried two eggs for breakfast the next morning, bound and determined to use up some of the eggs Gloria had given him. They were excellent eggs, still fresh, but there were only so many of them a guy could eat.

He came up with a brainstorm as he was washing up. He would bring the excess eggs to Victor Paul. He'd been so generous lately, he would offer Gloria's farm-fresh eggs to Victor as a gesture of gratitude and friendship. He never thought he would ever include *Victor* in the same sentence as *gratitude* and *friendship*, not to mention *generous*, but times change and he had to be ready to roll with them.

He carefully packed two dozen eggs into the front seat of the pickup and drove slowly down to YC. The lights were on in the store, and the door unlocked, but there was no Victor or Janelle. "Victor?" He called, loud enough to be heard in the back office.

He set the eggs on the counter and called out, "Hello? Janelle?" He noticed Victor's cell phone next to the register, which was strange. Victor always had his cell phone on his belt, like a gun in a holster.

The back door was open, another unusual occurrence. He rounded the counter and headed out the back door. The walk-in cooler took up most of the parking behind the store. As a teenager, Beans remembered when the cooler was brought in on the first barge of the season. Victor acted like he was welcoming another baby to his household, he was so proud. The cooler had survived a few decades of Yukon River winters and looked a little scraped and dented, but it hummed just as loudly as it did the first time Victor fired it up. Beans circled the cooler and was heading toward Victor's truck when he heard it. A faraway voice and muffled pounding.

Beans yanked at the door handle. At first it stuck, then he set his feet and pulled it again. It sprang open with a sucking sound, and Victor staggered out.

"Jesus Christ! Thank God you came by!" Victor put a hand on Beans's shoulder to steady himself.

"Are you all right? Shit, you could have suffocated in there!"

"Fucking handle. And stupid fucking me, left my phone in the store."

"You gotta fix that, Victor. That's not safe! How long were you in there?"

"Oh, about twenty minutes. Could have been worse. On Fourth of July, I was locked in there for thirty-five minutes! Everybody at the parade, bands playing and all that—Janelle couldn't hear me in there! That time, I left my phone in the truck! Jesus, maybe I'm losing my mind."

Victor shook himself, as if to warm up, and patted Beans on the shoulder. "Thanks, Havi. Jesus, Janelle's at the washeteria this morning, and Tammy's not due in until ten. I could have been in deep shit."

They walked slowly toward the back door, Beans alongside Victor in case he needed steadying.

"So, promise me you won't go in there unless you tell somebody. And for crying out loud, prop the door open," Beans said.

"I did! I had a shim in there, but then I tripped over it and it came out."

"Prop the door open with something bigger, like a rock, or a heavy milk crate." A small wooden shim could break or easily be kicked away.

Victor stared at him in disbelief. "What, and let all the cold air out?"

Beans stared back, then started laughing. Victor surprised him by laughing too, and slapping him on the back.

Inside, Beans gave him the nearly forgotten eggs, which Victor took gratefully. He offered to pay for them, but Beans said, "No, these are on the house this time—thanks for all the complimentary treats. But Fee might want to sell you eggs in the future—Gloria's hens are great layers, and Fee has way more eggs than she needs."

Victor said it sounded like a fine idea and he would talk to Fee about it. He forced a half dozen packs of sugar-free gum into Beans's hand and thanked him again for rescuing him from the cooler. Beans thought with amusement how much fun he would have telling Piper that he'd saved Victor Paul's life.

It wasn't until he was in his truck heading for the Public Safety Building that he realized that for thirty-five minutes during the Fourth of July Parade, *not everybody had an alibi.*

In the cab of his pickup truck, he told Fee about rescuing Victor from his walk-in cooler and the time he was in there during the parade. "What this means is Janelle does not have an alibi for those thirty-five minutes."

"There was nobody else at the store?"

"Nope. Tammy Underwood by then would have been helping out at Andreas's truck."

It only took a moment for Fee to digest this. "Thirty-five minutes is plenty of time to grab my mother from the parade, bring her to the house, jab her with some insulin, and get back to YC to let Victor out."

"She's not diabetic, though. Where would she get the insulin?" Beans wondered.

Fee chewed on her thumbnail. "And why? She's always been so kind to Mom. Why?"

"Janelle was there at Victor's, when your Mom said she saw Lloyd die," Beans pointed out.

"Yeah, but so was most of the town, and most of them hated Lloyd."

"Did they hate him as much as she did? She watched him steal from their parents, squander her inheritance, for years. And still he was their favorite, their golden boy. I'm willing to bet that nobody hated Lloyd as much as Janelle did."

Fee fell back in her seat. "But—enough to kill her own brother?"

"Wouldn't that give her a motive to want your mom silenced? If Gloria actually did see something that night?" Beans turned to meet her eyes.

"What if my mom was only yammering? She would have been killed for nothing," Fee looked into the dusty street in front of them, leaning her head against the passenger window.

"If Janelle killed Lloyd, she wouldn't want to take the chance, though, would she?"

Fee turned to him, her eyes wide. "These are people we grew up with, Havi. Bernie Waterman? Caleb Redfern? Janelle Mangold? I mean, these are people we've known our whole lives!"

At that moment, it almost seemed to Beans that there were two Galenas—one the benevolent small town he remembered; the other the malevolent flip side—where villagers were pod-grown Invasion of the Body Snatchers-like versions of themselves, dark and twisted, evil. He wondered to himself what kind of take Conrad the movie buff would have on this as he put the truck in gear. "I know. It makes it so much harder."

"Where are we going?"

"To talk to Junior Mangold."

37

Beans

Summer 2024

Junior Mangold was where he usually was, at the fuel dock, manning the pumps. Beans began to wonder if he had a life anywhere other than here—wearing the same grease-stained coveralls over a once-white T-shirt. He was reminded again of the contrast between Junior and his wife, Janelle, who was always tidily dressed in floral blouses and capris.

He smiled with tobacco-yellowed teeth, then spat. "Hi, Havi, Fee. Boy, you've been busy these last few days, haven't you?"

"Do you have a few minutes to chat, Junior?" Fee asked.

"Sure, sure. Let me cash this guy out, then let's find a spot in the shade."

Junior had set up a battered plastic patio table and umbrella at one corner of the dock property, and surrounded it with four equally decrepit plastic chairs. He scurried about, wiping the chairs down with a marginally cleaner rag and gestured for them to have a seat.

"As you know, we're following up on the events of the Fourth of July and what happened to Gloria Gunnerson," Beans said. He and Fee had agreed that, to avoid any conflict of interest issues, Beans would take the lead in these interviews.

"Sure, sure." Junior looked genuinely concerned. "I'm sure fond of your mom, Fee. It's horrible what happened to her. Is she doing better?"

Fee nodded and smiled. "Much better, thanks, Junior."

"Well, like I told you earlier, I was here working, so not sure how I can help you."

"Right. We're thinking now that what happened to Gloria might have something to do with events on the night Lloyd disappeared, eighteen years ago."

Junior's eyes darted to the pumps and back. "I don't know what Lloydie's disappearance has to do with that?"

"Frankly, we're not sure we do either, Junior. But I think we should run through it again. Why don't you just tell us what you remember about that Friday before Mother's Day, which would have been the twelfth of May."

"Wow, that was a long time ago . . ." Junior looked up, as if skywriting could prompt his memory.

"Just think back and recall the best you can," Fee said in a calm voice. "You were working here at the fuel dock, right?"

Junior snorted. "I'm working here just about every day, aren't I?"

"Let's start with—what was the weather like?" Beans asked.

"It was pretty warm. Do you remember, we had that early breakup? The ice jam downriver had just broken, and it could have been dicey. Everybody was afraid of flooding that year, more than usual. But everything held, thank God. Anyway, the river was clear that day as far as you could see, but upstream ice moved in later. Yeah, I remember later, chunks of ice, big and fast as cars. It was pretty dramatic."

Beans nodded. Flooding was always a concern during breakup, and that year, they had had an exceptionally cold winter and a sudden early warming trend. "How late did you stay here at the fuel dock?"

"Maybe about six o'clock? Yeah, I remember now—Janelle was working late, and I had to go pick Charlene up at the day care, 'cause they charge you if you keep your kid there past six. So I left just a few minutes before six."

"What happened after that?"

Junior scratched his head with the stub of the pencil he kept behind his ear. "I picked Charlene up and brought her home. Fixed her a sandwich since we needed to keep a tight schedule with her meals, and I didn't know when Janelle was getting home."

"Did you leave the house after that?"

"Nah. I opened a beer and watched ESPN like usual. I put Charlene to bed about eight o'clock."

"Janelle hadn't returned home by then?"

"No, she said that she was going to be busy at the store, it being just before Mother's Day and all."

"Did you see Lloyd at all that day?"

Junior pursed his lips as he thought. "Sure, sure, like I told you before, he dropped off his truck and skiff at the barge landing. Bernie and me loaded him. To tell the truth, I had had enough of Lloydie those last few days. Going on and on about how he was offered some great opportunity that he couldn't tell anybody about, but it was going to make him a fucking millionaire—oh, excuse me, Fee." He winced apologetically. "Anyway, I was sick and tired with him jawing on about his windfall."

"Do you remember what time Janelle got home?"

"I think I'd fallen asleep in front of the TV. I woke up when she walked in the door and a fishing show I like was on—so it must have been sometime around eleven o'clock." Junior squinted. "Yeah, around eleven."

"Did she leave the house after that?"

"No. It took her about a half hour to find room in the fridge for the huge turkey she brought back from the store. She was going to cook that up Sunday to bring to her folks'. Then she said she was beat and went to bed." He looked from Fee to Beans and shrugged. "That's all I remember."

As they drove from the fuel dock, Beans said, "Well, for what it's worth, I don't see Junior having any part in Lloyd's death, annoyed or not. Or Gloria's insulin poisoning either."

"Me neither," Fee said, chewing her thumbnail. "But he does give us a better idea of Janelle's timeline on Lloyd's last night. She was out until eleven."

"Lloyd didn't leave our house that night until about eight o'clock."

"You were at our house just after eight to get stitched up, I remember."

"How could you possibly remember that?" He turned to stare at her.

"You bled all over our garage. Your mom was almost unrecognizable. You guys were like The Night of the Living Dead. It's not likely I would ever forget that." Fee shuddered.

* * *

He wasn't looking forward to interviewing Victor Paul, especially with their newfound camaraderie, but it had to be done. Victor welcomed Beans and Fee, and told Fee he would be happy to buy her excess eggs from her. They agreed upon a rate of exchange, then Beans said, "We're beginning to think that what happened to Gloria has something to do with Lloyd's disappearance. Would you mind answering a few questions on your memories of that day eighteen years ago when Lloyd disappeared?"

Victor stared at Beans, then Fee. "Doc and Gloria were good friends to Dolores and me, you know that, Fee. And I'm so sorry about your mom. But I'm not sure Lloydie's—death—has anything to do with what happened to Gloria."

This was the first time Beans had heard Victor refer to Lloyd's death in those words. Maybe he was finally, after all these years, coming to terms with it. Beans hated even more having to revisit that event.

"We're not sure either, Victor, and we hate to bring up painful memories—"

Victor shook his head. "No, if it'll help, I'll answer any questions you have."

"Thank you, Victor. I really appreciate it," Fee said. "That night Lloyd disappeared, the Friday night before Mother's Day 2007, what do you remember about it?"

Victor shrugged. "It was crazy busy. Friday, anyway, which is always a busy day. And the Friday before a holiday? We could hardly catch our breath."

"Who was working there with you, on that Friday?" Beans asked.

"Well, Janelle, of course, and we had a part-time gal, Hannah, and me."

"Was Lloyd there?"

"Nah, Lloyd didn't work at the store much. He was probably at the washeteria."

Or at our house, getting shot. "And what time did you close the store?"

"We stayed open later that day, until nine, and still people hung around, trying to get their shopping done." Victor snorted. "Why people wait until the last minute—"

"And after you closed, you had other things to do, right?"

"Oh yeah, it's not just ringing stuff up, you know. Janelle and Hannah did some cleaning up, and I reconciled the cash."

"What time was it when everyone left and you locked up the store?"

"Oh, I think it was probably close to eleven o'clock. I gave Janelle and Hannah each a turkey for a Mother's Day and job-well-done gift." He patted the cash register as if it were a faithful dog. "And we all left."

"Did you go straight home?"

"Oh, yeah. Dolores, you remember, had health issues, and I needed to get home to spell the caregiver." Beans remembered that Victor's wife had been a frail woman who suffered for years from fibromyalgia and other autoimmune disorders.

"Did you see Lloyd at any time that night?"

"No. He was all full of this new enterprise that was going to make him a wealthy man. It was a big secret, though." Victor sighed. "Wouldn't even tell his old man about it."

* * *

They found Janelle in the back office of the washeteria, swearing in frustration at the QuickBooks program on her screen. The room looked a lot different than when Beans was sixteen and it had been Zach Green's office, where he regularly exchanged a few dollars for generic vodka. Janelle had cleaned it up and modernized it since then, with a newer laptop and monitor, and a laser printer on a credenza.

"Dad doesn't pay me enough to do the accounting for these businesses. I don't know why the hell he doesn't at least hire a bookkeeper!" Her freckled face was flushed and sweaty. "Cheap bastard," she muttered under her breath.

Once again, Beans took the lead, and Fee positioned herself near the door. "As you know, we're trying to narrow down everyone's activities on the Fourth of July, the day that Gloria was found unconscious."

"Of course, but I'm not sure why . . . ? I'm sorry about your mom, Fee, but she has been very ill." Janelle put on a funeral-attending face, nodding solemnly.

"Yes, she has been. But what put her in the hospital was an insulin overdose," Beans said.

"An insulin overdose? Well, I'll be. Is Gloria diabetic?" Janelle was politely inquisitive.

"No, she isn't," Fee said.

"Well then, I don't understand how she could have overdosed herself." Janelle's eyes widened in innocent disbelief.

"She didn't. Someone administered to Gloria, who is not diabetic, a potentially fatal dose of insulin."

Janelle swiped a hand across her damp bangs. "You must be mistaken. Who would do that to Gloria?"

"Where were you on the Fourth of July, for those thirty-five minutes that your father was trapped in the cooler?" Beans kept his tone pleasant, conversational.

"Why, I was in the store, of course. I couldn't have possibly heard him back in the cooler, especially with the door closed." The color began to rise in Janelle's face.

"Can anyone corroborate that?"

"No, Havi! Everybody else was either at the parade or trapped in the cooler!" Janelle stood suddenly, and Beans was acutely aware of what a big woman she was, strong and sturdy, like her father. He was suddenly grateful for the comforting but frightening weight of the Glock in its shoulder holster. "What are you accusing me of?" Her hard dark river rock eyes, so like Victor's, narrowed to slits.

Heller's comment leapt to his mind. *Even in a town the size of Galena, there has to be more than one diabetic.* That and something Junior said clicked definitively, like a key in a lock.

"How long has Charlene suffered from diabetes?"

Janelle's reddened face suddenly turned ashen. "Charlene?"

"Yes, your daughter. For how long has she been taking insulin?"

Janelle seemed to collapse against the desk. "Since she was a child. But you can't possibly think—"

"I'm not sure what to think. But I bet if we opened Charlene's refrigerator, she'd have a couple of week's supply at least. Who else had access to insulin? Who else had opportunity?"

"Charlene couldn't—she was in the parade! And why would she want to hurt Gloria?" She shook her head in disbelief.

"Maybe she had an accomplice. Maybe she was working with someone—she supplied the insulin, while the accomplice administered it."

"No! This is insane! Charlene had no reason to want Gloria dead!" Janelle held her large hands up in denial.

Beans pushed the office chair back toward her and gestured her to sit. "No, Charlene didn't. But you did, didn't you?" His tone was gentle.

Janelle seemed to deflate in front of his eyes. She collapsed into the chair and held her head in her hands.

"Do you want to tell us what happened?"

* * *

She did, and no, she didn't want an attorney. "But Charlene cannot be implicated. She had nothing to do with this, nothing."

Janelle had already taken a preloaded syringe from Charlene's refrigerator when she had driven her daughter home after Lloyd's funeral. After her father had locked himself in the cooler, and with most of the town at the Fourth of July Parade, she thought this would be the opportunity to silence Gloria.

"If only she hadn't said anything at Lloyd's reception," Janelle said tearfully. "I never wanted to hurt her. But she just wouldn't shut up. Going on and on about how she was there when Lloydie died."

It was easy enough to wait until Anita was distracted, then promise Gloria some punch back at the house. Gloria loved punch, and went with her without argument.

"Weren't you afraid someone would notice you kidnapping my mom?" Fee asked, with barely contained anger. Beans cautioned her with a glance.

"Everybody was distracted by the parade. If anybody noticed, I would just say I'm taking her for a snow cone or to the bathroom."

"Then you brought her home?" Beans asked.

"I wanted her to be home, in her familiar surroundings. Look, what I did was horrible, I know, but I had to, because I knew that she must have seen me that night . . . with Lloydie. I wanted her to be comfortable. Well, as comfortable as she could be."

Gloria wanted to collect eggs, she said. Janelle jabbed her with a syringe of insulin in the back of her neck as she was exiting her chicken coop. "I had lots of experience giving Charlene injections, so I promise, she hardly felt a thing," she said to Fee, as if a pain-free injection somehow mitigated her actions.

"But it was me—all me," Janelle went on. "Charlene had nothing to do with it. She doesn't even know she's missing a syringe. She gets three months at a time, and probably won't even know she's short until the time is almost up. Please—Charlene is innocent."

Beans nodded. "Other than being the source of the insulin—yeah, I believe you."

"But how did you know that Charlene was diabetic? She doesn't even have a local doctor," Janelle asked, her eyes tearful and desperate.

"I didn't really—until something Junior said about having to keep strict mealtimes with Charlene as a child. And the fact that she sells nothing but sugar-free pastries in her coffee shop made me take a stab in the dark that she was diabetic."

Janelle reached a hand toward Fee, but then thought better of it. "Please believe me, until the day of Lloyd's funeral, I never planned on doing anything to Gloria. But I just couldn't have her keep talking about that night, and what she saw." She swiped at her eyes with her bare arm and slumped into the chair. "So help me, before then, I never wanted to hurt her."

"The night Lloyd disappeared." Beans glanced toward Fee, who nodded. "Tell us about that night."

Janelle sighed and picked at a small hole in her shirt. "Fucking Lloydie."

"Tell us what happened that night," Beans said again. "We know that you worked late that Friday evening."

Janelle nodded. "Dad refused to close the store while there was still a buck to be made. By the time we had locked everything up, it was eleven o'clock. I was dead on my feet, had to work the next day, and the thought of having to do all the cooking for Mother's Day just pissed me off, you know? I mean, I don't blame Mom, it's not her fault she's sick, but the fact that I always have to do everything just put me in a foul mood."

"So what did you do after you closed up?" Beans sat on a corner of Janelle's desk. He didn't dare look at Fee, who hovered, restless, near the door.

"Dad gave Hannah and me a turkey. A turkey! Lloydie cleans out Dad's bank account, and all the change from the washeteria, and I get a fucking turkey! And it's a turkey I gotta cook on Sunday, along with everything else!" Janelle pounded herself on the chest for emphasis.

"And then where did you go?" Beans asked. His glance caught on a Yukon Commercial calendar on the wall behind Janelle's desk with a photo of Victor, Janelle, Charlene, and Lloyd, waving and smiling in front of the store. The caption read: "Your family grocery store."

"Dad and Hannah said good night, and they took off. Then I remembered that Junior had the truck, since he was picking Charlene up at day care. Our land line was out of commission until Alaska Comm could get out the next week. I called him on his cell but he didn't answer, probably because he left it at the fuel dock again. It was Junior's first cell phone—Lloyd's old Nokia—and he kept forgetting it somewhere. I was much younger then, and wouldn't have minded walking home, but I had this fucking turkey with me. What the hell, I'd martyr myself and make him feel guilty. I started to regret it right away—I mean, this is a fifteen-pounder. I tried calling Junior again, just as I'm passing the fuel dock—and I can hear the stupid thing ringing in the office. Shit. Then, guess who I saw, staggering around the dock?"

"Who?"

"My brother, the late Lloyd Paul."

38

Mari

May 2007

The river was high but clear of ice, silty and swirling in the darkness. Mari parked the truck under cover of a stand of scraggly hemlock and walked down to the fuel dock in the pale moonlight, Jimmy Beans's pistol heavy in her jacket pocket. The dock office was dark, but a phone rang, then stopped, then rang again, insistently. Each time, Mari halted, listening for someone to answer, but no one did.

Her eye throbbed where Lloyd had struck her. She pulled the gun out of her pocket and felt the cold reassuring steel against her cheek.

Just then, she caught sight of something moving at the end of the dock, barely visible in the thin light. It had a familiar loping gait, jingling. *Lloyd Paul.* Lloyd Paul with his pocketsful of laundromat change, drunk, probably bleeding all over the dock called out into the darkness, "Hey. I'm waiting."

She heard heavy steps behind her and ducked into the shadow of a propane tank, groping for the gun in her pocket.

The phone started ringing in the dock office again. Seven, eight, nine times. Then it stopped. The footsteps approached her, and she stayed hidden, holding her breath.

"Jesus, is that you, Janelley-belly?" Lloyd called out. "Shouldn't you be home getting your beauty sleep?"

Janelle Mangold appeared, plodding across the creaking dock, carrying a turkey or maybe a ham in a mesh bag. "What are you doing here, you little shit?"

"I'm waiting for my ticket to paradise," Lloyd slurred.

"Christ, what happened to you? You're bleeding, you moron."

"It's merely a flesh wound," Lloyd said in a passable imitation of a character from Monty Python.

"Maybe you should get to the clinic. Junior's not going to be happy about cleaning your mess off this dock."

"No time for that, Sis. Say goodbye to baby brother. I'm blowing this doghole."

"Oh sure. Big talk for a small man." Janelle rested the turkey on the dock. "Don't forget it's Mother's Day Sunday. For a reason I can't fathom, the folks would get their panties in a knot if you don't show."

"Nope. Not going. Not ever again. And I'm leaving with some cash parting gifts." Lloyd's voice was triumphant.

"What do you mean?"

"I'm sure Dad would have wanted me to have some seed money for my new enterprise, so I cleaned out the machines." He jangled the coins in his pockets.

Janelle snorted. "So what else is new?"

"And the joint account."

"What? That's Mom and Dad's! Just because you *can* access that money doesn't mean you *should*, you asshole!"

"A mere technicality. It's a done deal." Lloyd went to the end of the dock and peered upriver. "Hope they can land before the upriver ice shows up." He turned back to Janelle. "What's that you have there, Nelly-belly? A turkey? A Butterball from the YC freezer section?" Lloyd started laughing, cackling hysterically. "I get the cash, and you get . . . meat. Who loves you now, baby?" He bent from the waist, trying to catch his breath.

Janelle moved more quickly than Mari would have thought possible. While her brother was still bent over, she reached him, brought her arm back, the turkey hanging heavily from it, and swung it forward. As if on a pendulum, the frozen bird struck Lloyd squarely in the back of the head with a sickening crunch. A rattling cough escaped him. He staggered, teetered at the edge of the dock, then fell with a heavy splash into the water. Unconscious and weighed down with the quarters in his pockets, Lloyd sank without another sound and was swallowed by the dark, frigid river.

"Oh, shit," Janelle said softly.

She stood immobile for a full minute, silently looking down into the blackness lapping at the edge of the dock. Then she hooked up the hose and sprayed Lloyd's blood off the boards. She rinsed off the turkey too. She trod heavily back up to the road, the turkey still hanging from her arm. Janelle passed within three feet of Mari but never noticed her.

When she was sure that Janelle was out of sight and earshot, Mari crept out of her hiding place and went to the end of the dock. The river was swift and swollen. She half expected to see Lloyd's pale accusing face, but when she looked down saw only the bottomless river.

She should tell someone, Arvid maybe, what she just saw. But then she would have to explain why she was driving around in the middle of the night with the gun in her truck. She would have to explain that Janelle did just what Mari had planned to do, only Janelle did it with a turkey, where Mari would have done it with Jimmy's Colt.

She took the gun from her pocket. Its serial number was filed off and it was illegal as hell, and had slumbered in the piano for years. *Until this night when my boy used it to put a bullet through that bastard Lloyd Paul.* She gave the cold metal a grateful kiss, drew her arm back, and flung it into the river as far as she could. It splashed with finality and disappeared. She and the river would keep Janelle's secret.

39

Beans

Summer 2024

Janelle seemed more relaxed now, as if a great weight had been taken from her. Her words came out in a rush. "I told him he was a thief and an asshole. He came at me then, with that hunting knife. He was going to cut me for sure. I hit him with the only weapon I had—the turkey." She took a deep breath. "I just wanted to keep him away from me, but he fell off the dock. He went into the water, deep and moving fast with breakup. With all the coins in his pockets, he sank like a stone." She exhaled, finally looking up to meet Beans's eyes. "I couldn't have pulled him out if I wanted to."

"Did you want to?" Beans asked.

"I called for him, and threw a line in, but he was gone." She put her face in her hands. "I saw that look in his eyes. He wanted to kill me. I did the only thing I could to protect myself."

"Did you think about calling Arvid, or the fire department?" Fee asked.

"I did, but then I thought—he told everybody he was leaving town, right?" She looked from Beans to Fee and back again. "They could go on believing that, and be none the wiser."

"Weren't you afraid that your brother's body would wash up?" Beans was incredulous that Janelle could have lived with this secret for so long.

"Oh sure, I sweated it that year, and every spring breakup for several years. But as time went on, I was more certain that he was just—gone." She made a magician's "poof" motion with her hands. "Mom and Dad thought he became some rich dude who didn't have time for them and never called, which was fine with me."

She went on to confess that it "scared the bejeezus" out of her when Lloyd's leg was discovered washed up on the beach. "And I was even more freaked out when Dad hired the divers to look for his head." She grimaced. "And then, when Gloria went on and on about seeing Lloyd die that night, I started thinking—well, she's old and sick, and usually doesn't know what day it is. Maybe it's better for everyone, merciful even, especially for you, Fee, if I—"

"Wait." Beans felt his temper rise. "You were going to kill an innocent woman out of the kindness of your heart?" He turned away, disgusted. "Not buying it, Janelle."

"I have to know, Janelle," Fee broke in, sounding surprisingly calm. "Did you see my mother at the fuel dock that night?"

Janelle shook her head, not meeting Fee's eyes. "No, I didn't see anyone except Lloyd. I heard something though, behind the propane tank. That must've been Gloria."

Or not. Almost killed for nothing.

* * *

The Mangold family was shattered. Janelle, who had been the pleasant, efficient face of most of Victor Paul's businesses, now sat, morose and silent, in the holding cell at the Public Safety

Building. For Junior, it was business as usual at the dock, but he was nervous and inattentive, pumping fuel with trembling hands. Charlene appeared to be in shock, keeping Charbucks open despite the plunge in her already meagre business, but only to stare dead-eyed into space from behind the pastry counter.

The community was horrified at Janelle's confession to Gloria's attempted murder by insulin poisoning, but their reaction was mild compared to the response to her admission of fratricide. Janelle's confession to having killed Lloyd that night eighteen years ago, however unintentionally, ignited the Galena gossip network like summer lightning, even without Bernie there to fan the flames. The town had long since come to terms with the likelihood that Lloyd was probably dead, and everyone admitted that more than a few people wanted to see him that way. But nobody could have imagined that his own sister had killed him, in self-defense or not. Unlike Victor and Lloyd, Janelle had been universally liked and respected by her neighbors—so it would have been inconceivable that she could have killed her brother, then cooked and served the murder weapon to her family for Mother's Day dinner.

The hardest hit by Janelle's confession was Victor Paul. He seemed to shrink and age, like watching him in time-lapse photography, his gait suddenly stumbling and uncertain. Beans felt heartsick for him—intentionally or not, his one remaining child had killed his precious son. Still, Victor put on a brave but haggard face for the community.

He hired the most expensive criminal attorneys in Anchorage to work on Janelle's behalf and rented an apartment where she stayed while out on bail that he posted. Through the heartbreak and expense of Janelle's indictments, bail hearings, and plea bargains, Victor kept the YC store open. He bought eggs from Fee.

He installed a new safety handle on his walk-in cooler. Charlene finally closed Charbucks until further notice to help her grandfather out at the store and the washeteria. A win-win situation, Fee said to Beans, since her coffee was so shitty.

Beans had called his mother before someone else from Galena told her about Janelle.

A long silence on the line until Mari said, "Janelle? Killed Lloyd in self-defense? Well, he came after you with that very same knife, you remember." After a moment, she added, "It doesn't surprise me that Janelle would lash out against her brother. It's surprising she didn't do it sooner. She was the one at Victor's beck and call, and all the while, his Precious Boy Lloydie did nothing but steal from him. And her too, ultimately. Still, I feel sorry for Victor. Both children are lost to him." Mari sighed. "But it's hard to forgive her for trying to kill Gloria. How is she doing?" It sounded like his mother was once again in California traffic. He heard honking horns.

"She's pretty much recovered from her brush with insulin poisoning. It hasn't done a thing for her dementia, of course, but she's back to whatever's normal for her."

"Good. Neither Gloria nor Fee needs something else to worry about. Oh, and I wanted to let you know—I sent a Facebook Message to Yvonne Olsen, you know, George Lindeman's daughter? I hope I have the right Yvonne Olsen, it's such a common last name but we'll see. Her status is divorced, once married to a William Olsen—sheesh, another common name. I'm waiting to hear back from her. Oh, I got Piper on another call. I'll let her know about Janelle. Bye, baby."

Who needs social media when Piper and Mari are part of your family?

His phone barked. "Yo, Hellboy."

"Update on bypass mail kingpin Donovan Ching. We think we tracked him to a Dylan Chang traveling on an American passport. He boarded in San Diego a—get this—Disney Cruise Line ship for a Seven-Night Mexican Riviera Cruise. Anyway, the feds were ready to board at Puerto Vallarta, but last night," Heller started chuckling. "Minnie Mouse went overboard."

"What?" Beans wasn't sure he heard Heller right.

"Someone, presumably Dylan Chang, wearing a Disney costume went over the rail—a couple of almost sober passengers saw it. It was dark, and like I said, these witnesses were somewhat inebriated. So by the time they sounded the alarm and the boat came about, only the costume was found floating on the water. They searched for a while, brought in the Coast Guard, but so far, no Dylan Chang/Donovan Ching. He could've drowned, I guess. But feds are speculating that he might have had a boat pick him up."

"Not the happiest place on earth, then?"

"Trapped on a floating amusement park with a thousand screaming kids? I'd have jumped."

Beans hung up with Heller and focused his attention back on the list of missing women who had been wearing denim and possibly jewelry. There was still a death that needed to be solved—that of the Jane Doe, whose shallow grave was found at White Rock Lodge.

A sex worker who was picked up by Donovan Ching on the streets of Anchorage or Fairbanks to entertain his business associates? A girlfriend? A runaway? A witness who needed to be silenced?

Fee came in and slumped into her chair, tossing a packaged pastry onto her desk. "It's horrible. Victor won't even look me in the eye. He gave me way too much money for the eggs—and he gave me a Hostess fruit pie. It's like he feels personally responsible for what Janelle did." She sighed. "I liked him better before, when he was an asshole."

"Look at it from his point of view. The Pauls used to be the big shots of Galena, right? Everyone was so afraid of offending them. Overnight, this scandal has made them not just everyday people, but pariahs."

"And his precious Lloyd was a crook, supposedly part of Outport's drug enterprise." Fee shook her head. "I never thought I would feel sorry for him, Victor, I mean."

"Yeah, me too." Beans made a note to himself to stop by to talk to Victor. "He must be feeling very alone right now."

"Any luck with Jane Doe of White Rock Lodge?" Fee asked.

"Cam's shortened the list, but it's still plenty long."

"Here, give me some of that. I can work them in between my thousands of calls for lost dogs and stolen four-wheelers."

Smiling, he handed her a few printout pages. He knew he would miss working with Fee when it was time to leave Galena.

* * *

Even the bell on the door of the YC store sounded tinny and sad. The store had a deserted feeling—Victor was behind the counter as usual, but business had definitely suffered since the town had found out about Janelle.

Beans picked out a bag of barbecue potato chips and a Diet Coke and went up to the counter. "How are you doing, Victor?"

He waved around the nearly empty store. "See for yourself."

"It'll get better once the trial's over. Things will settle down."

Victor looked at him with haunted eyes. "I put everything into these businesses, Havi. I can't afford to wait until things settle down."

"You're a good businessman. You'll weather this." Beans didn't know what else to say.

"How come I didn't know? How come I couldn't see what Janelle had become? A murderer? Shit, and Gloria used to babysit Charlene sometimes. I can't even look at the Gunnerson girl now. And how come I didn't know that Lloydie was letting them bring their poison in with my groceries? And then dealing them out of my washeteria!" He jabbed a finger in the direction of the building that housed the now-closed post office and the laundromat. "I know what everybody says, that I spoiled him rotten, and maybe that's so. But he was my only boy . . ." Victor gazed down an empty aisle, "So help me, Havi, I didn't know about the drugs. Son or not, there would have been hell to pay if I had found out."

"I believe you, Victor. They were very clever about keeping it quiet."

"I guess that's why they were paying Lloydie. So he would keep his fool mouth shut." Victor slid Beans's money across the counter at him. "Just take the chips and pop."

Beans slid the money back at him. "Victor, you've got to let me pay."

Victor smiled sadly. "You know, you work all your life to build something you can pass on to your kids. And then your kids break your heart, one way or the other. So now I wonder, what was it all for?" He sniffed. "What the hell. I just should have let you and your brothers have those fucking candy bars." He surprised Beans by chuckling, his eyes watery.

Beans was munching on potato chips in the truck when a call came through from Mari.

"Are you eating in my truck?" she asked.

Shit. How did she know? "No." He dusted chip crumbs off his lap. Mari had forbidden anyone eating in her truck since a few years ago when a family of mice had set up house there, gnawing through the wiring.

Mari was chatty and cheerful. "I've had a wonderful email conversation with Yvonne Olsen. I did find the right Yvonne—she's George Laskin's/Lindeman's daughter. My cousin, well, half-first-cousin! Her dad's sharp and in good health, she says. Of course, she's heard her father talk about my grandfather and hers, Kazuhiro Yamane. She said she would scan a few photos and send them. Your Grandpa Ben didn't keep any photos of his father—my guess is his mother destroyed them? I'm going to send Yvonne some photos of my dad, who would be her uncle, or half-uncle? I've been telling her about the drawings and cartoons our grandfather drew for your Grandpa Ben, and she would love to see those, she says. She wants to see pictures of you kids too. She sounds delightful. I'm thinking now that I might make a stop in Juneau on my way home from the Bay Area. I could see Otter and meet these nice folks too."

"Sounds great, Mom," he said, distracted by the barbecue chip that he had just smashed into dust under the accelerator pedal.

"So, have you and Fee stemmed the tide of crime in Galena?" she asked, over the sound of horns honking.

"Pretty much. There is a Jane Doe we're trying to identify at White Rock Lodge, though. We think it has something to do with Waterman's group, Outport Enterprises."

"In your dad's day, White Rock was owned by a California investment group—it was quite the swanky spot then. Your dad flew me up there once for our anniversary. It was spectacular." Her voice sounded dreamy and nostalgic.

"Caleb says that he flew our Jane Doe up there with the Outport boys—not sure in what capacity, but you can imagine—somehow, she died or was killed and she's buried there. We only just found bone fragments a few days ago, but she's been there a while."

"She couldn't have been a local girl—we'd have known about it," Mari said.

"No, we think Caleb brought her up from Anchorage or Fairbanks."

"Poor thing. Someone has to be looking for her, don't you think?"

"We're going through the lengthy list of missing women now. It's really depressing."

"Do you think Caleb killed her?"

"You know, I don't think so. He's been almost too forthcoming about everybody he's attempted or conspired to kill. I figure he's got nothing to lose by 'fessing up here—but he's adamant. He flew someone in that he didn't fly out."

"So, Bernie and his cohorts?" Mari asked, a shudder in her voice.

"Kind of looks that way. At the very least, they disposed of her body. There's not enough of her there to figure out how she died, I don't think."

A pause, then Mari said, "You know, I was really looking forward to going home, and now I'm not so sure."

Beans laughed. "It'll all be wrapped up by the time you get home."

"I certainly hope so."

"How are things in California?"

"Your grandma is very gradually making a dent in the sorting out she has to do. She doesn't want to rush into anything, you know. I keep reminding her that I will be leaving for home in less than a month now. After we go to the ballet."

"Shit! The ballet!" With everything going on, he had totally forgotten that he promised to take them to Amy's world premiere.

"Don't forget. Grandma is really looking forward to it."

"I'll get on it right away."

More horns honking. "On the plus side, I think I'm really getting a hang of this freeway driving."

"You grew up in California, Mom. It should be second nature."

"But I've been away from it for so long. It's not exactly the same as riding a bicycle, you know. And there are, I don't know, *thousands* more miles of freeway and a *million* more cars since I lived here."

As he hung up with her, he made a mental note to self: (1) ballet tickets, (2) vacuum the barbecue chip crumbs from the pickup.

40

Beans

Summer 2024

The first thing he did when he got back to the house was to get on line and buy expensive orchestra-level opening night tickets to Amy's ballet and airline tickets to get him there. He would buy his mother and grandmother dinner, as well, and make a night of it. While he was still feeling virtuous, he pulled out the shop vac and cleaned out the truck. He smugly noted that he was not the only one who had eaten in Mari's truck—there were indistinguishable crumbs, gum and candy wrappers, an empty yogurt container, and several desiccated apple cores. *It's like a first-grader's vehicle.*

That done, he turned on a Mariners baseball game and opened the refrigerator to forage for something to eat. *Anything but eggs.* Other than eggs, though, there was precious little other than condiments and Japanese beer. He thought about calling Fee and going out for "not-so-shitty" pizza. He was about to text her when he was struck by a kind of wistfulness that his time in Galena was growing short. It was already mid-July. He just bought tickets for the July 25 performance in Oakland. He would need to leave soon.

When Fee had first called him, he had been less than enthused about coming to his hometown. He had seen it then as a debt to the Gunnersons for their discretion and silence that long-ago night he had been slashed by Lloyd's knife and his mother assaulted, one that he suspected was now repaid. Now he was surprised to admit, he'd enjoyed his time here. He didn't carry a badge, so didn't need to follow its rules. *Hell, he even carried and fired another cop's gun.* The small-town informality was, when not annoying, refreshing. No one had to explain their history. Everyone knew everyone, and everyone knew everyone's business. He'd reconnected with his buddy Conrad, and had established a friendship with his former nemesis Victor Paul, as bizarre as that seemed.

And then there was Fee. He had come to depend on her, not only as a professional colleague, but for congenial company. There was a sense of safety and security in hanging out with someone you had known your entire life. Warm and funny, Fee's familiar presence was comfortable, like a worn pair of slippers. *Am I comparing a girl to footwear?* It was probably just as well that he was leaving soon, he thought, before he got too attached. But maybe he already was?

He jumped a little when his phone barked. *Fee.* "You in the mood to get not-so-shitty pizza with Mom and me?" she asked him. "I haven't shopped for ages, and all I got is eggs and a Hostess fruit pie."

After pizza, which Fee proclaimed was "better than usual," they went back to Beans's house to further study the missing women's list. Fee parked Gloria in front of the TV where she became engrossed in *Dancing With the Stars.* Beans spread the pages out on the dining room table, while Fee grabbed a beer from the fridge.

"I know we're close on this," Fee said, scanning the list. "She's here somewhere in these pages. Come on, Jane, talk to us."

Beans circled the table several times, reviewing the list alphabetically, then in reverse. On his third time around, a name jumped out at him. Why hadn't he noticed this sooner?

Olsen, Christine. A common surname, especially in Alaska, with its large Scandinavian population. *Northern European, Native Alaskan, and Asian.* Reported missing by her father, William Olsen of Anchorage. Also a common name, but what were the odds?

Beans picked up his phone and called his mother. "You said Yvonne had a daughter named Christine?"

"Hello to you, too. Yeah, after the divorce, the girl went to live with her father in Anchorage, and they lost touch. I got the impression there was an estrangement, so I didn't get details. Why?"

"Ask her if her ex-husband reported Christine missing in 2008."

"You think the Jane Doe at White Rock . . . ?

"They're common names, but it's too much of a coincidence. I'll stand by."

Fee alternately chewed her thumbnail and peeled the label off her beer bottle while they waited. Beans paced around the dining room table, opened the freezer for ice cream, realized he didn't have any, then closed the freezer door.

After what seemed like hours, Mari called back, her voice subdued. Beans switched to a speaker setting on his phone. "Yvonne gave me the whole sad story on Christine. Soon after the divorce, which was a pretty nasty one, she said, William moved to Anchorage. He wanted to take Christine with him, but Yvonne wanted to keep her in Juneau, and George doted on his granddaughter.

"Christine and Yvonne butted heads from day one—she was too much like her mother, Yvonne said. Finally, when Christine was fourteen, she ran away to live with her dad in Anchorage, and Yvonne didn't contest it. Even there, she was wild, and her dad couldn't control her. Yvonne lost contact with Chrissy, who refused to talk to her mother—she only got occasional updates from William, who called his ex-wife every now and then for money."

"Is that Mari?" Gloria called from the living room sofa.

"It's me, Gloria," Mari answered. "I hope you're well."

"Trev in the septic truck, then the hospital, all I remember. Oh look, it's the guy who used to be on *The Brady Bunch*." Gloria pointed at the TV screen.

"Who?" Mari asked, confused.

"No it's not, Mom," Fee said, exasperated. "Sorry, Mari."

"Did William report her missing?" Beans asked, trying to get back on track.

"I'm getting to that, Havi. Losing contact with her daughter was very painful for Yvonne, as you can imagine. The last communication she had with William was when Chrissy was about sixteen. Her ex said he heard that Chrissy had had a baby and given it up for adoption. He thought she might be living with a boyfriend or on the street and only contacted him when she needed money. Like father, like daughter, Yvonne said. She had no idea if William reported her missing or not."

"So, as far as she knows, William is still living in Anchorage?" Fee asked.

"She found out from a mutual acquaintance that he died in 2010 in a car accident."

Silence both on Mari's end and Beans's. Finally, Beans said, "Do you think Yvonne would be willing to give us a DNA sample for comparison?"

"She told me she would do anything to bring Chrissy home."

* * *

A technician at the Juneau Police Department sent Yvonne Olsen's buccal swab to Anchorage and Heller fast-tracked it through the system. Beans was watching coffee drip into the Black & Decker carafe when his partner called.

"Sorry, guy. There's no familial relationship. Your Jane Doe is not Christine Olsen."

With a sigh of disappointment, Beans tapped on Mari's number. While this development did nothing to help identify their Jane Doe, at least there was a chance that his long-missing relative Chrissy Olsen could still be alive.

41

George Lindeman

Summer 2024

"Dad?" Yvonne's voice sounded very far away, even though she was just across the channel in the wheelhouse of their purse seiner *Vixen*. He could tell by the muffled shouts of the crewmen, the chugging of the diesel engine, the grinding sound of the power block hauling in net. He held his breath.

"Dad? Mari called. The DNA test came back. It's not Chrissy. The girl at White Rock is not our Chrissy."

He released his breath in a long exhale. "Well, then."

"Yeah. Listen, Dad. This means she could still be alive, right?" Yvonne's voice sounded hopeful.

"Sure, sure, honey." *The cherished nut-brown child who sat on his lap and called him "Gamps." The fearless gap-toothed girl who took her mother's car for a joyride when she was eleven. The same girl who was caught in the backseat of the same car with the neighbor boy when she was thirteen.*

Chrissy was never easy. Willful and fiercely argumentative from the moment she could talk, things always had to go her way. The unplanned child of a couple far too young to be parents, she became a bargaining chip between the two of them when their marriage fell apart. Then, sensing that she was an unpleasant reminder of her parents' failures, she disappeared from their lives. *She wasn't the body at White Rock but could be in another shallow grave. Scattered by foxes. Feeding fish.* But maybe not.

George reached for the small wooden heart in his pocket, its carved surfaces worn smooth from years of rubbing. He had planned on giving the little carving to Chrissy, but now who would he give it to?

George had no memory of ever being without this little totem, a gift from the mother he couldn't remember. His earliest memories were fond, fleeting ones of being carried on his Grandpa Otto's shoulders through the snow. Later ones were more troubling: stumbling in the darkness with only a pillowcase of clothing and the cold wooden heart in his pocket, pulled by the wrist by a towering woman in a musty-smelling wool suit. Ketchup on stale white bread and powdered milk. Having the heart stolen by one of the bigger girls at the foster home, and biting her to get it back.

Everything changed when the limping man came for him that day. He said he was George's father, sent for by Grandpa Otto. He remembered wondering how could that be, since he knew that Grandpa Otto was dead. The man bowed and apologized for not coming for George sooner. George didn't care and put his small hand into the man's, his other gripping the pillowcase of clothes.

For ten years the heart sat in George's pocket while he grew taller and stronger. He devoured his father's *onigiri*, rice balls with a sour *ume* or shaved smoked salmon in the center, the warm grains sticking to his dimpled cheeks. He learned how to say several Japanese phrases, including "Happy New Year." He could count to a hundred and knew the days of the week in Japanese. They rescued a blue-eyed black puppy they named Sumi, the Japanese word for "black ink." They went up the Taku River to camp and fish and jump beaver dams in their skiff while Sumi howled in the back of the boat. He learned to shoot and dress ptarmigan and grouse. His father had a bad leg, but liked to snowshoe in the winter, even if he couldn't go very far.

His father worked for the newspaper, and they could afford to rent a small house in town. George chopped wood for their stove and got even taller and stronger while his father seemed to shrink as he watched him.

His father often talked about his other son, Ben. He wrote many letters, but never got any in return. Even as a child, George could tell that this made him sad. George knew that his father had sacrificed much to be with him, and he seemed to sag under the terrible weight of this burden. Sometimes George felt like his own guilt weighed on him almost as heavily.

His father's final job was as a watchman at a fish processing plant in Hoonah on Chichagof Island. There was no nearby school, but his father monitored his correspondence studies diligently. During the long dark winter nights, when they had run out of books to read, George learned *hiragana* and *katakana*, the two basic Japanese alphabets, and a few *kanji* characters as well. On the long summer days after he was done with his mess hall duties, he tossed a stick for Sumi, who ran joyfully in and out of the surf, while his father sat bundled up on the shore, drawing in his sketchpad.

His father was an accomplished artist, George thought. He captured the spirit of the wildlife on the island, the rocky beaches, the smiling faces of the Tlingit women on the canning line. One charcoal drawing of his dog, Sumi, in the back of the skiff George still treasured, decades after both dog and artist were gone.

George's childhood with his father was idyllic until one day, it suddenly wasn't. Breathless from lugging a pailful of salmonberries up to the watchman's house, he burst through the door to find his father collapsed on the floor. He was deathly pale and feverish, his bad leg twisted under him.

The doctors in Juneau said that his appendix had ruptured and peritonitis had set in. Despite their efforts, George's father and grandfather died in the same hospital wing, ten years apart.

This time, though, there was to be no big white woman in a smelly suit, dragging him off to foster care. George hardly had time to grieve before Ivan Lindeman, a seine boat owner and friend of George's father, folded the boy into his family's embrace. Ivan and his wife, Joan, a warm, maternal presence, helped George with funeral arrangements and insisted that George, and Sumi too, come to live with them. Before long, they approached George about adopting him. They had three grown daughters, and were anxious for him to join their family and become their only son.

So at the age of fourteen, George Laskin became George Lindeman. The Lindemans were kind and generous, but he would have given anything to have had more time with Kazuhiro Yamane. His father had rescued him. For this and other reasons, he would always hold his father dear to his heart.

But who would rescue his Chrissy? He felt for the carved wooden heart that seemed to pulse painfully in his breast pocket.

42

Beans

Summer 2024

One thing Beans knew for certain—Jane Doe didn't bury herself in that shallow grave. Whether she died by her own hand or was killed, either Donovan Ching, Bernie Waterman, or one of their shady colleagues had dug her grave and put her in it.

Jane Doe was not Christine Olsen, but now at least they had a DNA profile that could be compared against possible relatives. They could continue working the missing persons list and maybe through Investigative Genetic Genealogy eventually get a familial hit. Like Mari said, "Someone must be looking for her."

The last player in the Outport Enterprises drama remained missing. Zach Green's gun had been found, but not Zach, the weed dealer who had sabotaged Jimmy Beans's plane. Local legend said he boarded a plane south, but after that he disappeared.

Caleb, still the proverbial squeeze bottle of information, swore he couldn't verify where Zach was but had no problem voicing his opinion. "You want to know what I think? Zach never got over his part in that crash. It ate him up, man, leaving Jimmy's kids fatherless. And after he got fired from the washeteria ..." Caleb sighed. "Zach went into the river the same time his gun did. Can't prove it, but that's what I think."

"And still no sighting of Donovan Ching or Dylan Chang," Heller said. "I bet his Mexican connections spirited him away. Unless they get tired of him or he slips up, he's gone. In the meantime, the feds have seized the floatplane and White Rock Lodge."

With the arrests of Waterman and Caleb Redfern and the disappearance of Donovan Ching, Outport Enterprises dissolved and the distribution points on their drug network quickly vanished. The United States Postal Service transferred a new postmaster to the Galena office—a no-nonsense middle-aged woman from Bethel. Beans lay Arvid's Glock in its holster and what was left of Gloria's eggs on Fee's desk. "Permission to leave, Officer Gunnerson."

She looked up, her eyes wide. "What? You're leaving me?"

"Of course I'm leaving you. I got a real job to go back to. One that pays me. I gotta help my grandmother move. I gotta go to a ballet, for crying out loud." He was beginning to feel overwhelmed by the tasks that needed to get done before he went back to work.

"Oh right, the girlfriend." Fee rolled her eyes.

"Yeah, whom I haven't seen in weeks! And my dog and cat probably don't remember what I look like."

"They like Piper better anyway," Fee muttered.

He kept forgetting that Fee and Piper were social media friends. Piper probably posted endless Instagram reels of Archie and Elwood fawning over her.

"I did what you asked me, Fee. I came up here when you called. I think we're even."

She nodded. "We're even." She busied herself rearranging papers on her desk.

"So, what are you going to do, Fee?"

"I got first-grade Stranger Danger training in about a half hour."

"No, I mean, long term. Are you going to stick around?" He leaned against her desk.

She sat back in her chair. "I don't know, Havi. I don't mind it, and as long as Mom's here, it's OK. But it's not exactly, you know, 'the bigs.'"

"Hey, we've seen as much serious crime these last few weeks as Arvid did in his entire career here, I bet."

She gave him her wide bright smile. "No shit."

"And you even got shot."

"Still got a bruise." She rubbed her side.

"Solved two almost twenty-year-old cases. That's nothing to sneeze at."

"How would things have been different if Lloydie's leg had never washed up?" Fee asked, chewing her thumbnail. "You would have gone to California. Bernie Waterman and company would still be running their drug operation out of Galena. Your dad's death would still be a horrible accident. Lloyd Paul would still be missing."

All true, Beans thought—different, but not necessarily for the better.

* * *

"It would have been better if that fucking leg had never washed up," Victor Paul said from behind the counter at the YC store. "Fee wouldn't have asked you up here. Things would be normal. I would still have my family," his voice broke. He pulled out a plaid handkerchief and swiped at his eyes. "No offense, it was good of you to come up to help Fee. But it would have been better if that stupid leg had never showed up."

But then, he would never have known that his father was murdered, and hadn't carelessly crashed his plane, Beans thought. And the drug-dealing would still have been going on. But he didn't say that.

Beans had stopped by the YC to say goodbye to Victor before returning to Anchorage. Charlene hovered near the back office, still barely speaking to him since the arrest of her mother. With the exception of Victor, Charlene, and Beans, the store was empty. Victor came around the counter to shake his hand and give him a pack of gum and a candy bar. "For the flight—I know how you Beans kids love your chocolate."

Beans arrived back at the house to pack and do some minor housework. Mari was going to have to be happy with clean sheets, light vacuuming, and a cursory scrub of the toilets. He didn't want her to come home to a dirty house, but he wasn't prepared to spring clean either.

He was putting the damp sheets into the dryer when his phone barked. The call was from a number with a 907 area code, but one he didn't recognize. Thinking it might be someone from the airlines, he answered it.

The reedy voice of an elderly man. "Hello, is this DeHavilland Beans?"

"Yes. And you are . . . ?"

"Please forgive me, I got your phone number from your mother, Mari. This is George Lindeman. Let's see if I can get this right. I'm your grandfather's half-brother."

Beans collapsed onto the sofa. "Wow. Mr. Lindeman—it's great to meet you, or hear your voice, anyway."

George Lindeman chuckled. "Oh, please call me George. May I call you Havi?"

"Yes, of course." Beans liked the man's throaty laugh, his slow, deliberate speech.

"Havi, first I want to thank you."

Beans felt a lump in his throat. "It wasn't the outcome we had hoped for."

"No, but we—Yvonne and I—really appreciate your efforts. I guess we can go back to clinging to the fantasy that Chrissy may still be alive somewhere."

Beans was struck by the parallel to Lloyd Paul, who for years hovered in that purgatory somewhere between missing and dead.

"Now, second, I would like to ask you a favor. I know this is an imposition, and if it's not possible, please let me know. Chrissy's father thought she had a baby when she was sixteen and gave it up for adoption. We don't want to disrupt this child's life in any way. But it would mean a lot to us—Yvonne and me—to know what has become of Chrissy's baby."

"You know that most adoption records are private and sealed, right?"

"Of course. But your mother also told me that you used your police resources to find out who had adopted me so that she could find out more about this—thorny branch of the family," he chuckled again. "Thank you for that, too! It's been delightful connecting with Mari!"

Oh, right. My Little Robot research project. "I can't promise anything, George, but I'll give it a try."

"That's the most we can hope for. Thank you so much." George gave Beans the approximate date and presumed location of the adoption in Anchorage. He expressed his desire to meet Mari and the entire family in person in the near future and hung up.

While the sheets thudded through their drying cycle, Beans shot a quick email off to Cam Kristovich: "Hi, Cam. I have another Priority Five task for you. Please research adoption records of a child born to Christine Marie Olsen in Anchorage sometime in 1997 through 1998. I don't know if it makes a difference or not, but Christine Olsen was probably sixteen at the time the child was born. The child was given up for adoption soon after birth, probably in Anchorage, but that's not certain. I need to know the names of the child and the adoptive parents, and where they are living now. Thanks, Cam. I'll see you soon."

August 5, 1955
Ben Yamane
c/o Setsuo Sawada
45 11th St.
San Francisco, California

Dear Ben,

We've never met, but I'm your half-brother George Laskin. I'm writing to let you know that our father, Kazuhiro Yamane, died on June 15 of this year. We were at the plant in Hoonah when his appendix burst and caused a terrible infection that even the doctors in Juneau couldn't cure. He is buried in a cemetery here in Juneau. I'd be happy to show you where if you want to visit.

Dad spoke of you often, Ben. I know that his leaving to come up here caused you and your family so much pain, and for that I'm so sorry. But he spoke of you all the time, and drew really neat charcoal sketches of you and your mom, and your life in camp. Each time he mailed a letter to you, he said "This will be the one that gets answered."

You are probably in university now—our father said you were always so clever, and good at your studies. I'm not as smart, I'm afraid! But I run a boat pretty good, and our family friends the Lindemans have me help out on their fishing boats.

I hope you will answer this letter, Ben. We are brothers, and we both of us lost our father. In case you're thinking that our dad favored me over you, you need to think again. On his last day, I was at his hospital bed, putting a cold towel on his forehead. He looked right at me, smiled, and said, "You've come, Ben." And those were the last words he said to me or anybody else.

Well, I can honestly say this is the longest letter I've ever written. Please write me back at the Lindemans' address below, or call, collect even, at their phone number. Lindemans said it was OK.

I hope I'll hear from you soon.

Your brother,
George Laskin

43

Beans

Summer 2024

Fee was subdued when she picked Beans up to take him to the airport. She waited in the truck while he left a brief note for Mari, then locked up the house. He felt nostalgic as they pulled away from his childhood home—this was the longest stretch of time he'd spent in Galena since he'd left for college. As he slid into the passenger seat, he felt something press against his tailbone.

"Hey, you're sitting on your present." Fee pulled the truck out of the driveway and headed to the airport.

The lumpy package was wrapped in crumpled birthday wrapping paper and was roughly the size of a cue ball.

"Should I unwrap it now?"

She shrugged. "It's up to you."

The misshapen gift consisted of the head of a Barbie doll with black hair braided into twin plaits. Beans guessed it was supposed to look Native American. "Is this supposed to look like you? Indigenous Barbie?"

"Doesn't it, kinda? I wanted to give you something to remember me by."

"It's not likely I'd forget you, Fee." He stuck the Barbie head on the tip of his pinkie and waggled it at her. "I'll treasure it always." He knew just where he'd put it. On his Buddhist shrine, next to his family's photos, and his Grandpa Ben's carved wooden gun—where he'd light incense and say a daily sutra for her health and safety.

"You'd better."

At the airport, Beans slipped the Barbie head into his pocket and stepped out of the truck.

Fee did the same, and stood beside him. "Well, I don't know how I'm supposed to get anything done without my best unpaid deputy."

"I'm your only unpaid deputy."

"Another technicality." She looked up at him, her dark eyes glistening. "I didn't realize until you came up here, how much policing is a collaborative thing. How much I missed working with a partner. I'm going to miss you, Havi."

"Me too. It's been a productive partnership."

Like the impulsive Fee from his childhood, she flung her arms around him and hugged him tightly. Then, unlike the Fee from his childhood, she gave him a lingering, fragrant kiss on the lips and whispered in his ear, "See you, partner." Her scent was like tropical fruit and flowers, probably from the gum she chewed and her hair conditioner. He found it comforting and familiar, and at the same time, provocative. He waved and smiled at her as she drove off, feeling more than a little bit off balance. *Oh Jesus. This is Conrad's sister.*

* * *

Heller picked him up at the Anchorage airport and drove him to the office where Lieutenant DuBois returned his gun and badge to him. "You're a few days early, but who's counting?"

Beans reminded DuBois that he still planned on taking time to travel to the Bay Area to help his grandmother for a few days.

"Fine, but don't forget to schedule those psych sessions."

By the time Heller dropped him off at home, Piper was already there, throwing a tennis ball in the backyard for Elwood. His dog was happy to see him, prancing on his big feet and flipping the ball into the air, while Archie the cat wove between his legs, yowling.

"They've really missed you," Piper said, kissing him on the cheek. "Me too."

"No, they haven't. They're getting fat and spoiled living with Auntie Piper."

"Well, that too."

He told her of his plans to fly down to the Bay Area to help Grandma and attend Amy's ballet. "So, can you stay for a few extra days and watch the boys?"

Piper draped the ginger cat across her shoulders. "Oh, I suppose. They're almost out of food, though."

Elwood snuffled in Beans's pocket and pulled out Fee's Barbie head. He tossed it gleefully in the air, catching it between his jaws.

"Hey! Drop it, Elwood!"

Piper shrieked. "What the hell is that?"

Elwood did drop it, eventually, but not before the doll's hair was unbraided and frizzy, and there were puncture marks on its slimy smiling face.

Piper picked it up by the hair. "Fee gave you this?"

"Yeah. Just before I left. You remember how she had all those headless Barbies. I guess she did keep a few heads somewhere."

"Hmm." Piper hummed wisely.

"What's that supposed to mean?"

"Nothing, just that I was her best friend in Girl Scouts, and she never gave me a Barbie head."

"Oh, for crying out loud." He felt his face flush as he headed toward the house to get the keys to the Explorer. "I'm going to buy pet food."

He was in Back to Nature Pet Foods pushing a cart containing a twenty-five-pound bag of special Gastrointestinal Diet for Active Dogs, and a five-pound bag of Salmon and Sweet Potato Feline Formula, when his phone barked.

It was Heller, sounding small and faraway. "Hey, where are you?"

"Back to Nature Pet food store, you know, on the same block as the 'groovy sandwich place' where Amy works. Why?"

"Oh good, you're close to the shop. Do you mind swinging in for a few minutes?"

"Yeah, sure. What's up?" He thought maybe there was a development in the Donovan Ching situation, but he couldn't figure out why Heller didn't just tell him.

"Nothing to worry about. I'll see you when you get here."

Fifteen minutes later, he was walking through the doorway to the Violent Crimes Division. Heller waved him over into a conference room, and Beans was surprised to see Cam Kristovich already sitting there, his hands folded and fingers laced on a legal pad.

"Hi, Cam, I didn't think you were scheduled to work until tomorrow morning."

"Hello. I had some extra time, so I worked on that Priority Five task you gave me the other day."

Heller seemed hardly able to contain himself, and even Cam seemed fidgety and uncomfortable.

"OK, great. Did you have any luck with that?"

Cam looked over at Heller, who nodded. Cam consulted his yellow legal pad. "You asked me to research the records of Christine Marie Olsen's child, adopted in 1997 or 1998. It was a boy. I was able to access the names of the adoptive parents. He was adopted in Anchorage by Carl and Mildred Kristovich. They named him Cameron." Cam looked up from his legal pad to a point somewhere over Beans's left shoulder. "I am that boy, Detective Beans."

After a few seconds of stunned silence, the first thing Beans could think of to say was, "I didn't know you were adopted."

Cam nodded. "My parents adopted me when I was just a few days old."

"I had no idea—I'm sorry about springing this on you, Cam. This must have been a real—shock—learning about your birth mother, I mean—and you had no time to prepare for it . . ." He knew he was babbling. If this news floored Beans, he could only imagine what it did to Cam.

"It's OK, Detective Beans. My parents are and always will be Carl and Mildred Kristovich. They are the ones with 'skin in the game,' like Detective Heller says sometimes."

Heller chuckled. "That's my boy."

"You know what this means, don't you?" Beans asked.

Cam shook his head. "No."

"It means we're related!" Beans couldn't believe how glad this made him. He was fond of the young man, and now they shared more than just an affinity for police work.

A small smile seemed to play at Cam's lips. "I am an only child."

"Right, but now you have half- or quarter-cousins or whatever—me, and my sister Piper, Otter, and Herc . . . my mom would be some kind of great-aunt, I think. Remember that George Laskin adoption you looked up for me?"

"Priority Five George Lindeman?"

"Yes! George Lindeman is Christine Olsen's grandfather. And he and my grandfather are half-brothers! They share the same father!"

Cam looked Beans in the eye. "Will I meet them sometime?"

Beans started, since eye contact with Cam was very uncommon. He was surprised to see that his eyes were brown with flecks of green, almost the same color as Beans's own.

"Well, my grandfather died last year, but of course you can meet everybody else. And we—you—have relatives in Juneau. Yvonne Olsen is your grandmother and George Lindeman is your great-grandfather. Of course," Beans hurried to add, "any further contact is entirely up to you."

Cam was silent as he absorbed this information. "This is kind of like Christmas, isn't it?" he said, finally. The corners of his eyes crinkled, much like Beans's did, in a rare smile.

44

Beans

Summer 2024

Like many of the perpetrators he had apprehended during his ten years on the force, Beans returned to the scene of his crime. He had not returned to Ma's Family Grocery since that hellish night he had shot Willis Helms dead in front of Sophie Ma, under the store's unsteady fluorescent lighting. He had put it off as long as possible. Returning to the store was not going to be a pleasant task, but was something that he needed to do to somehow reset his karmic balance.

When he pulled up, his college friend Frankie Ma was sweeping the sidewalk in front of the displays of fresh vegetables. Frankie had aged visibly in the last few years, wearing glasses now, his black hair flecked with gray, his back a little stooped as he swept. Beans suspected the stress of paying off his gambling debts had contributed to his premature aging.

They had been inseparable in college, both playing basketball at the University of Alaska, both embracing the party-boy lifestyle that included lots of drugs and alcohol. Until the morning that Beans woke up, failing every class but P.E., seeing the haggard, hungover face of his dead brother Lindbergh when he looked in the mirror. Beans had then sworn off the booze and drugs, while Frankie had not.

Frankie looked up as Beans approached, his face breaking into a wide smile.

"Beans! Jesus, it's good to see you!" He pumped Beans's hand. "I never had a chance to thank you for being there for Mom, for fucking saving her life, man. We—Allison and me—can't thank you enough. I don't know what would have happened if you hadn't been here."

Beans suspected that Frankie had been at a high-stakes poker game or at a cockfighting ring in the Valley the night his mother had been threatened by Willis Helms, but didn't say so. Frankie's older sister, Allison, had been and still was in Seattle in a heated custody battle with her estranged husband for their two kids.

"I'm just glad I was here." *Was he?* He was glad that he was able to come to Sophie Ma's aid, but he would have preferred that it had ended differently.

"Come on in. Mom would love to see you." Frankie ushered Beans past the open crates of eggplant and tomatoes.

Beans hesitated a little as he crossed the threshold. The tile flooring had been returned to its usual dingy yellow, without a trace of blood or root beer. The glass cabinet that had been shattered during the altercation had been replaced by a newer, larger one. The bullet hole in the ceiling had been patched—by Frankie, Beans assumed, since it looked haphazard and had not been painted over yet.

"I figured we should leave it that way," Frankie said. "A conversation piece. And a warning as well, you know—don't mess with Mom." He chuckled, unaware that the bullet he had dug out of the ceiling had been fired out of Willis' gun and not his mother's.

Sophie Ma bustled out of the back room, trailing a long ribbon of adding machine tape. "Frankie! Did you make the deposit?"

Beans remembered that Mrs. Ma's interrogation techniques rivaled those of seasoned investigators and could tell that she was gearing up to start a session with her son. Then she spotted Beans.

The questioning of Frankie forgotten, she rushed to hug him. "Beans! I'm so glad to see you! You OK?" Her bright eyes searched his face as she patted his hands. "Thank you, thank you! You saved me, you know. I am in your debt."

Beans was embarrassed. Sophie and her husband, Coleman, had given Beans a cheap place to live, the apartment above the store at the time. He had been welcomed in their home and eaten at their table at least once a week for the whole time he was in college. "No, Mrs. Ma. Let's say we're even."

Mrs. Ma took him on a guided tour of the store improvements. "Do you like the new cigarette case? Nice, huh? Insurance paid. We got new cameras, too." She pointed to the ceiling. "Frankie plugged the hole but needs to paint." Her face fell as she passed the freezer case against which Willis had slumped and spent the last few seconds of his life. "Poor Willis. He used to come in all the time, buying chips or pop. Kind of, you know, crazy, but never made trouble. Except the last time, with the gun." She shook her head. "We made a donation to the Grace Mission in memory of Willis."

"That's a good idea." Beans made a note to do the same.

"Come, come, let's have tea." Mrs. Ma ushered him into the small office behind the store and plugged in a hot water kettle. "You sit." She pushed a wheeled stool in his direction.

Beans watched as she scurried back and forth, putting tea bags in mugs, placing almond cookies on a plate. He knew that given the same circumstances again, he wouldn't hesitate to protect this woman, almost as dear to him as his own mother. He was meant to be here in the store, he realized, on that day at that time, to fire the bullet that would kill Willis and allow Sophie Ma to live. So she would be here to make him tea and chatter about Allison's divorce and the price of eggs, and the bullet hole in the ceiling, while Frankie swept the sidewalk and the sun began to set on this endless summer day.

Epilogue

The mist lay heavily on the river the August morning that Beans and Piper arrived in Galena for Gloria Gunnerson's memorial service. Mari was there to meet them at the airport, throwing her arms around them and bundling them into the pickup. Herc wanted to be there, she said, but was out on the fishing grounds. Otter also sent his regrets, as he was part of a gubernatorial contingent steaming up the Inside Passage on a cruise ship. "Our tax dollars at work," Piper muttered.

Gloria had died quietly in her sleep, less than a month after she had nearly succumbed to an overdose of insulin administered by Janelle Mangold. Conrad had insisted on an autopsy, and one was performed by Chuckie Hefner, the medical examiner in Anchorage. Gloria's death was natural, caused by a hemorrhagic stroke, common among Alzheimer's patients. Conrad and Fee speculated that the insulin overdose could have contributed to the stroke, but Chuckie couldn't or wouldn't confirm that theory. How ironic, Beans mused as he mourned the woman who had cheerfully served him endless gallons of lemonade, that Gloria should survive a murder attempt but be felled by a more insidious killer.

Cam Kristovich had offered to stay with Elwood and Archie while Beans and Piper were gone. The animals seemed to love him, and Beans knew that there was no better caretaker to stick to a pet's routine than Cam, his newfound second cousin once removed.

Beans had been unsure about how Cam's parents would accept the news of his newly discovered relatives, but he needn't have worried. The Kristoviches were delighted that Cam had connected with the Beans and Lindeman families, and were looking forward to meeting everyone as well.

Beans's trip to the Bay Area had been productive, but bittersweet. He and Mari, with the help of Mari's brother, Roy, and his son, Ethan, successfully moved Michiko into her new retirement apartment. Beans enjoyed getting to know the Yamane side of the family, and they parted company trading contact info and promising to keep in touch.

Amy Chandler was stunning as the lead in the newly choreographed ballet of Benjamin Britten's *The Turn of the Screw.* After the performance, she invited them backstage, and Mari and Michiko were starstruck by the sets and the costumes. The ballet was so well-received that the Houston and Denver ballets, among others, had invited the company for guest engagements. While a major feather in her cap and boost to her career, it meant that Amy would be on the road for the better part of six months. They both knew what this meant. They would see each other on those rare occasions when they were in the same town, then less and less, until not at all. As they left a shaded sidewalk café in Sausalito, she gave him a tearful "Later, copper" kiss that they both knew meant "Goodbye."

* * *

The current plan for a "family reunion" was for Cam to travel to Juneau and spend a few days with the grandmother and great-grandfather he had never met, with Beans, Mari, and Piper joining them later. George and Yvonne were in total agreement with this and suggested that they organize the gathering for late September, before the weather got too rainy in Southeast. Otter lived in Juneau and could easily interrupt his hectic man-about-town lifestyle to join them. Herc would be done fishing for the season, and could bring his kids over from Sitka. Together, they would visit Kazuhiro Yamane's grave, not far from where Ivan and Joan Lindeman, George's adoptive parents, were buried. By then, Mari said she would have all of Kazu Yamane's artwork and comic strips as well as the charcoal sketches from George's collection scanned and in a book form, so that each member of the family could have a copy. She would also bring Kazu's intricate wood carvings to distribute among his descendants. The little wooden gun that his Grandpa Ben had meant for him to have already rested on Beans' Buddhist shrine, next to the black and white photo of his grandfather with the same gun in his child-sized holster.

As part of their itinerary, George offered to organize a boat trip to Funter Bay on Admiralty Island, to visit the site of the camp where he, his mother, and grandfather had been imprisoned, and where Otto and Addy were buried.

So many family graves to visit, Beans thought, but not unhappily.

* * *

By the time Beans, Mari, and Piper arrived at the dock, the mist had risen from the river, and most of the town had gathered at the water. Gloria Gunnerson had been a much-beloved teacher's aide at the elementary school, and many of her former students had come to pay their respects. A pair of cackling geese bobbed offshore, seemingly unconcerned by the large crowd at the water's edge.

Conrad was there with his diminutive but feisty Japanese wife, Yuki, and their young children, Theo and Madison. Victor Paul seemed to have weathered the stagnant business cycle and ostracizing by the community. Slowly, people were coming back, he said. His granddaughter Charlene had a new boyfriend, the same cargo worker who had earlier whistled at Fee at the airport, and decided to start speaking to Beans again. Junior Mangold surprised everyone by showing up at the dock he manned during the workweek in a tan sport coat, white shirt, and XtraTuf boots, his frizzy red hair neatly trimmed. Beans couldn't help but wonder if the pending media attention surrounding Janelle's trial had caused Junior's grooming about-face.

Fee seemed to float through the crowd, not in her khaki uniform, but in a pale blue sun dress, looking sophisticated and pretty, her hair in what Piper said was a French twist. His sister ran over to Fee and the friends embraced, tearing up over Gloria. Fee gave Beans a quick hug and a swift kiss, smiling as she met his eyes. "Hey, partner." There was that scent again—tropical fruit and flowers, familiar and provocative and once more, the world seemed to tilt on its axis.

The service was short and informal. Conrad said a few words from the family, then friends were invited to share stories about his mother. Who'd have thought there would be so many racy and funny stories about Gloria, even before her dementia, Beans wondered. The attendees laughed so hard that many were in tears.

Finally, Conrad and Fee, hand in hand, walked to the end of the dock and cast Gloria's ashes into the water—into the river that had taken her husband, Jimmy Beans, and maybe Zach Green into its embrace. The river that had consumed Lloyd Paul but spit out his leg. The same river that had taken guns and secrets into its quiet, discreet depths. The cacklers skimmed the water then took to the air, while the river lapped and sang at the shore.

Acknowledgments

A huge debt of gratitude to Matt Sweetsir with Ruby Marine—absolutely the best barge service on the Yukon River—for supplying specific, insightful information on water and weather conditions, bypass mail, and village life. For reasons that were evident, I elected to use a fictitious barge name in the book—although in reality, it's Ruby Marine that provides economical, efficient seasonal barge service to Alaskan villages on the Yukon, Koyukuk, and Innoko Rivers. Any and all departures from reality or accuracy are my responsibility exclusively.

Many thanks to Dr. Judith A. Berg, who has once again been my advisor on all things medical. Mark Carpenter and his fellow pilot/docents at the Heritage Flight Museum in Burlington, Washington were so generous with their time and expertise, providing technical info on the DeHavilland Beaver floatplane. I'm pretty sure I've got the medical and aeronautical details right, but if not, any inaccuracies are on me.

Thank you again to my editor Sara J. Henry for her patient guidance, gracefully wielding her editing pen like a velvet rapier. Everything she touched is *astronomically* better for the attention she gave it. The entire team at Crooked Lane Books has again designed a dynamite cover and has been, as always, the epitome of patience and a joy to work with for this old author.

Critique group members Judith Kirscht and Serena DuBois supplied much-needed moral support. Trusted friend and sometime collaborator Becky Warden did a thorough beta-reading and gave me, as she always does, thoughtful feedback.

Finally, thanks to my husband Jon Black, who at the very least deserves a medal for living with me through yet another authoring endeavor.